THE MARQUESS'S MOVE

The Marquess slowed his pace, and Judith followed
suit. She turned to him and fixed her eyes on the
top button of his greatcoat as his gloved hands cupped
her face. She lifted her hands and rested her palms
against his chest. And she lifted her eyes to his and
then closed them as his mouth came down to
cover hers.

He was the man she had feared for so long. She
tried to remember the impression she had had of
his face until now—harsh, the eyes steel-gray,
the lips thin. It was he who was kissing her,
she told herself.

*Was this the face of love? The face of hate? And
did she, in this moment of abandoned ecstasy,
any longer care?*

MARY BALOGH, who won the *Romantic Times* Award for
Best New Regency Writer in 1985, has since become one
of the genre's most popular and bestselling authors. She also
won the Waldenbooks Award for Bestselling Short Historical
in 1986 for *The First Snowdrop* and the *Romantic Times*
Reviewer's Choice Award for Best Regency Author in 1988,
the Waldenbooks Award for Bestselling Short Historical in
1989 for *The Obedient Bride* and a *Romantic Times* Lifetime
Achievement Award in 1989.

Christmas Beau

by
Mary Balogh

A SIGNET BOOK

SIGNET
Published by the Penguin Group
Penguin Books USA Inc., 375 Hudson Street,
New York, New York, 10014, U.S.A.
Penguin Books Ltd, 27 Wrights Lane, London W8 5TZ, England
Penguin Books Australia Ltd, Ringwood, Victoria, Australia
Penguin Books Canada Ltd, 10 Alcorn Avenue, Toronto, Ontario, Canada M4V 3B2
Penguin Books (N.Z.) Ltd, 182-190 Wairau Road,
Auckland 10, New Zealand

Penguin Books Ltd, Registered Offices:
Harmondsworth, Middlesex, England

First published by Signet, an imprint of New American Library,
a division of Penguin Books USA Inc.

First Printing, December, 1991

10 9 8 7 6 5 4 3 2 1

1

It felt strange to be dressing up to go out again. And strange to be wearing a blue gown. She had gone straight from black to colors when her year of mourning had ended the week before, with no intermediate stages of gray or lavender.

Not only strange. It felt somehow wrong to be dressing to go out to enjoy herself with the children in bed in the nursery. Especially since she had during the past week denied them what might have brought them great pleasure. She had refused to go to Scotland with her parents in order to spend Christmas with her sister. The journey would be too tedious for the children, she had decided, especially Kate, who was scarcely three years old.

A whole month before that she had refused an invitation to spend Christmas with Andrew's family at Ammanlea, although there was the country estate for the children to run free on and several other children for them to play with. She had refused because she had always felt almost as if her identity was swallowed up by their large numbers. And because she did not particularly want any reminders of Andrew.

The thought brought further guilt. He had been her husband, after all, and father of her two children.

It seemed that they would be spending Christmas alone together in London, the three of them, with Amy. It was a bleak prospect, though preferable to either of the two alternatives.

Blue. Judith Easton ran her hands lightly over the soft silk of her new evening gown and looked down at the flounces at the hem and the blue silk slippers beneath. Her favorite color. How very delightful it was to look down and not see unrelieved black. Even after a week the novelty of being out of mourning had not worn off.

Her fair hair had been looped down over her ears and dressed in ringlets at the back of her head. It was an elegant style, she thought, though perhaps she should be donning a turban as more in keeping with her age and widowed status.

She was twenty-six years old. Did she look it? she wondered, glancing in the mirror. She did not feel that old. Being back in London again and living in her parents' home while they were in Scotland, the years seemed to roll away. It did not seem as if almost eight years had passed since her come-out Season. Though there were two children in the nursery to prove that it was indeed so.

She turned from the mirror and picked up her cloak and fan. She did not want to think of her come-out Season. The memories made her shudder with shame and embarrassment. The only consolation had always been that she had escaped from a dreaded marriage. But then, the one that had replaced it had quickly brought disillusion and heartache.

She tiptoed into the nursery, but Rupert was sitting up in bed frowning over a book, and even Kate was still awake, her cheeks flushed, her dark eyes wide.

"Mama," she asked, her lower lip wobbling, "don't be gone long."

"By the time you wake in the morning," Judith said, bending over the child to kiss her, "I shall have been home a long time. Nurse will be close by. You have nothing to fear. And Aunt Amy will be in the house."

"Mr. Freeman will not still be here tomorrow, Mama, will he?" Rupert asked with a frown, looking at her over the top of his book.

"He is being obliging enough to escort me to Lady Clancy's this evening," Judith said, crossing to her son's bed and kissing the top of his head. "That is all."

"Good," Rupert said, ducking his head down behind his book again.

Claude Freeman was a former acquaintance of Andrew's, who had come to pay his respects to her when she came to London two months before and had called at regular intervals ever since. He was a large man with a pompous manner.

Unfortunately, his overhearty efforts to befriend her children had met with no success.

"I must go," Judith said, straightening up and smiling at both children. "Mr. Freeman will be waiting downstairs for me. Sleep well."

"Mama," Kate said, "you look pretty."

Judith smiled and blew a kiss.

She still felt guilty as she went down the stairs. She and Andrew had lived in the country for all of their married life. The only social occasion she had known for several years had been the dinners and assemblies there, and they had not been numerous. Though it would be more accurate to say that *she* had lived in the country all that time. Andrew had frequently spent weeks and even months alone in town.

Claude was in the hallway, looking large and imposing in his evening cloak and silk hat. He looked even larger in comparison with Amy, who was tiny and birdlike. A battle with smallpox as a child had left her pale and undergrown, her complexion marred by a few pockmarks. She had been made for marriage and motherhood, Judith had always thought, but both had eluded her thanks to the cruelty of fate. She was Andrew's elder sister. Judith had invited her to live with them after his death since no one else in the family appeared to want her. Amy had accepted with unexpected eagerness.

"Judith," Amy said as Claude took her cloak from her hands and wrapped it about her shoulders, "how lovely you look again. Black is really not your color."

Nor was it Amy's. She did not need black to sap her of the last vestiges of color. Even her hair was a faded blond. Amy must be thirty-six years old, Judith thought. Time marched on.

"My sentiments exactly, Mrs. Easton," Claude said, standing back and making her an elegant bow. "I shall be the envy of the *ton* this evening."

Judith smiled. There was a definite excitement about going out again to a *ton* event, even if it was only a soirée and not a full ball. She had had a few invitations during the past month. She had chosen her first appearance with care.

Yes, there was a lifting of the spirits. There was no deny-
ing it. But there was also an apprehension that was making
her stomach churn rather uncomfortably. She supposed that
such a feeling was natural for someone returning to society
after eight years away. But there was more to it than that.

Would the old scandal be remembered? she wondered.
Would she be snubbed? She did not really believe it would
be quite as bad as that. Surely she would not have had any
invitations at all if she were still considered to be in disgrace.
And Claude would not be so eager to escort her if she was
to be ostracized.

But there would doubtless be some who would remember
that she had been formally betrothed for all of two months
during the Season seven and a half years ago and that she
had broken off that betrothal abruptly and without any public
announcement—or any private explanation to her
betrothed—in order to run off to the country to marry
Andrew.

She had acted very badly. Even at the time, she had known
that. But she had been so young, so terrified, so bewildered.
She had found herself quite unable to face the consequences
of her change of heart—no, there had been no change of heart
since there had been no love or even affection involved in
that betrothal. But however it was, she had been unable to
do things properly. She had fled with her sister and her maid,
leaving her parents to find the note she had left behind and
to smooth things over as well as they were able before
following along after her.

She smiled determinedly at Claude and took his arm. That
was all eight years in the past, a girl's gaucherie. She was
a different person now, with a different name. And she was
about to begin her life without Andrew.

She was free. There was exhilaration in the thought.

"You are quite sure you will not come too?" she asked
Amy. It was a foolish question to ask when she was ready
to step out the door, but it was not the first time she had
asked.

"I have never attended a *ton* event, Judith," Amy said. "I would positively die and not know where to hide myself. You run along and have a lovely time. I shall stay here in case the children need me. And I shall imagine all the conquests you are making."

Judith laughed. "Good night, then," she said. "But one of these times I shall drag you out with me, Amy."

Her sister-in-law smiled, and looked wistful only as the door closed behind Judith and Mr. Freeman. How she sometimes wished . . . But she was far too old for such wishes. And she must count her blessings. At last she had a home where she felt wanted and useful. And she was in London, where she had always wanted to be.

Amy turned and climbed the stairs to her sitting room.

Judith's exhilaration continued. Lord and Lady Clancy received her graciously, and Claude took her about their drawing room on his arm until they stopped at a group where she found the conversation particularly interesting. Soon Claude had wandered off, and she felt as thoroughly comfortable as if she had never been away.

For perhaps the span of ten minutes, anyway.

At the end of that time, the lady standing next to Judith stood back with a smile to admit a new member to the group.

"Ah," she said, "so you did come after all, my lord. Do join us. You know everyone, of course. Except perhaps Mrs. Easton? The Marquess of Denbigh, ma'am."

Was it possible for one's stomach to perform a complete somersault? Judith wondered if her thoughts were capable of such coherence. Certainly it was possible for one's knees to be almost too weak to support one's person.

He had not changed, unless it was possible for him to look even harsher and more morose than he had looked eight years before. He was very tall, a good six inches taller than Andrew had been. He looked thin at first glance, but there was a breadth of chest and of shoulders that suggested fitness and strength. That had not changed with the years either, one glance told her.

His face was still narrow, angular, harsh, his lips thin,

his eyes a steely gray, the eyelids drooped over them so that they might have looked sleepy had they not looked hawkish instead. His dark hair had the suggestion of gray at the temples. That was new. But he was only—what? Thirty-four? Thirty-five years old?

The sight of him and his proximity could still fill her with a quite unreasonable terror and revulsion. Unreasonable because he had never treated her harshly or with anything less than a perfectly correct courtesy. But then, there had never been any suggestion of warmth either.

She had always wanted to run a million miles whenever he came into a room. She wanted to run now. She wanted to run somewhere where there would be air to draw into her lungs.

"Mrs. Easton," he said in that unexpectedly soft voice she had forgotten until now. And he bowed stiffly to her.

"My lord." She curtsied.

"But of course they know each other," a gentleman in the group said with a booming laugh. "I do believe they were betrothed once upon a time. Is that not so, Max?"

"Yes," the Marquess of Denbigh said, those steely eyes boring through her, not the faintest hint of a smile on his face—but then she had never ever seen him smile. "A long time ago."

"I think not, Nora," the Marquess of Denbigh had said three evenings before the night of the soirée. He had called to pay his respects to the Clancys between acts at the theater.

"We scarcely see you in town, Max," Lady Clancy protested. "It must be two years at the very least since you were here last. And yet even when you are here, you refuse to go about. It is most provoking. I am considering disowning you as my cousin."

"Second cousin," he corrected, putting his quizzing glass to his eye and gazing lazily about the theater at all the boxes. "And I am here tonight, so I can hardly be accused of being a total recluse."

"But alone in your box," she said. "It is inhuman, Max.

One word and you might have come with us. Are you sure you cannot be persuaded to come to my soirée? It would be a great coup for me. Word that you are in town has caused a considerable stir, you know. If you are intending to remain for the Season, you will be having a whole host of mamas sharpening their matchmaking skills again.''

"They would be well advised to spend their energies on projects more likely to bring them success," he said, still perusing the other boxes through his glass.

"One wonders why you have come to town at all," she said rather crossly, "if not to mingle with society."

"I have to call on Weston among others," he said. "I have fears that after two years I may no longer be fashionable, Nora."

She made a sound that was perilously close to a snort. "What utter nonsense," she said. "You would look elegant dressed in a sack, Max. It is that presence you have. Are you looking for someone in particular?"

He dropped his quizzing glass unhurriedly and clasped his hands behind his back. "No," he said. "I was only marveling at how few faces I know."

"They would begin to look far more familiar if you would just do more with your invitations than drop them in a waste basket," she said. "That is what you do with them, I presume?"

"Ah, not quite," he said. "But I do believe that is what my secretary does with them."

"It is most irritating," she said. "December is not a month when society abounds in London, Max. But it seems that there is no reasoning with you. There never was. And there—you have made me thoroughly cross when I am normally of quite sanguine disposition. You had better return to your box and be alone with yourself as you seem to wish to be. The next act must be due to begin."

Lord Clancy had turned from his conversation with a lady guest who shared his box. He laughed. "Nora has been quite determined to be the first and only hostess to lure you out this side of Christmas, Max," he said. "She has forgotten that since this morning there has been good reason for you not to come.''

"Quite right. I had forgotten," Lady Clancy said, "though it all happened such a long time ago that I daresay it makes no difference to anyone now. Mrs. Easton sent an acceptance of her invitation this morning. Judith Easton, Max. Lord Blakeford's daughter."

"Yes," the marquess said, looking down into the pit of the theater, his hands still at his back, "I know who Mrs. Easton is."

"I thought she would have gone to Scotland with Blakeford and his wife," Lord Clancy said "They have gone for Christmas apparently. But she has stayed here. Nora sent her an invitation to her soirée. It is an unfortunate coincidence that she should be in town at the same time as you, Max. She has not been here for more years than you, I believe. In fact, I do not recall seeing her here since she ran off with Easton."

"That is all old news," Lady Clancy said briskly. "You had better take yourself off, Max. I am planning not to talk to you for a whole month if you will not come to my soirée—not that I am likely to see you in that time to display my displeasure to you, of course."

The Marquess of Denbigh sighed. "If it is so important to you, Nora," he said, "then I shall look in for half an hour or so. Will that satisfy you?"

She smiled and opened her fan. "It is amazing what a little coercion can accomplish," she said. "Yes, I am satisfied. Now, will you take a seat here, or are you planning to insist on returning to your own box?"

"I shall return to my own," he said, bowing to the occupants of the box.

But he did not return to his box. He left the theater and walked home, his carriage not having been directed to return for him until the end of the performance.

So she was coming out of hiding at last. She was going to be at Nora's. Well, then, he would see her there.

Eight years was a long time—or seven and a half to be more accurate. He supposed she would have changed. She had been eighteen then, fresh from the schoolroom, fresh from the country, shy, sweet, pretty—he never had been able to find the words to describe her as she ahd been then. Words made her sound uninteresting, no different from dozens of other young girls making their come-out. Judith Farrington had been different.

Or to him she had been different.

She would be twenty-six years old now. A woman. A widow. The mother of two young children. And her marriage could not have been a happy one—unless she had not known, of course. But how could a wife not know, even if she spent all of her married life in the country, that her husband lived a life of dissipation and debauchery?

She would be different now. She was bound to be.

He wanted to see the difference. He had waited for it a long time, especially since the death of her husband in a barroom brawl—that was what it had been despite the official story that he had died in a skirmish with thieves.

He had waited. And come to London as soon as he knew that she was there. And waited again for her to begin to appear in public. And finally, it seemed, she was to appear at Nora's soirée.

He would be there too. He had a score to settle with Judith Easton. Revenge to take. He had a great deal of leftover hatred to work out of his heart and his soul.

He had waited a long time for this.

His eyes found her immediately when he entered Lord Clancy's drawing room three evenings later. Indeed, he hardly needed the evidence of his eyes that she was there. There had always been something about her that appealed very strongly to a sixth sense in him.

"Come," Lady Clancy said, linking her arm through his and noting the direction of his gaze. "You do not need to be embarrassed by her presence, Max. I shall take you over to Lord Davenport's group. Caroline Reave is there, too. Conversation is never dull when she is part of it."

"Thank you, Nora," he said, resisting the pressure of her arm, "but I can find my own way about. I have not forgotten how to do it in two years away from town."

She shrugged and smiled. "I might have known that you would confront the situation head to head," she said. "Perhaps I should have warned Mrs. Easton as I warned you."

Ah, so she had not been warned, he thought as he strolled across the room toward the group of which she was a part.

Yes, she was different. She was slender still, but with a woman's figure, not a girl's. Her hair was more elegantly dressed, with ringlets only at the back, not clustered all over her head as they had used to be. She carried herself proudly. He had not yet seen her face.

And then Dorothy Hopkins saw him and stood aside to admit him to the group, and he was able to stand right beside her and turn and make his bow to her, since Dorothy seemed to have forgotten the old connection and mentioned her particularly by name.

"Mrs. Easton," he said.

It was impossible to know her reaction. She spoke to him and curtsied to him, but her expression was calm and unfathomable—as it had always been. He had not known at that time that she hid herself behind that calmness. Her flight with Easton had taken him totally by surprise, had shattered him utterly.

Yes, her face had changed too. She had been pretty as a girl, with all the freshness of youth and eagerness for an approaching womanhood. She was beautiful now, with some of the knowledge of life etching character into her face.

"A long time ago," he said in reply to a remark made by someone in the group.

He did not take his eyes off Judith Easton or particularly note the embarrassment of the other members of the group, who had just been reminded of their former connection. He hardly noticed that their embarrassment drew them a little away from the two of them, so that soon they were almost isolated.

She was not looking quite into his eyes, he saw, but at his chin, perhaps, or his neckcloth or his nose. But her chin was up, and there was that calmness about her. He had dreamed once of transforming that calmness into passion once they were married. He had not known that behind it she was totally indifferent to him, perhaps even hostile.

It had been an arranged match, of course, favored by his father and her parents. He had been a viscount at the time. He had not succeeded to his father's title until three years before. But she had shown no open reluctance to his proposal. He had attributed her quietness to shyness. He had dreamed of awakening her to womanhood. He had dreamed of putting an end to his own loneliness, his own inability to relate to women, except those of the wrong class. He had loved her quite totally and quite unreasonably from the first moment he set eyes on her.

They had been betrothed for two months before she abandoned him, without any warning whatsoever and no explanation. They were to have been married one month later.

"Eight years, I believe," he said to her.

It was seven years and seven months, to be exact. She had been to the opera with him and two other couples. He had escorted her home, kissed her hand in the hallway of her father's house—he had never kissed more than her hand— and bidden her good night. That was the last he had seen of her until now.

"Yes," she said. "Almost."

"I must offer my belated condolences on your bereavement," he said.

"Thank you." She was twisting her glass around and around in her hands, the only sign that her calmness was something of a facade.

He made no attempt to continue the conversation. He wanted to see if there would be any other crack in her armor.

She continued to twist her glass, setting one palm against the base while she did so. She raised her eyes to his mouth, drew breath as if she would speak, but said nothing. She lifted her glass to her mouth to drink, though he did not believe her lips touched the liquid.

"Excuse me," she said finally. "Please excuse me."

It was only as his eyes followed her across the room that he realized that a great deal of attention was on them. She had probably realized it the whole time. That was good. He was not the least bit sorry. If she was embarrassed, good. It was a beginning.

He did not know quite when love had turned to hatred. Not for several months after her desertion, anyway. Disbelief had quickly turned to panic and a wild flight, first to the Lake District, and then to Scotland. Panic had turned to numbness, and numbness had finally given way to a deeply painful, almost debilitating heartbreak. For months he had dragged himself about on his walking tour, not wanting to get up in the mornings, not wanting to eat, not able to sleep, not wanting to live.

He had continued to get up in the mornings, he had continued to eat, he had slept when exhaustion claimed him. And eventually he had persuaded himself to go on living. He had done it by bringing himself deliberately to hate her, to hate her heartlessness and her contempt for honor and decency.

And yet hatred could be as destructive as heartbreak. He had found himself after his return to London hungry for news of her, going out of his way to acquire it—not easily done when she never came to town. He had found himself viciously satisfied when it became evident that Easton was returning to his old ways. She had preferred Easton to him. Let her live with the consequences.

Finally he had had to take himself off to his estate in the country to begin a wholly new life for himself, to try to stop the bitterness and the hatred from consuming him and destroying his soul.

He had succeeded to a large extent. He had focused the love she had spurned on other persons. And yet always there was the hunger for news of her. The birth of her children. The death of her husband. Her return to London.

And overpowering all his resolves, all his common sense, the need to see her again, to avenge himself on her, to even the score. He had been horrified at himself when he had heard of her arrival in London and had realized the violence of his suppressed feelings. Despite the meaningfulness, the contentment of his new life, they had been there the whole time, the old feelings, and they had proved quite irresistible. They had driven him back to London to see her again.

The Marquess of Denbigh turned abruptly and left both the room and Lord Clancy's house.

2

The weather was bitterly cold for December. Although there had been only a few flurries of snow, there had been heavy frost several mornings and some icy fog. And it was said that the River Thames was frozen over, though Judith had not driven that way to see for herself.

One was tempted to huddle indoors in such weather, staying as close to the fire and as far from the doors as possible. But Judith had lived in the country for most of her life and loved the outdoors. Besides, she had two young and energetic children who needed to be taken beyond the confines of the house at least once a day. It had become their habit to take a walk in Hyde Park each afternoon. Amy usually accompanied them there.

"One stiffens up quite painfully and feels altogether out of sorts when one stays by the fire for two days in a row," Amy said. "So exercise it must be. Old age is creeping up on me, Judith, I swear. Although sometimes I declare it is galloping, not creeping at all. I had to pull a white hair from its root just this morning."

Amy was a favorite with Kate because she was always willing to listen gravely and attentively to the child's often incomprehensible prattling. She had always seemed to know what Kate was talking about, even in those earlier days when no one but Amy—and Judith, of course—had even believed that the child was talking English.

"I just wish," Judith said, her hands thrust deep inside a fur muff as they walked along one of the paths in the park two days after Lady Clancy's soirée, "that taking one's exercise was not so utterly uncomfortable sometimes. I would be convinced that I had dropped my nose somewhere along the way if I could not see it when I cross my eyes. It must be poppy red."

"To match your cheeks," Amy said. "You look quite as pretty as ever, Judith, have no fear."

"I just hope I will not have to appear at the Mumford ball tonight with ruddy cheeks and nose," Judith said. "Indeed, I wish I did not have to appear there at all. Or I wish you would come too, Amy. Won't you?"

"Me?" Amy laughed. "Maurice once told me that I would be an embarrassment to gentlemen at a ball since I scarce reach above the waist of even the shortest of them. Henry agreed with him and so did Andrew. They made altogether too merry with the idea, but they were quite right. Besides, I am far too old to attend a ball in any function other than as a chaperone. And since you do not need a chaperone, Judith, I shall remain at home."

Judith felt her jaw tightening with anger. How could Amy have remained so cheerful all her life, considering the treatment she had always received from her family? They were ashamed of her, embarrassed by her. They had always liked to keep her at home, away from company, where she would not be seen.

Judith had tackled Andrew about it on one occasion, before she had learned that he did not have a heart at all. She had accused him and his brothers of cruelty for persuading Amy against attending a summer fair in a neighboring town.

"We have her best interests at heart," he had said. "We don't want her hurt, Jude. She might as well stay with the family, where her appearance does not make any difference."

"Perhaps one day," she said now, "we can drive down to the river to see if it is true about the ice. Claude says that if it thickens any further there will be tents and booths set up right on the river and a frost fair. But I am sure he exaggerates."

"But how exciting it would be," Amy said. "Booths? To sell things, do you think, Judith? But of course they would if it is to be likened to a fair. Perhaps we can buy some Christmas gifts there. I have not bought any yet, and there are only three weeks to go."

Amy entered into the excitement of the prospect and pushed

from her mind the mention of the ball. Balls were not for her. It was too late for her. There had been a time when she had dreamed of London and the Season and a come-out. It was true that her glass had always told her that she was small and plain, and of course she had those unfortunate pockmarks on her forehead and chin. But she had been a girl and she had dreamed.

Her father had never taken her to London. And finally it had dawned on her that he considered her unmarriageable. She had gradually accepted reality herself. She was an old maid and must remain so. She learned to take pleasure from other people's happiness and to love other people's children.

"Run along, by all means," she said when Kate tugged at her hand. "Aunt Amy is quite incapable of breaking into a run." She released her niece's hand and watched her race forward to join Rupert.

Judith watched the two children ahead of them. Rupert was a ship in full sail and was weaving and dipping about an imaginary ocean. Kate was hopping on first one leg and then the other.

It was hard to believe that Christmas was approaching. There was no feel of it, no atmosphere to herald the season. Christmas had always been a well-celebrated occasion in her family, and for a moment she regretted having decided against the long journey to Scotland and her sister's family. It would have been good once they had arrived there.

And in Andrew's family, too, it was always a big occasion. It was traditional for the whole family to gather together at Ammanlea, and she had been expected to join them after her marriage and abandon her own family's traditions. She had always hated it. Almost the only activities had ever been card playing and heavy drinking.

Even last year. They had all been in deep mourning for Andrew and the nursery had been the only room in the house to be decorated. But the drinking and the card playing had gone on unabated despite the blackness and the gloom of all their clothing.

She had come almost to hate Christmas for seven years.

"We must decorate the house," she said. "We must find

a way of celebrating and making Christmas a joyous occasion for the children, Amy, even though there will be just the four of us and the servants.'' She looked at her sister-in-law with some concern. ''Are you sure you do not want to go home, Amy? You have never been away at Christmas, have you?''

''I am sure.'' Amy smiled. ''I will miss all the children. I must admit that. But there are some things I will not miss, Judith. It will be lovely to be quiet with you and Rupert and Kate. Yes, we will decorate the house and go to church and sing carols. Perhaps carolers will come to the house. Does that happen in London, I wonder? It would be very pleasant, would it not?''

Yes, it would be pleasant, Judith thought. Strangely, although the prospect of their very small gathering seemed somewhat bleak, she was looking forward to Christmas for the first time in many years.

Invitations continued to arrive at the house daily. She could if she wished, she knew, be very busy and very gay all over Christmas. And she was determined to go out, to meet society again, to enjoy herself, to feel young again, of some worth again. But not too much. She would not sacrifice her children's happiness at Christmas for her own. And she would not leave Amy at home night after night while she abandoned herself to a life of gaiety.

Besides, she was a little afraid to go out. In some ways she was dreading that evening's ball. Would he be there again? she wondered.

It was a question she tried not to ask herself. There was no way of knowing the answer until the evening came. And even if he were, she told herself, it would not matter. For that very awkward first meeting was over, and they had had nothing whatsoever to say to each other and would be at some pains to avoid each other forever after.

There was no reason for the sleeplessness and the vivid, bizarre dreams of the past two nights and the breathless feeling of something like terror whenever her thoughts touched on him.

It was all eight years in the past. They had grown up since

then—though he, of course, had been her present age at the time it had happened. And they were civilized beings. There was no reason to wonder why he had made no effort to make conversation when they had been awkwardly stranded together at Lady Clancy's. It was merely that he was morose by nature, as he always had been. It was absurd to feel that she should have rushed into some explanation, some apology.

It had been a shock to realize that it had been the first time she had set eyes on him since that night of the opera, when her flight with Andrew had already been planned for the following day. That night she had sat through the whole performance without once concentrating on it, anxious about the plans for the morrow, breathless with the knowledge that the viscount, seated slightly behind her in the box, had been watching her more than the performance with those hooded and steely eyes. And she remembered wondering if he suspected, if he would do something to foil her plans, something to force her into staying with him and marrying him after all.

"He is slowing down," Amy said, and Judith realized with a jolt that her sister-in-law had been commenting on the approach of a rider and expressing the hope that he would not gallop too close to the children.

And looking up, Judith felt that disconcerting somersaulting of her stomach again. The rider, with a billowing black cloak, drew his equally black stallion to a halt, removed his beaver hat, and sketched them a bow.

"Mrs. Easton," the Marquess of Denbigh said. "Good afternoon to you."

She inclined her head. "Good afternoon, my lord," she said, expecting him to move on without further delay. She was surprised he had stopped at all.

He did not move on. He looked inquiringly at Amy.

"May I present my sister-in-law, Miss Easton, my lord?" she said. "The Marquess of Denbigh, Amy."

Amy smiled and curtsied as he made her a deeper bow than the one with which he had greeted Judith.

"I am pleased to make your acquaintance, my lord," Amy said.

"Likewise, ma'am," he said. "I did not know that your brother had any sisters."

"I have always lived in the country," Amy said. "But when Judith came to London and needed a companion, then I gladly agreed to accompany her. I have always wanted to see London."

"I hope you are having your wish granted, ma'am," he said. "You have visited the Tower and Westminster Abbey and St. Paul's? And the museum?"

"Westminster Abbey, yes," Amy said. "But we still have a great deal of exploring to do, don't we, Judith? We are going to drive down to the river tomorrow, or perhaps the day after since Judith is to attend a ball this evening and is likely to be late home. Have you heard that it is frozen over, my lord?"

"Indeed, yes," he said. "There is likely to be a fair in progress before the end of the week, or so I have heard."

"So it is not idle rumor," Amy said, smiling in satisfaction. "What do you think of that, Judith?"

Judith was not given a chance to express her opinion. The children had come running up, Kate to grasp her cloak and half hide behind the safety of its folds, Rupert to admire the marquess's horse.

"Will he kick if I pat his side, sir?" he asked. "He is a prime goer."

A prime goer! The phrase came straight from Maurice's vocabulary. It sounded strange coming from the mouth of a six-year-old child.

"Stand back, if you please, Rupert," she said firmly.

"He is a prime goer," the marquess agreed. "And I am afraid he is likely to kick, or at least to sidle restlessly away if you reach out to him in that timid manner and then snatch your hand away. You will convey your nervousness to him."

Rupert stepped back, snubbed.

"However, you may ride on his back, if you wish," the marquess said, "and show him that you are not at all afraid of him despite his great size."

Judith reached out a hand as Rupert's eyes grew as wide as saucers.

"Really, sir?" he asked. "Up in front of you?"

The marquess looked down at the boy without smiling so that Judith felt herself inhaling and reaching down a hand to cover Kate's head protectively.

"I don't believe a big boy like you need ride in front of anyone," Lord Denbigh said. And he swung down from the saddle, dwarfing them all in the progress. He looked rather like a rider from hell, Judith thought, with his black cloak swinging down over the tops of his boots, and his immense height.

"I can ride in the saddle?" Rupert gazed worshipfully up at the marquess. "Uncle Maurice says I am a half pint and must not ride anything larger than a pony until I am ten or eleven."

"Perhaps Uncle Maurice was thinking of your riding alone," the marquess said. "It would indeed not be advisable at your age to ride a spirited horse on your own. I shall assist you, sir."

And he stooped down, lifted the boy into the saddle, kept one arm at the back of the saddle to catch him if he should begin to slide off, and handed the boy the reins with the other.

"Just a short distance," he said, "if your mama has no objection."

Judith said nothing.

"Oh, how splendid," Amy said. "How kind of you, my lord. I am sure you have made a friend for life."

They did not go far, merely along the path for a short distance and back again. Judith stood very still and watched tensely. Her son's auburn curls—he was very like Andrew— glowed in marked contrast to the blackness of the man who walked at the side of the horse. She was terrified for some unaccountable reason. It was not for her son's safety. The horse was walking at a quite sedate pace, and the man's arm was ready to save the child from any fall.

She did not know what terrified her.

"There," the marquess said, lifting Rupert down to the ground again, "you will be a famous horseman when you grow up."

"Will I? Did you see, Mama?" Rupert screeched, his face

alight with excitement and triumph. "I was riding him all alone."

"Yes." Judith smiled at him. "You were very clever, Rupert."

"Do you think so?" he asked. "Will I be able to have a horse this summer, Mama, instead of a stupid pony? I will be almost seven by then. Will you tell Uncle Maurice?"

She cupped his face briefly with her hands and looked up to thank the marquess. And then she froze in horror as she saw him looking down at a tiny auburn-haired little figure who was tugging at his cloak.

"Me too," Kate was saying.

"No," Judith said sharply. And then, more calmly, "We have taken enough of his lordship's time, Kate. We must thank him and allow him to be on his way."

"Pegasus does not have a saddle for a lady," the marquess said. "But if you ask your mama and she says yes, I will take you up before me for a short distance."

"Please, Mama." Large brown eyes—also Andrew's— looked pleadingly up at her.

But was Kate not terrified of the man? Judith thought in wonder and panic. How could she bear the thought of being taken up before him on the great horse and led away from her mother and her aunt and brother? Kate was not normally the boldest of children.

"Very well," she said. She fixed her eyes on his chin. "If it is no great inconvenience to you, my lord."

He swung back up into the saddle again and reached down for the child, whom Judith lifted toward him. His hands touched her own briefly and she felt that she must surely suffocate. She stepped back as he settled Kate on the horse's back before him, and her daughter stared down at her with eyes that seemed as large as her face.

"How very kind of him," Amy said quietly as they rode away along the path. "There are not many gentlemen who would have such patience with children, Judith—including these children's own uncles."

"Yes," Judith said. "It is kind of him. And also unutterably embarrassing."

He took his leave of them and rode away as soon as he had returned with Kate and handed her down into Judith's waiting arms.

"What a very unfortunate meeting," she said when he had ridden out of earshot and the children's excitement had died down enough that they rushed ahead along the path again.

"Unfortunate?" Amy said. "Oh, no, Judith. You must not feel embarrassed. He was under no compulsion to be so kind to the children. But where did you make his acquaintance? At Lady Clancy's?"

"Yes," Judith said. "And before, Amy. He was—and I suppose still is—the Viscount Evendon."

"Evendon?" Amy was quiet for a moment. "The man to whom you were betrothed, Judith? Really? It is very good of him to be so civil, then." She stared back along the path at the disappearing figure of the marquess.

"Yes," Judith said.

And it was good of him. He had been remarkably civil to take such notice of her children. Why, then, did she feel frightened, almost as if he had attempted to kidnap them? Why did she not feel at all that an olive branch had been extended?

Was it just her guilt? Or was it something else?

It had been impossible to discover if she intended to go to the Mumford Ball short of asking the question of Mumford himself. And even he probably would not know since he had expressed a certain distaste for all the elaborate preparations Lady Mumford was making and a determination to stay within the safe walls of White's until he could stay there no longer.

The Marquess of Denbigh did not ask Mumford. He merely spent his days at White's and kept his ears open. It was amazing what gossip passed within the walls of the club. The story of his coming face to face with Judith Easton at Nora's had become common knowledge, of course. Some men avoided the topic in his presence, assuming that he would be embarrassed by a reminder of the way he had been jilted eight years before.

Fortunately, some gentlemen considered that he needed consoling.

"I hear you ran into Mrs. Easton at Clancy's," Bertie Levin said. "Unfortunate that, old chap."

The marquess shrugged. "Ancient history has no particular interest for me," he said.

"Too bad that you had to return at just the time when she is here," Bertie said. "Easton never brought her, you know."

"Is that so?" The marquess polished his quizzing glass.

"She might have interfered with his other pleasures," Bertie said with a chuckle.

"Yes," the marquess said. "They were well known."

"Though why he would want to get into the muslin company when he had such a looker for a wife eludes my understanding," Bertie said. "She is well rid of him if you were to ask me."

"To be uncharitable," the marquess said, "I would have to say that perhaps the world is well rid of him."

"She don't go about much, by all accounts," Bertie said. "It was unfortunate that you ran into her at Clancy's. Especially since you don't go about much yourself." He laughed heartily.

"Yes," Lord Denbigh said.

"She is a model mother, according to Freeman," Bertie said. "Cannot be pried from her children and all that. Walks them in the park every afternoon despite the weather. That would certainly not suit Freeman." He chuckled again. "At least you can be warned about that, Denbigh, and avoid the place."

"Yes," the marquess said, dropping his quizzing glass on its black ribbon. "Though ancient history, as I said before, does not excite me."

"Well," Bertie said, getting to his feet, "I never could understand why she dropped you for Easton, Denbigh. Most females would kill for a chance at you. Maybe money and titles and all that did not interest the chit. And Easton was a handsome devil, one must admit. I have to fetch my mother from my aunt's. She will shoot me with a dueling pistol if I am late.''

The marquess inclined his head and watched Bertie leave the room. Then he consulted his watch. Scarcely past luncheon time. At what time during the afternoons? he wondered. Early or late? He supposed that the only way he would find out was to ride to the park himself both early and late. He got to his feet.

He was fortunate enough not to have to ride there for longer than an hour. Obviously, early afternoon was the time for their walk. Four of them. Judith Easton herself, the two children, who both resembled Easton to a remarkable degree, and the little bird of a woman who was introduced to him as Easton's sister.

He rode away after giving each of the children a brief ride, well satisfied with the encounter. He knew now for certain that she was indeed planning to attend the Mumford ball. And he knew something else, too, something about her children and something about her sister-in-law.

And something about her, too. Clearly, her children were everything in the world to her.

Perhaps he could make something of those facts. The desire for revenge had burned in him with increased fervor since he had seen her again at Nora's.

Since the park was empty at that time of the day and of the year, he increased his horse's speed to a canter. Fortunately, he would not have to sit around any longer, wondering how he was to come upon her again. He would see her again that evening.

He could scarcely wait for the hours to pass.

The Mumford ball was not what might be called a great squeeze—not of the kind, anyway, that Judith had known in her come-out Season. But then, as Lady Mumford explained to her almost apologetically before the dancing began, it was the wrong time of year for grand *ton* events. Even those people who spent the winter in town were beginning to take themselves off for Christmas parties in the country.

Judith did not lament the lack of crowds. There were quite enough guests present to make it a pleasant occasion. Claude led her into the opening quadrille, and Lord Clancy was waiting to dance with her the set of country dances that followed.

And he was not there, she thought with some relief as the second set began. The Marquess of Denbigh was not there. Perhaps it was as well that Amy had mentioned her own plans in his hearing that afternoon, though she had been alarmed at the time. If he had intended to come, surely he would have changed his mind after that.

But her early pleasure in the evening dissipated halfway through the second set while she was laughing at something Lord Clancy said as he twirled her down the set.

He was standing alone in the doorway of the ballroom, dressed in black evening clothes and immaculately white linen and lace. He was the only gentleman clad in black. He looked more than ever like a hawk or some other bird of prey.

He would be as intent on ignoring her, she told herself as another gentleman twirled her back down the set, as she would be on ignoring him. She was not going to let him spoil her evening. She looked very deliberately across the ballroom at him just to prove her theory to herself.

He was staring back, his eyes hooded and intent.

She whisked her eyes away from him and made some remark to Lord Clancy and smiled broadly at him. And she kept her attention on the dance for all of five more minutes without giving in to the urge to look back to the doorway.

He would have moved away from there, she persuaded herself at last. He would have found a group of people with whom to converse. She turned her head to look.

He stood in exactly the same place. And he was still looking steadily at her.

By the time the set came to an end almost ten minutes later, Judith felt quite unnerved. She could not walk without feeling that her movements were jerky. She could not smile without feeling as if she were behaving artificially. She could not laugh without hearing the trill of her own voice. And she could not talk without losing the trend of her own words or listen without suddenly realizing that she was not hearing a word.

And each time she turned her head, sometimes deliberately, sometimes under the pretense of looking elsewhere close by, he was standing in the same place. Lady Mumford joined him there, but still he looked quite steadily at her, Judith found.

She had not realized that the ballroom was quite so hot and stuffy.

3

She was wearing an apricot-colored gown of simple but elegant design. It was neither too low nor too high at the bosom, and it was fashionably high-waisted, falling in soft folds to the scalloped hemline. She wore white lace gloves and white slippers. Her hair was dressed as it had been at the soirée.

She looked beautiful, as she had looked in the park that afternoon with reddened cheeks and nose and hair somewhat windblown beneath her bonnet.

The Marquess of Denbigh stood in the doorway of Lord Mumford's ballroom looking at her. If she had been grief-stricken at the death of her husband, then she had recovered her spirits in the year since. She was laughing quite merrily.

He watched her until he knew she was aware of his presence. And then he continued to watch her, knowing that his gaze would disconcert her. He knew that even when she was not darting glances at him she was aware of his steady scrutiny. And he knew that when she looked at people or objects close to him, smiling in apparent enjoyment of the evening, she was really seeing him out of the corner of her eye. He knew that when she looked full at him it was in the hope that his attention had been taken by someone or something else.

He watched her even when he knew that other people must be noticing the focus of his attention and even when Lady Mumford came to speak with him to apologize for the fact that she and Mumford had not been at the door to greet him. He knew he was late, he explained to her. He did not expect them to stand at the door all evening merely in order to greet latecomers.

Finally, after he had stood in the doorway for well over half an hour, a set ended and Judith Easton joined a group

of guests and deliberately turned her back on him. It was
a very straight back. If she was uncomfortable—and he knew
very well that she was—then she was going to do nothing
outwardly to show it.

She had always had that control over her emotions even
as a girl. Unfortunately, at that time he had mistaken control
for sweetness and shyness.

He strolled toward her. Nothing in her posture suggested
that she knew he had moved from his position in the doorway.
But as he approached another lady said something to her and
she turned her head sharply just as he came up to her. He
nodded a greeting to the whole group and turned to her.

"Mrs. Easton," he said, "will you do me the honor of
waltzing with me?"

She inhaled visibly as she lifted her eyes to him.

"Oh, I say," said a florid-faced gentleman with whom
the marquess was not acquainted, "I was just about to ask
you myself, ma'am."

"Thank you," she said, ignoring the florid-faced gentleman, seeming in fact not even to have heard him. She stepped
away from the group. He felt himself also inhaling slowly
when the music started and he touched her for the first time
in almost eight years. Her waist was still small and supple
beneath the folds of her gown—even after two children. Her
hand was still slim and soft. She wore the same perfume.
He could not identify it, but he knew instantly that he had
not smelled it since he had last been close to her. Long eye-
lashes, darker than her hair, still fanned her cheeks.

He had never waltzed with her before. The waltz had come
into fashion since their betrothal. But she danced it as well
and as daintily as she had used to dance the quadrille or the
minuet.

She looked up to his chin. "I want to thank you for letting
my children ride your horse this afternoon, my lord," she
said. "You gave them a great deal of pleasure."

"I am fond of children," he said, and watched her raise
her eyes briefly to his.

Perhaps she did not believe him. Probably she did not.
And of course he had not been motivated chiefly by his love

for children that afternoon, though he had liked the boy's enthusiasm and the girl's quiet trust.

What had he done wrong? he wondered as he had wondered hundreds—thousands—of times years before. Why had she preferred Easton to him? He had had the rank and the wealth and the prospects. It was true that Easton had been good-looking and charming with the ladies. But the man had also had a reputation as something of a rake.

Probably that had been it, he had concluded long ago. Perhaps it had been the eternal attraction of the rake. He on the other hand had always behaved toward her with perfect decorum and restraint. Perhaps she would have liked him better if he had displayed his feelings on occasion. But he had thought a display of feelings inappropriate before their wedding night. A night that had never come. Besides, he had never been easy with women of his own class.

"You are planning to make London your home?" he asked.

"For a while," she said.

"You are joining your husband's family for Christmas?" he asked.

She hesitated. "No," she said. "We are going to be quiet here alone for a change. My parents went to Millicent's in Scotland, but I decided that my daughter is too young for the lengthy journey. We are not going to stay with Andrew's family this year."

"Ah," he said. "London can be sparsely populated and a little lonely at Christmas."

"I have two young children and a sister-in-law," she said. "We will not be lonely."

That was the end of their conversation. He had found out what he wanted to know, and he had no wish to entertain her. He watched her as they waltzed, not taking his eyes from her face, totally unconcerned by the attention he must be drawing from the other guests—or by the embarrassment he must be causing her.

She remained calm, though he could feel a certain tightening of muscles beneath his hand at her waist.

Had she ever regretted jilting him? he wondered. Once

the stars had faded from her eyes and she had realized—as she surely must have done—what kind of man she had married, had she remained in love with him, loyal to the feelings that had sent her running guiltily to his arms?

Or did she sometimes regret the man she had wronged? He supposed the answer depended upon whether she had been hostile to him or merely indifferent. Perhaps she had been hostile. Having grown up in a womanless home, he had never learned that easy charm with women that seemed to come so easily to other men. Perhaps she had actively disliked him. Perhaps she had never for one moment regretted her decision. His jaw tightened and his lips thinned.

Toward the end of the waltz he thought that she would open the conversation again. She drew breath and looked up resolutely into his eyes. But whatever words she planned to say were not spoken after all. She let out the breath through her mouth and continued to look into his eyes as he gazed steadily back. And finally her own wavered and fell.

He felt almost like laughing. But it was far too early to gloat. His revenge had scarcely begun yet.

"Thank you, my lord," she said, smiling at his chin when he returned her to her group at the end of the set. "That was pleasant."

"The pleasure was mine, ma'am," he said, bowing to her as she lifted her hand from his arm.

And he sought out Lady Mumford, complimented her on the success of her ball, bade her good night, and left the house.

Judith awoke the following morning when a little figure climbed onto her bed carefully so as not to wake her, and burrowed beneath the bedclothes beside her.

"Mm," she said, reaching out a hand and ruffling auburn curls, "am I being an old sleepyhead?"

"Yes," Kate said. "Aunt Amy is painting with Rupert and Nurse is busy, and I escaped."

Judith chuckled. "Did you?" she said. "Have I slept the whole morning away?"

"Did you have fun, Mama?" the child asked.

Judith laughed again and swung her legs over the side of the bed. She sat up and stretched. Goodness, someone had been in and built up the fire without her even knowing.

"I had lots of fun," she said. "I danced all night until I thought I must have blisters on every toe." She turned and tucked the blankets under Kate's chin. "Are you going to have a sleep?" she asked. "Shh."

Kate chuckled and kicked the blankets away. She bounded to her feet and scrambled off the bed. "We are going to the river tomorrow," she said. "Aunt Amy said so. We can walk on it, Mama. It is all over ice." And she was gone from the room.

Judith smiled and noted that the water in the pitcher on the washstand was warm. She must have been very deeply asleep. She supposed it was not surprising. She had still been awake when daylight broke and had quite resigned herself to a completely sleepless night. But as so often happens on such occasions, she had fallen asleep with the coming of day.

She had had fun indeed, she thought, her hand pausing as it poured water into the china basin. Fun! She could not recall a worse disaster of an evening.

Except that that was a ridiculous assessment. Claude had been attentive without being annoyingly so. She had mingled with ease and renewed some old acquaintances and made some new. She had danced every set except the one she had sat out with Colonel Hyde. It had been a wonderful evening. She had always loved dancing more than any other social activity.

And yet when she had come home and lain down, humming to herself, determined to remember only the gaiety and the successes, it had been he she had seen as soon as she closed her eyes. The Marquess of Denbigh, standing motionless and dark in the doorway of the ballroom for what had seemed hours and for what had probably been close to one—staring at her with that harsh angular face and those hooded gray eyes.

Why? Was he so outraged at her return to town and his domain? Was he trying to make her so uncomfortable that she would leave for the country without further delay? He had been trying to make her uncomfortable, she was convinced. She could not subscribe to Mrs. Summerberry's assessment.

"Mrs. Easton," that lady had said, tapping her on the arm with her fan after he had left the ballroom not to return, "I do believe the marquess is still wearing the willow for you. Is there a chance that romance will blossom after all?"

Unfortunately, there had been other listeners, all of whom had turned interested eyes on Judith.

"Wearing the willow?" she had said with a laugh. "He never did. It was an arranged match, you know, and a mistake from the start. His feelings were no more engaged than mine. I believe he was just being civil dancing with me this evening, showing everyone that the past is in the past. And romance? I have experienced it once in my life and am now long past the age of such silliness."

But he was not being civil. She had lied when she said that. She knew that he was being anything but civil. Apart from those few words they had exchanged at the very start, he had made no attempt whatsoever to make conversation, and she had been feeling too tense to do so. And yet he had not taken his eyes off her. She had known it though for most of the time she had not had the courage to look up into his eyes.

Had he been gazing at her because he was wearing the willow for her, as Mrs. Summerberry had put it? No. She knew the answer was no. There had been a deliberate intent to embarrass her, to discompose her.

He had almost succeeded. She had almost cracked at the end and had looked up at him, determined to confront him, to demand an explanation of his behavior. But she had looked into his eyes, those keen gray eyes over which his eyelids drooped incongruously, giving an impression of sleepiness to an expression that was far from sleepy, and she had lost her nerve.

She had suddenly been even more intensely aware than she had been since the start of the waltz of his physical presence, of his great height and that impression of strength in his lean body that she was sure was no illusion, of some force—some quite unnameable force—that terrified her now even more than it had used to do.

For whereas eight years before she had considered him cold and unfeeling and had been afraid of being trapped in a marriage with a man she feared, now she could sense a very real animosity in him and felt like a weak victim being stalked by a bird of prey.

It was a foolish idea, a ridiculous idea. And yet, she thought as she rubbed a cloth hard over her face and neck, it had haunted her through what had remained of the night after she had arrived home. It had kept her from sleep.

At luncheon, which she and Amy took with the children, Judith announced that they would walk to St. James's Park that afternoon for a change.

"And the river tomorrow," she said. "We will see if it is safe to walk upon."

Judith was feeling pleased with herself when they arrived back from their walk in St. James's. She could not be at all sure, of course, that the Marquess of Denbigh had ridden in Hyde Park that day, but if he had—and she had a strange feeling that he had—then he would have been foiled. He would have taken a lone and chilly ride for nothing.

She hoped that he had ridden there. Perhaps he would have realized by now that she could not so easily be made his victim.

And it was strange, she thought, repairing the damage made to her hair by her bonnet before going downstairs to the drawing room for tea, how she was assuming that the meeting in the park the afternoon before had been no accident. But how could it not have been? How could he have known?

The thought made her shiver. It was time for tea.

"We must buy some holly and ivy and other greenery," Amy was saying to the children, who were also in the drawing room for tea, as had been their custom since arriving in town. "And how dreadful to be talking about buying when they have always been there for the gathering in the country.

But never mind. And we will need some bows and bells and other decorations.''

"We are going to buy them?" Rupert asked.

Amy frowned. "We must make as many as possible," she said. "It will be far more fun. There are boxes and boxes of decorations at Ammanlea. Here we must begin with nothing. But it will be fun, I promise you children. Perhaps we can even make a Nativity scene somehow." She smiled brightly.

"Perhaps after we have been down to the river tomorrow," Judith said, "we can go shopping and buy some length of ribbon to start making the bows and streamers. Shall we, Kate?"

The child's eyes grew round with wonder.

"I still think Christmas is going to be dull with no one else to play with," Rupert said dubiously.

Judith smiled determinedly. "We will play with one another," she said. "And there will be so many good things to eat and only the four of us to eat them that we will all burst and never be able to play again."

"We must sing carols while we make the decorations," Amy said. "I wonder if we could go carol singing about the square, Judith. Do you think the people here would think we had quite lost our senses? I will miss going caroling more than anything else."

Amy had a sweet voice and was always the most valued member of the carolers who traveled about the neighborhood at Ammanlea every Christmas. She would be missed that year.

"Perhaps," Judith said, but was interrupted by the appearance of her father's butler, who had come into the room to announce the arrival of a gentleman below asking if he might call upon Mrs. Easton and Miss Easton.

"Upon me too?" Amy said, brightening.

"The Marquess of Denbigh, ma'am," the butler said, inclining his head stiffly.

"We are from home," Judith said.

"Oh, famous," Rupert said, jumping to his feet. "Perhaps he has come to give me another ride, Mama."

"Riding," Kate said, clapping her hands.

"Oh, how very civil of him," Amy said. "Do show him up." But she flushed and looked at her sister-in-law. "I am sorry. Judith?"

Judith felt rather as if someone had punched her in the ribs. "He is calling on both of us?" she asked. "Then please show him up, Mr. Barta."

"Famous," Rupert said. "I think he is top of the trees, Mama."

Another of Maurice's phrases.

Kate moved from her chair to sit on the stool at Judith's feet. Judith stood.

"Good afternoon, my lord," she said, clasping her hands before her when he entered the room.

Amy swept him a deep curtsy and beamed at him. "How very civil of you to call, my lord," she said. "It is quite as cold outside today as it was yesterday, is it not?"

"It is indeed, ma'am," he said. "But I am afraid I played coward today and called out my carriage."

"Good afternoon, my lord," Rupert said.

Kate half hid behind Judith's skirt.

"Ah, the children are here too," the marquess said. "And good day to you, sir, and to the young lady who believes that she is invisible although I can clearly see two large eyes and some auburn curls."

Kate chuckled and hid completely behind Judith.

"Won't you be seated, my lord?" Judith said coolly. "The tea tray arrived a mere few minutes before you. I have not even poured yet."

"Then my timing is perfect," he said, seating himself as Amy resumed her place. "I came to assure myself that you have recovered from the exertions of last night's ball, ma'am."

"Yes, I thank you," Judith said. "It was a very pleasant evening."

He looked penetratingly at her while she looked coolly back. She scorned to lower her eyes in her own drawing room.

"And to assure myself that you took no chill from your

walk in the park yesterday, ma'am," he said, turning his attention to Amy.

"Oh, no," Amy said. "We walk every day, you know. And it is my opinion that it is fresh air and exercise that keeps a person healthy and free of chills. Huddling by a fire all day and every day is a quite unhealthy practice."

"My feelings exactly, ma'am," he said. "But sometimes it is very hard to resist the temptation to keep oneself warm and cozy."

"It is a hard winter we are having so far," Amy said. "My only hope is that the snow will not come to prevent travel before Christmas. There will be many disappointed families, I am afraid, if their members cannot journey to be together."

"Yes, indeed," he said. "I have some guests coming to my home in Sussex for the holiday. I do not have any close family, but even so I will be hoping that both my guests and I will be able to travel. Loneliness is always hardest at Christmas for some reason."

"Yes," Amy said. "I remember . . ."

And to Judith's amazement they were off on a comfortable and lengthy coze, the two of them, ignoring her just as if she did not exist. And his manner with Amy was easy and pleasant, though of course he came nowhere near smiling.

She was angry. And even more so when Rupert, his cake eaten, got to his feet and went to stand patiently beside the marquess's chair, waiting to be noticed. She tried to frown him back to his own place, but he did not look her way.

"And how are you today, sir?" the marquess asked eventually, he and Amy having finally come to a full agreement about the undesirability of being alone at Christmas.

"My grandpapa keeps the largest stable in Lincolnshire," Rupert said gravely. "And the largest kennels too. My papa would have taught me to ride but he died before I was old enough. Uncle Maurice was too busy last summer, but he will teach me when he has time. I am going to be a bruising rider."

The marquess set a hand on the boy's shoulder while Judith unconsciously held her breath. "I have no doubt of it," he said. "You sat Pegasus quite fearlessly yesterday."

Rupert almost visibly swelled with pride.

"I was not afraid either," an indignant little voice said from the stool at Judith's feet.

He looked across the room, his eyes touching on Judith for the first time for many minutes before dropping to Kate.

"I don't believe," he said, "I have ever seen a lady sit a horse with such quiet dignity."

Judith could not see Kate's reaction to his words. The child said nothing, but Amy was beaming down at her.

Everyone was having a perfectly amicable good time, she thought, controlling her anger and sipping on her tea. And if she had been furious the evening before at the way he had gazed so fixedly at her for an hour or longer, now she was indignant at the way he had so effectively ignored her almost from the moment of his entrance into her father's drawing room—*her* drawing room in her father's absence.

And what was his game? She could not believe this was the purely social call that it appeared to be.

No sooner had she had the thought than she discovered the answer—or doubtless a part of the answer, anyway.

"The ice is very firm on the Thames," he told Amy and the children. "Booths and tents are being moved out there constantly so that the river between the Blackfriar's Bridge and London Bridge is almost like a new busy thoroughfare. By tomorrow the fair will be in full swing, I am sure."

"Oh, famous!" Rupert yelled. "We are going there tomorrow."

"Yes," the marquess said. "I remember Miss Easton's saying so yesterday. And the thought occurred to me, sir, that you would have your hands very full indeed escorting three ladies to what will be a busy and perhaps rough celebration without some assistance from another gentleman. I have come to put my carriage and my person at everyone's disposal for tomorrow afternoon."

Judith felt herself turn cold despite the fact that the fire was roaring cheerfully in the fireplace.

"Famous!" Rupert said.

"How very civil of you indeed, my lord," Amy said. "And you are quite right, of course. It would not be at all

the thing for Judith and me to go there with the children and
no gentleman to escort us. I daresay there will be people of
all classes there and some rogues and pickpockets too. We
are very obliged to you, I am sure. Are we not, Judith?''

Judith found herself finally being regarded steadily from
those eyes, which were coming to unnerve her more than
she cared to admit.

"Yes," she said. "You are very kind, my lord."

His eyes remained on her until they dropped to Kate, who
had suddenly appeared, standing before his knees.

"We are going to buy ribbons," she told him. "For
Christmas bows. Mama said."

"Are you?" he said. "Perhaps we will find some at the
fair tomorrow. Yards and yards of ribbon and all colors of
the rainbow, especially red and green for Christmas."

Kate returned solemnly to her stool.

The marquess stood up. "That is settled, then," he said.
"I shall call for you ladies and gentleman after luncheon?"

"Thank you," Judith said, also rising to her feet.

"We will look forward to it immensely," Amy said. "It
is very civil of you to think of us and our safety, my lord."

Everyone spoke at once after the marquess had left. The
children were excited by the renewed certainty that they
would indeed be going to the river the following day and
by the fact that a gentleman was to take them there. Amy
was quite ecstatic.

"I must confess," she said, "that I had not really
considered the dangers of our going there alone, Judith. But
now we do not have to worrry at all, for I am sure that his
lordship would only have to level a look at any impertinent
fellow for him to melt into the ice. I shall feel quite perfectly
safe with him and I shall feel that you and the children will
be safe too."

"I cannot like it," Judith said. "He is a stranger to us
and has no obligation at all to put his time so much at our
disposal."

Amy beamed at her. "I do not know what happened all
those years ago," she said, "and I certainly cannot say I
am sorry that you chose Andrew, Judith. I would not have

known you else and the children would not exist. But I can see that his lordship is going out of his way to win your favor again. And he is such a splendid and such a very civil gentleman."

"Upstairs, children," Judith said briskly, turning to pull the bell rope to have the tea tray removed. "Nurse will be waiting for you. Amy, you have mistaken his motives quite. He has no interest in me, you know. Why, he did not even speak with me at tea. It is quite as likely that his interest is in you. You must be very close to him in age, after all."

Amy laughed as the children left the room. "What a thoroughly nonsensical idea," she said. "It was perfectly obvious that he had nothing but a purely friendly interest in me, Judith. And I would have to say that age is the only thing the Marquess of Denbigh and I have in common. No, it is you with whom he is trying to fix his interest, mark my words."

"Amy." Judith covered her mouth with her hands. "Don't say so. Please don't say so. He makes my flesh creep."

Her sister-in-law looked at her in amazement. "Oh, no, Judith," she said. "Surely not. He is such a splendid man. But how insensitive I am being. It has been only a little longer than a year since Andrew passed away, has it not? Of course it is a little early for you to think of any other gentleman in that way. But never fear. The marquess is perfectly amiable and civil. He will not press unwelcome attentions on you, I am sure."

Amy had given up hope of matrimonial contentment for herself, but she loved to see those she cared for happy. And she cared for Judith more than for either of her other two sisters-in-law. Judith had not had a good marriage, Amy knew, but she had always remained true to it. She had made Andrew a good wife, and she was a good mother—and a good sister-in-law too. Amy could imagine no greater happiness than seeing Judith well wed. Though of course, she thought a little sadly, when Judith remarried, then she would have to return to Ammanlea.

Judith used the excuse of the removal of the tray to leave the room herself in order to return to her own room.

He was stalking his prey. She could feel it. And he was clever enough to get to her through her unsuspecting sister-in-law and children.

Because after eight years he wanted her back? Because he wanted to fix his interest with her, as Amy seemed to think?

No, not that. There was a certain expression in his eyes when he looked at her. He was not stalking her out of any soft sentiments, of that she was sure. But why, then? Punishment? Had she so wounded his pride and sense of consequence that she must be punished even eight years after the fact?

It must be that, she thought. She had made him feel and look foolish all those years ago. Now she must be punished.

She wondered with some fear and some anger what constituted punishment as far as the Marquess of Denbigh was concerned. Only what she had suffered so far, but at greater length? Embarrassment? Discomfort? Enforced hours in his company?

Or was there something else?

She shivered and despised herself for feeling fear.

4

He liked her children. He supposed that it might have been easier if he had not done so, and he had not particularly expected to do so since they were hers—and Easton's. But then in many ways it was not surprising. He had something of a weakness for children.

He liked the sister-in-law too. She was unfortunately plain, with several pockmarks marring her complexion, and she was unusually small. He guessed that she was about his own age, well past the age of marriage for a woman. But there was an amiability about her and a kindness that he sensed. It was a pity that such women were so often denied the fulfillment of husbands and families.

Her friendliness, of course, and that of the children—even the little one could not maintain her shyness when there was something important to be said—could only make his task easier. It would all depend, he supposed, on the amount of power Judith Easton held over them and how well she liked to use that power even against their wishes. Her behavior of the afternoon before had suggested that making them happy was important to her. She had put up no fight against the proposed outing.

The Marquess of Denbigh rode out to the river and across the Blackfriar's Bridge during the morning. The icy fog that had gripped the city earlier was lifting and there was a magical, almost fairytale quality to the view below him on the river. Booths and tents were lined up in close and orderly formation on either side with a wide avenue of roughened ice between. Hawkers were loudly advertising their wares. Shoppers, sightseers, and the curious were wandering from stall to stall. There was a tantalizing aroma of cooking food wafting up to him.

It would do, he thought. He was fortunate that the rare

occurrence of the Thames freezing over had happened at such
an opportune time. He turned his horse's head for home
again.

By the afternoon the fog had lifted right away and the sun
was even trying, though not quite succeeding, to break
through the high cloud cover. There was no significant wind.
It was still cold, but pleasant for an outing. And the Eastons
liked daily outings.

They were all ready to leave when he arrived, and came
downstairs to the hallway without delay. The boy was openly
excited. The little girl clung to her mother's cloak and smiled
shyly at him from behind one of its folds until he looked at
her. Then she disappeared altogether.

He bowed to them and bade them a good afternoon.

"The air is crisp," he said. "But you are all dressed
warmly, I see. And there are warm foods and drinks down
on the river, I have heard, and even a fire where meat is
being roasted. I could smell it this morning."

"A fire on the ice?" Amy asked in amazement. "Will it
not all melt?"

"Apparently not, ma'am," he said. "The ice is very thick
indeed."

"Amazing!" she said.

He handed them into his carriage, lifting the little girl and
setting her on her mother's knee. The boy scrambled in
without assistance. Judith Easton had not said a word beyond
the initial greeting and sat quietly and calmly smoothing her
daughter's cloak over her knees.

"From my observations this morning," the marquess said,
seating himself opposite Judith, his knees almost touching
hers, and addressing his words to Amy, "it is quite a festive
scene. The sort of excitement such an occasion en-
genders can also serve to make one quite unaware of the
cold."

"To be quite honest," Amy said, "I would prefer extreme
cold to extreme heat if I had to make a choice. Very hot
summer days can quite sap one of energy."

The two of them carried on an amicable conversation
during the journey while Kate stared wide-eyed from one

to the other of them and Rupert sat with his face pressed to the window, watching what passed outside.

"Oh," he said eventually, stabbing a finger against the pane, "there, Mama. There, sir, do you see? Look, Aunt Amy."

And then they were all leaning toward the one window, gazing down from the bridge at London's newest street.

"May we get down?" Rupert demanded. "Oh, just wait until Uncle Maurice hears about this."

"We may," the marquess said. He looked across at Judith for the first time. The moss green of her bonnet and velvet cloak became her well, he thought. "Shall I instruct my coachman to return in two hours' time, ma'am?"

"As you wish," she said.

Two hours should be long enough for a start, he thought. He must not be impatient.

But the time passed quickly. There were vendors of everything one might want to buy from lace to boots, from books to smelling salts. And hawkers to persuade a person that he needed an item he had never felt a need of before. There were the tempting aromas of roasted lamb and pork pies and tarts and chestnuts and the less tempting one of cheap ale. And there were fortune-tellers and portrait painters and card playing booths and skittle alleys. There was everything one could possibly imagine for the entertainment of all.

Amy was enjoying herself. She was in London and at the very heart of its life and activity. And she was not alone but with her sister-in-law and nephew and niece. And they had the escort of a handsome gentleman. She felt more light-hearted than she had felt for years.

"I am going to have my fortune told," she announced recklessly when they came to the fortune-teller's booth.

Judith smiled at her.

"There can be nothing but good ahead for you, ma'am," the marquess said gallantly.

Amy stepped inside the dark tent and gazed about, fascinated. Oh, she had always loved fairs, though more often than not after her early girlhood she had been refused permission to go.

She sat down before the gaudy, veiled figure of the fortune-teller with her crystal ball and waited expectantly, feeling like a hopeful girl again and smiling inwardly at the thought.

But she was feeling disappointed a minute later—the fortune-teller must have mistaken her age, she thought—but only a little disappointed. She was in the land of make-believe and she refused to allow reality to intrude too chillingly.

Romance, the fortune-teller had predicted. With a gentleman she had not met yet but would meet soon. And children —lots of them. That was the detail that was most disappointing, since it was so obviously the most impossible.

But no matter. She would dream of her gentleman in the coming days and laugh herself out of melancholy when he failed to put in an appearance in her life. There was a whole fair waiting to be enjoyed outside the tent.

"Thank you," she said formally, getting to her feet.

"How very foolish," she said, laughing and blushing when she rejoined the others. "I am to find love and romance soon, it seems, with a gentleman I have never before set my eyes on, and am to live happily ever after. I wonder if she ever says anything different to any lady who is unmarried. One would, after all, feel that one had wasted one's money if one were told that there were only misery and loneliness ahead." She said nothing about the many children.

"Perhaps we should put the matter to the test," the marquess said. "Mrs. Easton must have her fortune told too."

"I have no wish to waste money on such nonsense," Judith said.

"Then I shall waste it for you," he said. "Come, we must find what delights life has in store for you."

"Yes, Mama," Rupert said, jumping up and down on the spot. "Go on."

"Go, Mama," Kate said.

She looked rather as if she were going to her own execution, the marquess thought, but she went. He in the meanwhile swung Rupert up onto his shoulders when the boy complained that he could not see for the crowds.

"You were quite right, Amy," Judith said when she came out of the tent. "My own fortune was remarkably similar to yours. As if I am looking for love and romance at this stage of my life!" Her tone was scornful.

"And what is he to look like?" Amy asked.

"Oh, tall, dark, and handsome, of course," Judith said, flushing. "What else?"

"Well, there our fortunes differ," Amy said. "Now it is your turn, my lord."

"It would be interesting, would it not?" he said. "I wonder how many tall, dark, and handsome ladies there are in England?"

Amy laughed.

"Down you go, then, my lad," the marquess said, setting Rupert down on the ice again. "I shall take you up again when I come out."

"I see much darkness in your life," the fortune-teller told him a few moments later. "And a great deal of light too. A great deal of light. But the darkness threatens it."

Lord Denbigh had never been to a fortune-teller before. He supposed that there were a few fortunes to be told and that each listener could be relied upon to twist the words to suit his own case. One merely had to be clever with vague generalities. He was amused.

"Ah," the fortune-teller said, "but Christmas may save you if you keep in mind that it is a time of peace and goodwill. I see a great battle raging in your soul between light and darkness. But the joy of Christmas will help the light to banish the darkness—if you do not fight too strongly against it."

Well. That was it? Nothing about romance and love and marriage and happily-ever-afters? That was to be reserved exclusively for the female customers? He rose and nodded to the fortune-teller. It would be a kindness to tell her, perhaps, that if all her women customers were to find the romance she promised them, then men should be alerted to their needs.

"Nothing," he said to the ladies when he went outside

again. "There is to be no romance in my future, alas. Only the promise of a happy Christmas if I do not do something to spoil the occasion."

"Ah," Amy said. "How disappointing, my lord. But I am glad that you can expect a good Christmas."

He leaned down and swung Rupert up onto his shoulders again. Judith watched him, her lips tightening.

The marquess bought the children each a tart and all of them a hot drink of chocolate. And when Kate spotted a stall that sold ribbons, he bought her long lengths of green and red over Judith's protests and Amy's exclamations on his kindness.

"It amazes me," Amy said when they paused to watch the portrait painter draw his likenesses, "how he can hold the charcoal and wield it so skillfully without freezing his fingers off. But the portraits are quite well done."

"Have your picture drawn with your good lady, guv'nor?" the artist's assistant asked, looking from the marquess to Judith. "And with the lovely children too, if you want, guv. 'Alf a sovereign for all four of you."

"No, thank you," Judith said quickly.

Rupert shouted with glee from his perch on the marquess's shoulders. "He is not our father," he exclaimed to the assistant.

Kate was tugging at Judith's cloak.

"Mama," she said when Judith looked down, "may I have my picture?"

"Your portrait done?" Judith said, smiling down at her and passing a hand beneath her chin. "You would have to sit very still and would get very cold."

"No longer than five minutes, mum," the assistant assured her briskly. "The child's likeness in five minutes, satisfaction guaranteed or your money back. Two and sixpence for the child, mum."

"A shilling," the marquess said. "One and sixpence if it is a good likeness."

"Done, guv," the assistant said. "And worth two shillings it will be if it's worth a penny. Let the little lady take a chair."

Kate smiled wonderingly up at the marquess and her mother and aunt and allowed Judith to seat her on the chair indicated. And she sat very still, her feet dangling a few inches above the ice, her hands clasped in her lap, only her eyes moving.

"How sweet she looks," Amy said. "Would you like to be next, Rupert?"

"Pooh," the boy said. "I don't want to sit for my picture." But he did squirm to be set down so that he could walk around to the side of the artist and watch the progress of the portrait.

Judith wandered to a book stall a few feet away after a couple of minutes. But she was not to be allowed to browse in peace. A man with one arm outstretched and draped from shoulder to wrist in necklaces of varying degrees of gaudiness accosted her and tried to interest her in his wares. Another man came up on her other side with a tray of bangles.

The marquess watched her laugh and shake her head, looking from one to the other. They moved in closer on either side of her, pressing their wares on her. Her reticule dangled from her right arm.

He walked toward her and set one hand lightly against the back of her neck. "You are not considering buying more baubles, are you, my love?" he asked, at the same time picking up her reticule and tucking it into the crook of her arm.

She looked around at him, her eyes wide and startled.

"These pearls for the lidy, guv?" the necklace seller asked. "Real pearls wiv a real diamond clasp? A bargain they are today, guv."

"I am sure they are," the marquess said. "Unfortunately the lady already has three different strings of pearls." He held up a staying hand. "And all the other jewels she could possibly wear in a lifetime."

The bangle seller had already faded away.

"You're missin' the bargain of a lifetime, guv," the hawker said, and he turned and made his way to a group of three ladies who had stopped nearby.

The marquess removed his hand from Judith's neck.

"That was one reason why you needed a male escort," he said.

"They were harmlessly trying to sell their wares," she said stiffly. "I did not need your interference, my lord."

"You would have been easy prey," he said. "They would not even have had to draw attention to themselves by racing off with your reticule. The bangle seller was lifting it so skillfully off your arm that you probably would not even have missed it until they had disappeared among the crowds."

She looked down at the reticule she now held against her side. "That is ridiculous," she said. "They were merely selling their wares."

"They were merely thieving," he said. "However, since no harm has been done, I suppose it does not matter if you do not believe me. But do be careful. This type of scene is a pickpocket's heaven."

"He was really about to steal my reticule?" she asked, frowning.

"As surely as the clasp on that pearl necklace was glass," he said.

She was looking directly into his eyes. He had never quite been able to put a name to the color of her eyes. They were not exactly green, not exactly gray. They were certainly not blue—not altogether so, anyway. But they were bright and beautiful eyes, the colored circle outlined by a dark line, almost as if it had been drawn in with a fine pen. He had once fancied it possible to drown in her eyes.

"Thank you," she said. She did not smile. He knew that it had taken her a great effort to acknowledge her gratitude. She turned abruptly to the portrait painter's booth.

The portrait was finished and Kate was holding it in her hands and gazing at it wide-eyed. Her aunt was exclaiming in delight over it while Rupert regarded it critically, head to one side.

"Look, Mama." Kate held out the portrait for her mother's inspection. Judith took it and the marquess looked at it over her shoulder. A little girl sat stiffly on a chair, her feet dangling in space, her hands in her lap. Two large dark eyes peeped from beneath the poke of a bonnet. It could have been any child anywhere.

"Oh, lovely," Judith said. "I will have to find a frame for it at home and hang it in my bedchamber. How clever of you to sit still all that time, Kate."

The marquess paid the assistant one shilling and sixpence. Kate was pulling on the tassel of one of his Hessian boots as he put his purse away in a safe inside pocket.

"Yes, ma'am?" he said, looking down at her.

She pointed upward and smiled at him. He stooped down closer to her.

"Ride up there," she said.

She weighed no more than a feather. He swung her up onto one shoulder and wrapped an arm firmly about her. She put one arm about his head beneath his beaver hat and spread her palm over his ear. And she sat very still and quiet.

It was his one regret. No, perhaps not the only one. But it was one regret of his life that he had not had children of his own. He had dreamed of it once, of course. When he was twenty-six years old he had been very eager to marry and begin his family. He had hoped that Judith would want several children. He had suffered too much loneliness himself from being an only child.

He should, he supposed, have shaken off his disappointment and his heartache more firmly and chosen again. He might still have found contentment with another woman and he might certainly have had his family.

But it seemed too late now at the age of thirty-four to begin the process of finding a woman with whom he might be compatible. He had loved once, and the experience seemed to have sapped all his desire to search for love again.

Rupert was holding his free hand, he realized suddenly, and telling him in his piping voice how he would skate like the wind if he only had skates with him. Faster than the wind. He would skate so fast that no one would even see him.

Judith walked to his side, her eyes on her children, almost as if she believed that he would disappear with them if she relaxed her vigil for one moment. Amy walked at his other side, still gazing about her with bright interest.

"I'm cold," Kate announced suddenly.

They were strolling back toward the bridge where the carriage was to meet them, and the slight movement of air was against their faces.

"It is chilly," Amy agreed, "though you were quite right in what you said earlier, my lord. The excitement of the occasion makes one almost forget that it is a cold winter's day."

"We will warm ourselves at the roasting fire," the marquess said, leading the way there.

And indeed the heat from the flames was very welcome. While Rupert dashed forward, his hands outheld, Lord Denbigh lifted Kate down carefully from his shoulder, stooped down behind her and unbuttoned his greatcoat to wrap about her, and held her little hands up to the blaze.

"Better?" he asked.

She nodded. He took her hands and rubbed them firmly together and then held them to the blaze again. He looked up at Amy.

"It feels good, does it not?" he said.

"Wonderful," she agreed.

He looked up at Judith. "Warm again?" he asked.

"Yes, thank you," she said.

"Only those wot's buyin' meat is welcome to warm their 'ands, guv," the man who was tending the cooking said, and he stretched out a hand to catch the shilling that the marquess tossed to him.

"Is that better?" the marquess asked Kate after a couple of minutes, rubbing her hands together again.

She nodded once more to him, turned, and raised her arms to him. He wrapped his coat more firmly about her and lifted her.

"I think the carriage will be waiting by the time we have strolled back to the bridge," he said. "Has everyone seen enough?"

"Oh, yes, indeed," Amy said. "This has been very wonderful, my lord."

"This has been the best day of my life," Rupert said.

"May I take Kate, my lord?" Judith asked. "She must be getting heavy."

"As light as a feather," he said, glancing down and realizing that the child had fallen asleep against his chest.

He had a strange feeling, almost as if butterflies were fluttering through his stomach. She was warm and relaxed inside his coat. He could hear her deep breathing when he bent his head closer. No, it was more than butterflies. He felt almost like crying.

She might have been his, he thought, if only things had turned out differently. She might have had his dark hair or her mother's fair coloring. He swallowed and shook off the thought.

Judith Easton had seen to it that that had never happened.

He allowed his coachman to help the ladies into the carriage and climbed in carefully himself in order not to waken the child. He shifted her in his arms so that she lay on his lap, her head on his arm. Her mouth fell open as her head tipped back.

"Poor Kate," Amy said. "She has tired herself out. But she has had such a very happy afternoon, my lord. I am sure she will not stop talking about this for days."

Judith Easton, the marquess saw as he looked steadily across the carriage at her, had her eyes on her daughter. She was biting at her lower lip.

"But there is so much in London to delight children," he said. "And adults too. You have not yet been to the Tower, Miss Easton?"

Judith's eyes lifted to his and held. He did not look away from her.

"No," Amy replied. "But we have been meaning to do so ever since we came to town, have we not, Judith? I am longing to see the Crown Jewels."

"The menagerie there is not as impressive as it used to be, I believe," he said. "But it is still worth a visit and is the delight of all children who see it."

"Yes!" Rupert said. "Is there a lion, sir?"

"There is," the marquess said. "And also an elephant."

"A lion!" Rupert said. "I wonder if it has ever eaten anyone."

"Oh, I don't believe so, dear," Amy said. "It must be in a safe cage."

Judith lifted her chin slightly. She knew very well what was coming, the marquess thought, his eyes still on hers. And she knew that she was powerless to avert it.

"There are all sorts of armor and torture instruments on display too," he said, "including the block and ax with which people's heads used to be chopped off. Children inevitably enjoy seeing them even more than they enjoy the lion."

Rupert made a chopping motion at his own neck with the side of one hand.

"Perhaps you would allow me to escort you all there one afternoon, ma'am," he said. "It would be my pleasure."

He watched her mouth lift in a half smile, though there was no amusement in her eyes. She said nothing.

"Yes!" Rupert said. "May we, Mama?"

"How extraordinarily civil of you, my lord," Amy said, delight in her voice.

"Thank you," Judith said softly, that half smile still on her lips. "It would be our pleasure, my lord."

"Then it is settled," he said as his carriage jolted slightly to a halt outside their home. "Shall we say three afternoons from now?"

She inclined her head.

Five minutes later he drove away alone, having laid the child in her mother's arms inside the hallway of the house and declined an invitation to go upstairs for tea.

So Judith Easton was divining his game, was she? He wondered if she had even a glimmering of an understanding of the whole of it. And he wondered if she would be able to guard against it even if she did.

He would see to it that she did not. For the plan was now whole in his mind and he was quite confident of its success. The sister-in-law and the children were eating out of his hand already. And she cared for their happiness.

He would make it succeed. For now more than ever, having seen her again, having had some of the old wounds aggravated again, he wanted her to suffer. Almost exactly as he had suffered.

Almost exactly.

Judith carried the still-sleeping Kate upstairs to the nursery and laid her down carefully on her bed. She loosened the child's bonnet and slid it from her head, unlaced her boots and eased them off her feet.

Well, she thought, the Marquess of Denbigh was doing very nicely for himself. If punishment was his motive—and it must be that—then he was succeeding very well. Not only was he ruining the days and the evenings of her return to town and society, but he was insinuating himself very firmly into the approval and even the affections of her sister-in-law and her children.

Amy was already looking upon him as something of a hero. If she heard her sister-in-law talk one more time about his great civility and kindness, Judith thought, she would surely scream. And if Amy one more time suggested, as she had done after he came to tea and again a few minutes before when the door had closed behind him, that he had a *tendre* for her, Judith, and was trying to fix his interest with her, she would—scream. She most certainly would.

He had already won the children's confidence. It was hard to understand how he had done it. The man never smiled, and he had those harsh features and that stiff manner that had always half frightened her. And yet she could not push from her mind the images of Rupert riding on his shoulder and Kate huddled inside his greatcoat, her small hands in his large ones held out to the blaze of the fire. Or of Kate on his shoulder and Rupert's hand in his, her son's voice raised in excitement. Or of Kate asleep inside his coat and on his lap in the carriage.

Judith smoothed a hand over the soft auburn curls of her daughter and tiptoed from the nursery bedchamber.

She hated him. All the old revulsion and fear had been intensified into hatred. He was playing a game with her and for the time she seemed quite powerless to fight him.

She thought suddenly of his hand coming to rest against

the back of her neck and the shudders and flames it had sent shooting downward through her breasts and her womb to her knees. And of his soft cultured voice calling her "my love." She fought breathlessness and fury.

Well, she thought, she could wait him out. If he thought that she would break, that she would lash out at him in fury—perhaps in public—and give him the satisfaction of knowing that his punishment was having its effect, then he would be disappointed. She could wait.

There was less than three weeks left before Christmas. He had said that he was going home to the country for the holiday. And it was unlikely that he would change his plans—he had mentioned the fact that he had invited guests. So she had perhaps two weeks at the most to endure. Probably less.

She could endure for that long. And when he returned to town after Christmas, he would find her gone. She would go back home to the country herself. Perhaps it would be cowardly to do so, but there would also be good reason for going. The children needed the greater freedom and stability of a country home in which to grow up, she told herself. It was all very well to have come to London for her own sake when her mourning period ended. But she would not be selfish forever. The countryside was the place for children.

Yes, she would endure for another two weeks. And after that he would be powerless to interfere further with her life.

And she would never give him the satisfaction of knowing that he had ruined this brief return to town for her.

5

During the next week she saw him four times in all. It was endurable, she told herself. Barely. Surely, soon he would remove to his country estate.

He was at Mrs. Colbourne's musical evening the day before he had agreed to take them to the Tower. She sat with Claude Freeman and a few other acquaintances, watching the pianist seated at the grand pianoforte in the center of the room, listening to his skilled renditions of Mozart and Beethoven, wishing that her fingers would obey her will as the pianist's did his.

And all the time she was aware of the Marquess of Denbigh at the edge of her vision to the right. He was staring at her, she thought, until her breathing became a strained and a conscious exercise and her concentration on the music disappeared almost entirely. And yet since he was on a different side of the room from her, it was just as likely that he was staring at the pianist. She could not bring herself to look at him.

She did dart a look finally, unable to bear the strain any longer. He was watching the pianist. And yet her look drew his and their eyes met for a moment before she withdrew hers.

Why was it, she wondered, that all the other guests within her line of vision seemed a blur of faces and color while he stood out in startling detail? He was not even wearing black tonight to make him noticeable. His coat was blue.

Was it that he was so much more handsome than any other gentleman present? Yet she had never thought of him as handsome. Quite the opposite, in fact. His face was thin and angular, his nose too prominent, his lips too thin, his eyes too penetrating, his eyelids too lazy.

No, he was not handsome. Distinguished looking, perhaps?

Yes, definitely distinguished looking in a cold, austere way. She thought suddenly of the fortune-teller's prediction about a tall, dark, handsome man, and shivered. And the woman had told her that she knew the man already, that her love for him would come upon her quite unexpectedly. There had been children in her future too. Several of them. She had once dreamed of having a large family.

She focused her eyes and concentrated her mind on the pianist and his music.

The marquess came during the interval to pay his respects and to ask after the health of Amy and the children. He did not stay longer than a couple of minutes.

"You say that Denbigh escorted you and your family to the ice fair?" Claude said with a frown when the marquess had walked away. "I wish you had called upon me instead, Mrs. Easton. I would, of course, have advised against the visit. It is a vulgar show, or so I have heard. I would not have considered it desirable to have you rub shoulders with ruffians and thieves. And the children might have been in some danger. But then, I do not suppose Denbigh even so much as noticed your children."

She wished he had not, Judith thought, seeing again the image of Lord Denbigh with Kate on his shoulder and Rupert holding his hand.

"He was being civil," she said.

"I should watch his civility, if I were you," Claude said. "You have crossed his will once, ma'am, if you will forgive me for reminding you. I do not believe he would take kindly to its happening a second time."

Judith looked up at him indignantly.

"Pardon me," he said. "But people are saying, you know, that perhaps you are regretting your former decision."

"Are they?" she said, her voice tight with anger. "Are they, indeed?"

But she caught herself just in time and turned from him to resume her seat. She drew a few deep and steadying breaths. She closed her eyes briefly. She had been about to rip up at Claude in an appallingly public place, to tell him exactly what she thought of his impertinent and interfering words and of the *ton*'s foolish opinions.

And yet her anger was not really against Claude at all, or against the *ton*. It was against the Marquess of Denbigh, who had arranged all this, who was stalking her relentlessly, and who was intent on making her look a fool in the eyes of society. A rejected fool.

Well, let him keep on trying. She would never give him the satisfaction of showing anger or any other negative emotion in public. And let people say what they would. People would gossip no matter what. She had no control over that, only over her own behavior. And she supposed that a little gossip was no more than she deserved. She did deserve some punishment for her less than exemplary behavior almost eight years before.

She did not look at the marquess again that evening.

They visited the Tower of London the next day and St. Paul's Cathedral two days after that. If she really had been setting her cap at the man, Judith thought, or even if she had liked him, she would have to say that both afternoons were a great success. Amy and the children certainly thought so.

Amy and Kate, hand in hand, watched the birds in the menagerie while Lord Denbigh and Rupert lingered over their perusal of the lion and the elephant and other animals. The marquess answered Rupert's questions about them, about where they were from, how they would have lived in those countries, what they would have eaten, how they would have hunted. He delighted the boy by giving all the gory details while Judith stood helplessly and disapprovingly beside them.

But her disapproval was foolish, she told herself. Boys enjoyed hearing of some of the crueler realities of life. And those realities existed no matter how sheltered she wished her children to be from them. Andrew, she knew, would have wanted his son to grow up a "real man," as he would have put it. And so would Maurice and Henry.

It was doubtless good for Rupert to be with a man

occasionally, instead of always with her and Amy. If only the man were not the Marquess of Denbigh! Perhaps she should have gone to Andrew's family for Christmas after all, she thought fleetingly.

Amy exclaimed over the Crown Jewels, and Kate, in Judith's arms, gazed at them silent and wide-eyed.

"Pretty, Mama," was all she said, pointing at a crown.

Judith looked at the armory and even at a few of the instruments of torture, which the marquess explained to Rupert and Amy. But she refused to look at the block and ax. She turned away with Kate while Rupert laughed and jeered.

"I should stay with you, Judith," Amy said. "All this is quite ghastly. But I must confess that it is also fascinating."

Somehow, as they were strolling away from the White Tower on their way back to the carriage, it happened that the children hurried ahead with Amy to gaze down into the moat and Judith was left walking beside the marquess.

"You have recovered?" he asked. "You looked for a few minutes as if you were about to faint."

"It is horrible," she said, "what human beings can do to other human beings."

"You do not believe, then," he said, "that criminals should be punished?"

"Of course," she said. "But torture? And execution by ax?"

"Many criminals have themselves used cruelty," he said. "Many have killed or betrayed their country. Do they not deserve to be treated accordingly? Do you not believe in execution, Mrs. Easton?"

"I don't know," she said. "I suppose I do. Anyone who kills deserves to die himself—I suppose. But what sort of an example do we set thieves and murderers when we return brutality for their brutality—in the name of law? It does not quite make sense."

"I would guess that you have never witnessed a hanging at Tyburn," he said. "Some people would not miss such an entertainment for all the world."

She shuddered and raised a gloved hand to her mouth.

And then her other hand was taken in a firm clasp and drawn through his arm.

"Your son loves animals," he said. "He was telling me all about his grandfather's dogs, particularly the one shaggy fellow which is allowed inside the house."

"Shaggy?" she said. "That is its name, you know. Sometimes it is difficult to know which end is which. There are a few dogs at home too, but I would not allow any to be brought with us because London is not quite the place for pets, I believe. Besides, my father would not have taken kindly to having his home overrun by the animal kingdom."

"It is one advantage of living in the country," he said. "A great advantage for children. Animals were almost my only companions when I was growing up. Your children are fortunate that they have each other."

She looked up at him, startled. He had just given her almost the only human glimpse of himself she had ever had. He had no brothers and sisters. She had known that. She had never thought of what that might have meant to him. Son of the late Marquess of Denbigh, his mother dead since his infancy. An only child. Animals had been his only companions. Had he been lonely, then? But she did not want to start thinking of him as a person.

And she realized that she was strolling with him, her arm drawn firmly through his, conversing just as if they were friends or at least friendly acquaintances. She was relieved to see the moat ahead and Amy and the children standing on the bridge looking down into the water. She used the excuse of Kate's turning to wave a hand at her to withdraw her arm from the marquess's and hurry forward.

At least Kate had not fallen beneath his spell that afternoon, she thought a little spitefully as the child lifted her arms to be carried the rest of the distance to the carriage.

But even that triumph was to be short-lived. When they were seated in the carriage, Kate wriggled off Judith's lap and climbed onto the marquess's. He continued naming to Rupert all the towers in the outer walls and pointing them out through the windows as they drove away. But he opened the top two buttons of his greatcoat, drew out his quizzing glass on its black ribbon, and handed it to Kate.

She played with it quietly for a while before lifting it to her eye and peering through it at her brother. Rupert shrieked with laughter.

"Look at her eye!" he said, and Amy and Judith laughed too as Kate gazed from one to the other, the glass held to one hugely magnified eye.

The children laughed and giggled for the rest of the journey. It was a merry homecoming.

Amy as well as Judith was one of Claude Freeman's party at the theater on the evening of the following day. The marquess was there too, and came to pay his respects between acts. Fortunately, Judith found, talking determinedly with Mrs. Fortescue, who was also one of their party, he directed his attentions and his conversation to Amy.

Amy was enchanted and as excited as any child being given a rare treat. She had never been to the theater before and had never seen so many splendidly dressed people all gathered in one place. Best of all, she thought, gazing about her, no one was staring at her. She was a very plain, very middle-aged lady, she told herself. Not a monster. Sometimes her family members had protected her—or themselves—so closely that she had felt as if she must be some freak of nature.

"I cannot believe all the splendor of it," she told the Marquess of Denbigh. "The velvet and gold and the chandeliers. And the acting. I was never so well entertained in my life."

"It is your first visit to the theater?" he asked, his eyes looking kindly at her.

And she realized that her reactions must appear very naive to him. But she did not care. The marquess, for all his splendor and very handsome looks and impressive title, would not laugh at her. He was a kind gentleman and she liked him excessively. If only Judith . . .

But Judith was pointedly talking to someone else and for some reason did not like the marquess. Or else she felt embarrassed about what had happened all those years ago.

But Lord Denbigh had clearly forgiven her for that and was quite as clearly trying to fix his interest with her no matter how hard Judith tried to deny the fact.

She wished she had Judith's chance, Amy thought a little wistfully. Not with the marquess, of course. That would be ridiculous.

"The play is about to resume, ma'am," Lord Denbigh said, getting to his feet. "I shall take my leave of you and look forward to escorting you to St. Paul's tomorrow."

He took her hand and raised it to his lips. Amy felt ridiculously pleased. She felt even more pleased when he glanced toward Judith, although Judith was studiously looking the other way.

At St. Paul's the following day they wandered in some awe about the nave, dwarfed by the hugeness and majesty of the cathedral. Judith had never been there before. She had never been comfortable with heights, but the Whispering Gallery did not look too high up when one looked from below—the dome still soared above it—so she agreed to Rupert's persuasions and climbed the stone steps resolutely. Amy stayed down below with Kate.

But she felt the bottom fall out of her stomach when she stepped out onto the gallery, which circled the base of the dome. The nave of the cathedral looked very far down, the people there like ants. She did not even look long enough to distinguish Amy and Kate.

Rupert was running around the gallery, the marquess strolling after him. She stood against the wall, her palms resting against it at her back, willing her heart to stop thumping and her legs to regain their bones. She took a few tentative sideways steps. She looked nonchalantly about her but not down. It still seemed a very long way up to the top of the dome and the Thornhill frescoes painted there.

"It has nothing to do with cowardice, you know." She had not even noticed the Marquess of Denbigh coming back toward her. "It is an actual affliction that some people have. Your head can tell you that the gallery is broad and well railed, that there is no possible way you can fall. But still you can be paralyzed with terror. A friend who suffers in the same way has told me that it is not so much the fear of falling as the fear of jumping. Is that right?''

He was standing in front of her, perfectly at ease, filling her line of vision. He spoke quietly, as he usually did. For once in his presence she felt her heart quieting.

''Yes,'' she said. ''It is a very annoying terror. One feels like the typical helpless woman.''

''The friend I spoke of,'' he said, ''is a man and weighs fifteen stone if he weighs an ounce and is as handy with his fives as any pugilist one would care to meet. Take my arm. Your son, you will see, is across from us, waving down to his sister and his aunt.''

Judith felt her stomach somersault again.

''He is perfectly safe,'' he said, ''and will be delighted if we join him there. Walk next to the wall and imagine that we are strolling in Hyde Park. Look at my arm, if you wish, or at my shoulder. You have a lively and curious son. You must look forward to nurturing his curiosity.''

No, she thought firmly as she told him of her own plans to employ a tutor for a few years and the plans of her brothers-in-law to send him to school when he was older— Rupert would after all be head of the family after the passing of his grandfather—no, she would not grow to like him. She would not mistake his behavior either here and now or briefly at the Tower for kindness.

There was no kindness in the Marquess of Denbigh. Only a cold, calculating mind. Only the desire to punish her by winning the affection of her children and by inflicting his unwanted company on her and by making her look foolish and rejected in the eyes of society.

She must not even begin to doubt what she had so strongly sensed from the first moment of seeing him again.

''Your son will want to test the theory that a word whispered at one side of the gallery can be clearly heard at the other,'' he said just before they came up to Rupert. ''But since you must whisper with your mouth to the wall and listen with your ear to it, that should pose no great problem for you.''

Despite herself she found herself relaxing. His words were reassuring. Even more so was his tall strong body between her and the rail of the gallery.

He took them to Gunter's for tea and cakes before returning them home. He spoke of Christmas and his eagerness to return to his estate.

"There is nowhere quite like the country and a houseful of people for celebrating Christmas," he concluded, while Amy gazed wistfully at him and both children were unusually silent.

"There were always lots of cousins at Grandpapa's," Rupert said at last.

"But this year we will have each other," Judith said briskly, "and will be able to do just as we please all day long."

His words had been ill-considered, she thought. If his intention had been to make her feel guilt at having deprived her children and her sister-in-law of other company over the holiday, then he had succeeded. But it was one thing to hurt her, and quite another to depress the spirits of her family.

He had miscalculated. It was his purpose, surely, to win over the others. She felt an almost spiteful satisfaction at his one slip.

And an even greater satisfaction at the realization that he must surely leave for the country within the following few days.

It was snowing in a halfhearted way. Enough to whiten one's hat and shoulders and to blind one's vision as one rode. Enough to remind one of the coming season. But not enough to settle on the traveled thoroughfares and obstruct traffic.

Even so, the Marquess of Denbigh frowned up at the sky as he rode through the park. Perhaps he was foolish not to have gone into Essex before now. He had guests to prepare for, after all. And even if the weather should prevent the arrival of his guests, there were plenty of other people who needed his presence at Denbigh Park and would be disappointed if he did not arrive. All the children were to stay at the house for two nights—on Christmas Eve and Christmas Day—as they had the year before, and were looking forward to the treat almost as if he had offered them a month in Italy, according to both Mrs. Harrison's and Cornwell's letters.

It would not do to be stranded in town by snow.

But he had not wanted to jump his fences as far as Judith Easton was concerned. He had been proceeding with those plans as slowly as he dared. Too slowly perhaps. He was maybe seeing too much of her. And too much of her children and that good-natured sister-in-law of hers. He was becoming too fond of them.

One danger he had become particularly aware of in the past few days: He must not allow himself to like Judith Easton in any way. It was true—he had played on the fact—that she cared for the happiness of her family and hated to deny them pleasure. And it was true that she was a good mother, spending much of her days with her children instead of abandoning them to a nurse's care. He approved of the way she did not try to overprotect her children, especially the boy.

And there was something admirable about her courage. She had walked the whole circle of the Whispering Gallery at St. Paul's with him, even though he had known from the slight tremor in her voice that she had been terrified, and she had looked down at her son's direction and waved to her daughter and sister-in-law in the nave below. She had unconsciously gripped his arm a little tighter at that moment. She had spent ten whole minutes testing the acoustics of the Whispering Gallery to please her son.

But knowing someone was courageous was not the same thing as liking that person or growing soft in one's intentions for that person. He had always known that she was a woman well in command of her emotions. Or at least, he had known it since that morning after the opera when her white-faced father had called on him to bring his betrothal to an end.

No, courage, control over emotions did not necessarily

make a person likable. And even the most vicious and degenerate of creatures were capable of showing mother love.

He rode in the direction of Lord Blakeford's home. The ladies would in all likelihood have returned from their afternoon's walk, if they had taken it in this weather. He hoped so, at least. This was the visit he had been building toward since his arrival in London. He drew some deep and steadying breaths. He hoped the children would be downstairs for tea. He would be far more confident of success if they were.

They were. In fact, the tea tray had not yet been brought in, and Lord Denbigh realized as he followed the butler into the drawing room that the ladies had only just risen from the floor, where a game of spillikins was in progress. Miss Easton was smoothing out the folds of her dress and laughing, rather flustered. Judith was busy sticking out her chin and clasping her hands calmly in front of her.

"Good afternoon, my lord," she said.

"How civil of you to call on us, my lord," Amy said. "Have you come to join us for tea?"

"I came to get myself out of the snow for a few minutes," he said, "and to assure myself that you are all well after our outing yesterday. But if I am being invited to tea, ma'am, I will most gratefully accept."

"Do you have Pegasus with you, sir?" Rupert asked.

"Yes, indeed," the marquess said, rubbing his hands together to warm them. "But he looked rather like a white-haired old man by the time we arrived here. He was quite covered with snow."

Kate chuckled. "Old man," she said.

Judith had no choice in the matter, as he had intended. Soon he was seated by the fire with Kate on his knee showing him some of the Christmas bows they had made already from the ribbons he had purchased at the river booth. Amy was telling him that they had forgone their walk that day in order to drive to Oxford Street to shop for their Christmas gifts.

"I bought Mama a—" Kate began.

"Sh," Amy said. "Secrets, love."

"—pair of scissors," Kate whispered in his ear, tickling it.

Judith was pouring tea from the tray, which had just arrived.

"She will be delighted with that," the marquess said, looking into the wide dark eyes gazing eagerly into his and resisting the urge to hug the child.

He let conversation flow of its own volition for a while. But matters were made easy for him. The children, and their aunt too, had Christmas very much on their minds.

"I do believe we will be able to buy greenery at the markets, my lord, will we not?" Amy asked. "It would not seem like Christmas without greenery. And we have several of the bows with which to decorate it made already. I regret that we will not be able to gather our own this year."

"Yes," he said, "I would find it strange too. There are masses of holly bushes at Denbigh Park. The soil must be very suited to them there. They are almost always laden with berries. And the pine trees are so thick that they do not miss the boughs cut from them. I have sometimes been accused of making my home look like an indoor forest at Christmas."

Amy sighed. "I was very happy to come here with Judith and the children," she said, "and I know I will not regret my first Christmas away from home. But if there is one thing I will miss more than any other it is the caroling. There is nothing that more joyfully conveys the spirit of Christmas, I always think, than going from house to house singing the old carols and seeing the smiles on everyone's faces and tasting the wassail and the cider and the fruit cake. I have suggested that the four of us go caroling here, but every time I do so Rupert looks scornful, Kate will only smile, and Judith looks embarrassed." She laughed.

"There was never a strong tradition of caroling in my neighborhood," he said, "until a lady new to the area began it two years ago. It has taken well, but most of her singers are children. She is always pleading for new adult voices to help lead the singing."

Amy sighed again.

"Last year," Rupert said, "Rodney had a whole boxful of tin soldiers and we set them up in the nursery and had a war that lasted for two whole days. You never saw such fun, sir. There were seven or eight of us playing all the time and sometimes the girls joined in too. My side won because we had Bevin playing with us. He is twelve years old.''

Kate had found the marquess's quizzing glass again and was quietly playing with it.

"My house is going to be overrun with boys and girls this year,'' Lord Denbigh said. "Twenty altogether—ten boys and ten girls. They were there last year too, and I am quite confident in saying that it was the best Christmas Denbigh has ever known. Of course, my guests have to be warned. Some people do not consider such boisterous fun to their taste. But no one refused last year and no one has yet refused this year.''

"Ten boys?'' Rupert said wistfully.

"The youngest five and the oldest eleven,'' the marquess said. "I imagine it will be a very enjoyable Christmas for everyone who will be there, adults and children alike.'' He looked at Judith for the first time since he had sat down. She was looking at him tensely, her cup stranded halfway between her saucer and her mouth. *Yes, my lady,* he told her with his eyes. *Oh, yes indeed.* "Holly. Ivy. Pine boughs. Decorations. A Yule log. Good food and drink. Games. Dancing. Caroling and church going. Outdoor exercise. Skating. Perhaps sledding and snowballs if the snow decides to come in earnest.''

"Skating,'' Rupert said, longing in his voice. "I can skate like the wind. Papa said so when we used to skate before he died.''

Kate was patting the marquess's waistcoat with her free hand. He looked down at her.

"Yes, ma'am?'' he said. "What may I do for you?''

"Can we come?''

"Kate!'' Judith's cup clattered back into her saucer.

"Actually,'' he said, "my very reason for coming here today was to invite you. Would you like to come?'' He looked from Kate to Rupert.

Rupert jumped to his feet. "Mama too?'' he yelled.

"Aunt Amy too?'' Kate asked.

"All of you," he said. "I cannot quite imagine Christmas without you. Will you do me the honor of coming, ma'am?" He looked directly at Amy. "Despite the shortness of the notice?"

"Oh." Amy clasped her hands to her bosom and looked across at Judith.

"Ye-e-es!" Rupert cried.

Kate looked fixedly up into the marquess's face.

"Ma'am?" Lord Denbigh looked at Judith, whose face had lost all color. "Perhaps I should have asked you privately? It looks as if your family will be disappointed if you say no and you would, very unfairly, seem to be the villain. But it will please me more than I can say if you accept."

"Oh, Judith," Amy said, "it would be so wonderful."

"Lord Denbigh's housekeeper will not be expecting four extra guests," Judith said in a strangled voice.

"My housekeeper is always ready for guests," the marquess said. "She has learned from experience that they may descend upon her at any time and in any numbers."

"But it must be your decision," Amy said. "I told you when I came to live with you, Judith, that I would go wherever you wished to go and do whatever you wished to do. I meant it."

Judith turned her eyes from the marquess's to look first at her sister-in-law's resigned expression and then at her son's tensely excited one. And at Kate, who was looking at her with wide, solemn eyes.

"Please, Mama?" Rupert said.

"It is extremely kind of you to invite us, my lord," she said. "We accept."

There was great jubilation in the room while she held the marquess's eyes for longer than necessary. *Yes, my lady,* he told her silently. *Now do you begin to understand?*

When he rose to take his leave five minutes later, she rose too and accompanied him from the room and down the stairs.

"Why?" she asked him quietly as they descended the stairs side by side. "Have you not punished me enough?"

"Punished?" He looked at her, eyebrows raised.

"You know what I mean," she said. "Please do not pretend innocence. You have stalked me ever since that evening in Lady Clancy's drawing room. You have done all in your power to make me uncomfortable, to make me the topic of gossip and speculation. And you have used my children against me. Today more than ever. Yes, of course you should have spoken with me about this invitation first. But you knew very well what your answer would have been. When is this punishment to end?"

He stopped at the bottom of the stairs and turned to frown down at her. "Punishment?" he said. "Is that how you see my attentions, Judith? Is that how you always saw them? I have used your children, yes, and your sister-in-law. That is somewhat dishonorable, I will confess. But I will use all the means at my disposal. I have waited almost eight years for my second chance with you. I do not wish to squander it as I did the first."

He held her amazed eyes with his own as he took her nerveless hand from her side and raised it to his lips.

She was still standing at the foot of the stairs after he had donned his greatcoat and gathered up his hat and gloves. He looked at her once more before nodding to her father's butler to open the outer door for him.

And he stood for a moment on the steps outside, smiling grimly to himself.

6

The Marquess of Denbigh left town two days later. Fortunately, the snow had done no more than powder the fields and the hedgerows beside the highways. And the weather remained too cold, some said, for there to be danger of much snow.

His guests were not due to arrive until three days before Christmas, but there was much he wished to do before then. He must make sure that invitations were sent out for the ball on Christmas Day. His neighbors would be expecting them, of course, since he had made it a regular occurrence since his assumption of the title. But still, the formalities must be observed.

And then he must make sure that all satisfactory arrangements had been made for the children. Ever since bringing them to the village of Denbigh two years before, he had tried to make Christmas special for them—having them to stay at the house for two nights, providing a variety of activities for their entertainment, filling them with good foods, encouraging them to contribute to the life of the neighborhood by forming a caroling party, making sure that they felt wanted and loved.

This year Cornwell and Mrs. Harrison had reported that the children were preparing a Christmas pageant. He would have to decide when would be the best time for its performance. The evening of Christmas Eve would seem to be the most suitable time, but that would interfere with the caroling and the church service.

Perhaps the afternoon? he thought. Or the evening before? Or Christmas Day?

He ran through his guest list in his mind. Sir William and Lady Tushingham would be there. They were a childless couple of late middle years, who boasted constantly and tediously about their numerous nephews and nieces but who seemed always to be excluded from invitations at Christmas. And Rockford, who was known—and avoided—at White's as a bore with his lengthy stories that were of no interest to anyone but himself, and who had as few family members as he had friends. Nora and Clement had agreed to come this year as their only daughter was spending the holiday with her husband's family. And his elderly aunts, Aunt Edith and Aunt Frieda, who had never refused an invitation to Denbigh Park since the death of his father, their brother, from whom they had been estranged.

And the Eastons, of course. He wondered how high in the instep Judith Easton was and how well it would please her when she discovered who all the children he had spoken of were. He wondered if she would approve of her son and daughter mingling with the riffraff of the London slums. He smiled grimly at the thought.

He had brought them to Denbigh a little more than two years before after sharing several bottles of port with his friend Spencer Cornwell one evening. Spence was impoverished, though of good family, and restless and disillusioned with life. He was a man with a social conscience and a longing to reform the world and the knowledge and experience to know that there was nothing one man could do to change anything. Cornwell had fast been becoming a cynic.

Except that somehow through the fog of liquor and gloom they had both agreed that one man could perhaps do something on a very small scale, something that would do nothing whatsoever to right all the world's wrongs, but something that might make a difference to one other life, or perhaps two lives or a dozen lives or twenty.

And so the idea for the project had been born. The Marquess of Denbigh had provided the captial and the moral support—and a good deal of time and love too. He had been surprised by the latter. How could one love riffraff—and frequently foulmouthed and rebellious riffraff at that? But he did. Spence had gathered the children—abandoned orphans, thieving ruffians who had no other way by which to survive, gin addicts, one sweep's boy, one girl who had already been hired out twice by her father for prostitution. And Mrs. Harrison had been employed to care for the girls.

They lived in two separate houses in the village, the boys in one, the girls in the other, six of each at first, now ten, perhaps twenty with more houses and more staff in the coming year. Two years of heaven and hell all rolled into one, according to Spence's cheerful report. In that time they had lost only one child, who had disappeared without trace for a long time. Word had it eventually that he was back at his old haunts in London.

The marquess wondered how Judith would react to sharing a house with twenty slum children for Christmas. He should have warned her, he supposed, told her and her sister-in-law the full truth. Undoubtedly he should have. He always warned his other guests, gave them an opportunity to refuse his invitation if they so chose.

He watched the scenery grow more familiar beyond the carriage windows. It would be good to be home again. He had been happy there for three years, since the death of his father. Or almost happy, at least. And almost not lonely. He had good neighbors and a few good friends. And he had the children.

Watching the approach of home, the events of the past two weeks began to seem somewhat unreal. And he wondered if he had done the right thing, dashing up to London as soon as word reached him that she was there. And concocting and putting into action his plan of revenge—a plan to hurt as he had been hurt.

But of course it was not so much a question of right and wrong as one of compulsion. Should he have resisted the urge—the need—to go? *Could* he have resisted?

The old hatred had lived dormant in him for so long that he had been almost unaware of its existence until he heard of the death of her husband. Perhaps it would have died completely away with time if Easton had lived. But he had not, and the hatred had surfaced again.

"When is this punishment to end?" she had asked him just two days before.

He rested his head back against the cushions of his carriage and closed his eyes. Not yet, my lady. Not quite yet.

But did he want her to suffer as he had suffered? He thought back to the pain, dulled by time but still bad enough to make his spirits plummet.

Yes, he did want it. She deserved it. She should be made to know what her selfish and careless rejection had done to another human heart. She deserved to suffer. He wanted to see her suffer.

He wanted to break her heart as she had broken his.

He opened his eyes. Except that his hatred, his plans for revenge, seemed unreal in this setting. He had found happiness here in the past few years—or near happiness, anyway. And he had found it from companionship and friendship and love—and from giving. He had found peace here if not happiness.

Would he be happy after he had completed his revenge on Judith Easton?

He closed his eyes again and saw her as she had been eight years before: shy, wide-eyed, an alluring girl, someone with whom he had tumbled headlong in love from the first moment of meeting. Someone whom he had been so anxious to please and impress that he had found it even more impossible than usual to relax and converse easily with her. Someone who had set his heart on fire and his dreams in flight.

And he remembered again that visit from her father putting an end to it all. Just the memory made the bottom fall out of his stomach again.

Yes, he would be happy. Or satisfied, at least. Justice would have been done.

Kate was asleep on Amy's lap, a fistful of Amy's cloak clutched in one hand. Rupert should have been asleep but was not. He was fretful and had jumped to the window twenty times within the past hour demanding to know when they would be there.

Judith did not know when they would be there. She had never been either to Denbigh Park or to that part of the country before. All she knew was that it would be an enormous relief to be at the end of the journey but that she wished she could be anywhere on earth but where she was going.

Her anger had not abated since the afternoon during which she had been trapped into accepting this invitation. But she had been forced to keep it within herself. Amy was quite delighted by the prospect of spending Christmas in the country after all, part of a large group of people. And the children were wildly excited. Judith had voiced no objections, realizing how selfish she had been to have decided against spending the holiday with Andrew's family that year.

Amy of course was delighted not only by the invitation but also by what she considered the motive behind it.

"Can you truly say," she had asked after the marquess had left the house, "that you no longer believe he has a *tendre* for you, Judith? Do you still refuse to recognize that he is trying to fix his interest with you?"

"I do not know why he has asked us," Judith had said, "but certainly not for that reason, Amy."

Her sister-in-law had clucked her tongue.

But Judith had lain awake for a long time that night. He had said that he had waited eight years for a second chance with her. He had called her by her given name. He had kissed her hand, something he had done several times during their betrothal.

She could not believe him. She *would* not believe him. And yet her breath had caught in her throat at the sound of her name on his lips and she had felt the old churning of revulsion in her stomach when he had kissed her hand.

Except that it was not revulsion. She had been very young and inexperienced when they were betrothed. She had called it revulsion then—that breathless awareness, that urge to run and run in order to find air to breathe, that terror of something she had not understood.

She had called it revulsion now too for a couple of weeks, from mere force of habit. But it was not that. She had recognized it for what it was at the foot of the stairs when he had kissed her hand. And the realization of the truth terrified her far more than the revulsion ever had.

It was a raw sexual awareness of him that she felt. A sort of horrified attraction. A purely physical thing, for she did not like him at all—and that was a gross understatement. She disliked him and was convinced, despite his words and actions, that he disliked her too. She distrusted him.

And yet she wanted him in a way she had never wanted any man, or expected to do. She wanted him in a way she had never wanted Andrew, even during those weeks when she had been falling in love with him and contemplating breaking a formally contracted betrothal. In a way she had never wanted him even after their marriage during that first year when she had been in love—the only good year.

And so if the Marquess of Denbigh was trying to punish her—and it had to be that—then he was succeeding. She was a puppet to his puppeteer. For the wanting him brought with it no pleasure, no longing to be in his company, but only a distress and a horror. Almost a fear.

Amy closed her arm more tightly about Kate and reached up for the strap by her shoulder. Rupert let out a whoop and bounced in his seat. The carriage was turning from the roadway onto a driveway and stopping outside a solid square lodge house for directions. But the coachman's guess appeared to have been right. The carriage continued on its way along a dark, tree-lined driveway that seemed to go on forever.

"Oh," Amy said, peering from her window eventually. "How very splendid indeed. This is no manor, Judith. This is a mansion. But then I suppose we might have expected it of a marquess. And then, Denbigh Park is always mentioned whenever the great showpieces of England are listed. Is that a temple among the trees? It looks ruined."

"I daresay it is a folly," Judith said.

The house—the mansion—must have been built within the past century, she thought. Or rebuilt, perhaps. It was a classical structure of perfect symmetry, built of gray stone. Even the gardens and grounds must be of recent design. There were no formal gardens, no parterres, but only rolling lawns and shrubberies, showing by their apparent artless-ness the hand of a master landscaper.

Their approach had been noted. The front doors opened as the carriage rumbled over the cobbles before them, and two footmen ran down the steps. The marquess himself stood for a moment at the top of the steps and then descended them.

And if she had had any doubt, Judith thought, tying the ribbons of her bonnet beneath her chin and drawing on her gloves and cautioning Rupert to stay back from the door, then surely she must have realized the truth at this very moment. Something inside her—her heart, her stomach, perhaps both—turned completely over, leaving her breathless and discomposed.

And angry. Very angry. With both him and herself. He looked as if he had just stepped out of his tailor's shop on Bond Street, and there was that dark hair, those harsh features, those thin lips, the piercing eyes and indolent eyelids. And she was feeling travel-weary and rumpled. She was feeling at a decided disadvantage.

The carriage door was opened and the steps set down and the marquess stepped forward. Rupert launched himself into his arms—just as if he were a long-lost uncle, Judith thought—and launched into speech too. The marquess set the boy's feet down on the ground, rumpled his hair, and told him to hurry inside where it was warm. And he reached up a hand to help Judith down.

"Ma'am?" he said. "Welcome to Denbigh Park. I hope your journey has not been too chill a one."

She was more travel-weary than she thought, she realized in utter dismay and mortification a moment later. She stepped on the hem of her cloak as she descended the steps so that she fell heavily and clumsily into his hastily outstretched arms.

A footman made a choking sound and turned quickly away to lift down some baggage.

"I do beg your pardon," Judith said. "How very clumsy of me." There was probably not one square inch on her body that was not poppy red, or that was not tingling with awareness, she thought, pushing away from his strongly muscled chest.

"No harm done," he said quietly, "except perhaps to your

pride. Is the little one sleeping?'' He turned tactfully away to look up at Amy, who was still inside the carriage. ''Hand her down to me, ma'am, if you will.''

Judith watched as he took Kate into his arms and looked down at her. The child was fussing, half asleep, half awake.

''Sleeping Beauty,'' the marquess said, ''there will be warm milk waiting for you in the nursery upstairs, not to mention a roaring fire and a rocking horse. But I daresay you are not interested.''

Kate opened her eyes and stared blankly at him for a few moments. Then she smiled slowly and broadly up at him while Judith felt her teeth clamping together. A long-lost uncle again. How did he do it?

''Do let me take her, my lord,'' she said, and felt his eyes steady on her as she relieved him of his burden.

He turned to help Amy down to the cobbles.

''What a very splendid home you have, my lord,'' Amy said. ''It has taken our breath quite away, has it not, Judith? Are we not all fortunate that there has been no more snow in the past week? Though of course it is cold enough to keep the ice on the lakes and rivers. I do declare, it must be the coldest winter in living memory. And it is only December yet.''

''I have snow on order for tomorrow or Christmas Eve,'' Lord Denbigh said. ''And plenty of it too. It cannot fail, ma'am, now that all my guests have arrived. And it has been trying so hard for the past two weeks or more that it surely will succeed soon.''

He had taken one lady on each arm and was leading them up the front steps and into the tiled and marbled great hall with its fluted pillars and marbled galleries. And if the approach to the house had not taken one's breath away, Judith thought, then this surely would. The hall was two stories high and dwarfed any person standing in it.

And yet it was unexpectedly warm. Fires blazed in two large marble fireplaces facing each other at either side of the hall.

The Marquess of Denbigh presented his housekeeper, who

was standing in the middle of the hall curtsying to them and smiling warmly from a face that must boast a thousand wrinkles, Judith thought, and turned them over to her care. Mrs. Hines smiled with motherly warmth at Rupert, clucked over Kate, and led them all upstairs to their rooms.

Tea would be served in the drawing room, she told them, after they had refreshed themselves. She would return to conduct them there in half an hour's time.

The children had been put into the care of a very competent nurse, who had been provided by the marquess. Judith sank down onto a small daybed at the foot of the high four-poster bed in her room and blew out two cheekfuls of air.

So it had begun. A week's stay at Denbigh. The final week of her punishment, doubtless. There was a week to live through before she could make arrangements to return to her own home in Lincolnshire and try to begin normal life again.

A week was not an eternity. It was a shame that it had to be the week of Christmas so that her first Christmas free of Andrew's family was to be ruined after all. In fact, it was more than a shame, it was infuriating. But nonetheless it was only a week. She must fortify herself constantly with that thought.

She frowned suddenly. All his guests had arrived, he had said. Where, then, were all the children he had promised Rupert and Kate? Had he lied to them on top of everything else?

She straightened her shoulders suddenly as there was a tap on her door and Amy's head appeared around it.

"Are you going to change your frock, Judith?" she asked. "Or are you just going to wash your hands and face?"

"Oh, let us change by all means," Judith said, getting briskly to her feet. She had already made a disaster of an opening scene—her mind touched on her clumsy stumble and the firm security of his arms and chest, and veered away again. At least she would face the next one in a clean and fresh dress and with combed hair. "There is a maid in my dressing room, unpacking my things already."

"Yes, and in mine too," Amy said. "I shall see you

shortly, then, Judith." She withdrew her head and closed
the door again.

Yes, shortly, Judith thought, drawing a deep breath and
walking through into the dressing room.

"We were facing that much-dreaded experience," Lady
Clancy was telling Judith during tea in the drawing room,
"a Christmas alone. Why is it, I wonder, that no one would
dream of pitying a married couple for having to spend any
other day of the year alone in each other's company whereas
any number of people would consider it a dreadful fate on
that one particular day?"

"Perhaps because Christmas is for families and sharing,"
Judith said.

"Oh, undoubtedly," Lady Clancy agreed. "Clement and
I have been assuring each other since November that it will
be delightful to spend one quiet holiday free of our daughter
and her family. But of course it was mere bravado, and Max
saw that in a moment. He always does. His home is always
filled with lonely persons at Christmas—first at his other
home and now here. Not that I am for a moment suggesting
that you are one of that number, Mrs. Easton. Your two
children are upstairs? They must be weary after the journey.
Carriages and children usually do not go well together."

Filled his home with lonely persons? Judith thought as she
answered Lady Clancy's questions. That did not sound at
all like the Marquess of Denbigh as she knew him.

"He used to fill his house to overflowing," Lady Clancy
said. "But last year and this there have been fewer invited
guests because he has been taking in the children for the
holiday. I daresay it will be very noisy once they arrive. I
am not sure whether to look forward to it or to plan my escape
tomorrow. But we have had plenty of warning, of course.
And I like the idea. I really do admire Max more than I can
say for actually doing it instead of merely talking about the
problems as most of us do. Are you in any way apprehensive about your children's mingling with them, Mrs.
Easton?"

Judith looked at her companion, mystified. "Lord Denbigh

mentioned that there would be children here," she said. "But where are they? And who are they?"

"He has not told you?" Lady Clancy laughed. "How naughty of him. They are children from the streets of London, Mrs. Easton, children who had no homes and no prospects for the future except perhaps a noose to swing from eventually. They are housed in the village and fed and clothed and taught. The older ones will be trained eventually to a trade and I am sure Max will see to it that they find suitable positions. From what I have heard, they also enjoy a great deal of recreation and merriment. They will be here, staying at the house, for Christmas."

"Ten boys and ten girls," the marquess's voice said from behind Judith's shoulder. She had not heard him come up. "And a more boisterous score of youngsters you would not wish to meet, ma'am. Did I neglect to explain to you in London who the children were? I did mention the children, did I not?"

He seated himself close to Judith and Lady Clancy and proceeded to engage them both in conversation. His manner was amiable, Judith found. He seemed at ease, relaxed. The country and his home apparently suited him.

Lonely persons? She had been introduced to everyone in the drawing room. Lord and Lady Clancy were without their daughter and her family that year and would have spent Christmas alone. The Misses Hannibal, his aunts, were elderly ladies, both spinsters, who would perhaps not have been invited anywhere else. Sir William and Lady Tushingham she did not know. But she remembered Mr. Rockford. She had been slightly acquainted with him during her come-out Season. Andrew and his friends had used to make ruthless fun of the man because no one could listen to him talk without falling soundly asleep after three minutes if they suffered from insomnia, they had used to say.

Was Mr. Rockford a lonely person too? Did he have no family? Or friends? Somehow it seemed unlikely that the Marquess of Denbigh was his friend. And yet he had invited the man to his home.

And Amy and the children and she. They would have been

alone too, lonely despite the fact that there were four of them. Was that why he had invited them? But no, she knew that was not the reason. Besides, she did not like to think of its being the reason for any of the invitations to his guests. The Marquess of Denbigh compassionate? She did not like the image at all.

But what about those children? The ones he had taken from lives of desperation in London and brought here. But she knew only Lady Clancy's version of that story.

The marquess and Lady Clancy had been left to talk alone, she realized suddenly. She was being ill-mannered and not doing her part to sustain the conversation.

Lord Denbigh was looking at her, his keen gray eyes holding hers. "Your children are contentedly settled in the nursery, Mrs. Easton?" he asked. "Mrs. Webber will make them feel quite at home. She was my nurse many years ago and was quite delighted to come out of retirement for the occasion."

"Thank you," Judith said. "Kate had eyes for nothing but the rocking horse before I left, and Rupert had spotted the books."

"But you must not feel that they are being confined to the nursery," he said. "You must allow them downstairs as often as you wish. I have never subscribed to the theory that children should remain invisible until they have grown as sober and dull as the rest of us. And at Christmas time especially children should always be allowed to run wild— or almost so, anyway."

"Thank you," Judith said again.

And she stared, fascinated, as he smiled at her. A smile that only just touched the corners of his mouth and brightened his eyes, but a smile nonetheless. And one that transformed his face for the moment from harshness to handsomeness.

Judith felt that growingly familiar somersaulting feeling within and concentrated on keeping her breathing even.

7

"Judith." Amy came bursting into her sister-in-law's dressing room the following morning after a quick knock. "Ah, you are up. His lordship is a magician or a prophet, I do declare. Have you seen?"

Judith had indeed seen and had had much the same thought. And also the thought that if it had only happened one day sooner, or better still, two, she might have been saved. *She*, not anyone else. Amy would have been disappointed and the children quite despondent.

"Yes," she said. "It must have been snowing in earnest all night for there to be such a thick covering already."

"And it is still coming down," Amy said. "Do you realize what this means, Judith? Snow for Christmas. It does not happen often, does it? Especially fresh white snow. It is going to be perfectly splendid for the children. Have you heard about the children? I do admire Lord Denbigh for doing such a thing. But will this snow impede their coming here tomorrow night, Judith? I do hope not, though of course it could be said that it is not at all the thing for such children to be brought into a house with guests. I think the idea quite charming, however. I hope you do not think it is in poor taste with Rupert and Kate here."

Amy was excited and enjoying herself already—Judith could see that. There was even a flush of color in her cheeks. The Misses Hannibal had taken her to their bosoms the evening before and Mr. Rockford had even tried flirting with her. Amy had never been made so much of in her own home.

"It will be a new experience," Judith said, swiveling about on the stool, her temporary maid having finished pinning up her hair. "I look forward to it. Shall we go down to breakfast?"

Amy's fears were put to rest very soon after breakfast. Rupert and Kate were very eager to be outside in the snow. Judith and Amy dressed themselves and the children warmly and descended the stairs. But when they emerged into the great hall, it was to find the front doors being opened and children of all sizes and descriptions pouring inside, all variously covered with snow, all seemingly talking at the same time. Two adults came in after them. The marquess was emerging from a downstairs room.

"Cor blimey," someone yelled, "it's three feet thick out there if it's an inch."

"Ow, luverly," someone else shrieked, "fires. Me fingers is froze off me 'ands." A thin girl detached herself from the mob and raced for one of the fires. Two others followed her.

"Ow, look," a tall and gangly boy said above the general hubbub of noise. " 'Oo are the nippers, guv?"

The Marquess of Denbigh stood with his feet apart and his hands clasped behind his back. "The nippers, Daniel, my lad," he said, "are Master Rupert Easton and his sister, Miss Easton. Could you children not have left at least some of the snow outside? Did you have to drag it all inside with you?"

A chorus of voices explained with varying degrees of coherence that there had been snowball fights to accompany the walk from the village.

"And Val got shoved in the snow by Toby," one of the larger girls said, "and Toby got shoved in by five of us girls and got 'is face washed in it too."

"Ah," the marquess said. "That explains it, then. Now, left turn the lot of you and march smartly into the salon. Mrs. Hines is having warm chocolate sent up for you."

"And cake too, guv?" Daniel asked, a cheeky grin on his face.

"Left turn," the gentleman who had arrived with the children said sternly. "And the 'guv' is 'my lord' to you, Daniel, as I have explained five thousand times at a conservatively low estimate."

As quickly as the hall had filled, it emptied again, leaving behind only the adults and Rupert and Kate.

"May I go too, Mama?" Rupert asked hopefully.

"Me too, Mama?" Kate tugged at her cloak.

"I shall take them in with me if you have no objection, ma'am," the lady who had come with the children said. She was plump and matronly and looked perfectly capable of dealing with the toughest urchin.

"Mrs. Easton," the marquess said, "Miss Easton, may I present Mrs. Harrison and Mr. Cornwell, the very capable and long-suffering guardians of the hurricanes who just passed through here?"

Mr. Cornwell was short and inclined to stoutness, though Judith guessed that there was a great deal more muscle than fat on his frame. Frost was melting from his sandy mustache and eyebrows. His fair hair was thinning.

"Ladies?" he said, bowing to them.

Mrs. Harrison curtsied. "Despite all the noise," she said to Judith, "the children are quite a harmless lot, ma'am. They will not gobble up your own children, I promise you." She smiled.

"I am afraid," Mr. Cornwell said, "that their elocution slips alarmingly whenever they get excited about something, Max. And this morning they are very excited." He turned and addressed himself to Amy. "One would hardly know that in the schoolroom they often speak something approximating to the English language, would you?"

"Go along, then," Judith said, relinquishing Kate's hand to the outstretched one of Mrs. Harrison.

The two children disappeared inside the salon. A moment later two maids followed them, each with a tray laden with steaming cups. A third maid was carrying a tray of cakes and muffins.

"Come into the library, Spence," the marquess said, "and breathe in some sanity for a few minutes. Ladies, will you join us? You are dressed for the outdoors, I see. I was about to send up to invite you and the children to accompany us once the party arrived from the village. This is the morning when we are to haul in the Yule log and gather the greenery for decorating the house. The task is now to be made more difficult and infinitely more exciting by the presence of the snow. Rockford should be down soon too.''

Amy clasped her hands tightly and beamed. "Oh," she said, "this is so much more pleasurable than being in town, shopping at a market. We would be delighted to come, would we not, Judith?''

Lord Denbigh ushered them all into a large and cozy library. Looking about, Judith guessed that he spent a great deal of his time there. There was an open book on a table beside a leather chair, she noticed. The desk was strewn with papers. It was obviously a room that was used, not just a showpiece.

Both gentlemen had a drink. The ladies refused.

Amy had been a little divided in her feelings about the invitation to spend Christmas at Denbigh Park. The lure of a country home was strong and she liked the marquess and looked with hope on what appeared to be a budding romance between him and Judith. But there was also the fact that they must leave London so soon after she had finally gone there.

She no longer had any misgivings. From the moment of her arrival the afternoon before, she had felt like a person. Judith had always made her feel that way, of course, and the marquess in the past few weeks had been very civil. But now she was in a country home with several other guests and she was being treated with respect. That silly Mr. Rockford had even tried flirting with her the evening before.

Amy realized in full just how much less than a person she had always been considered at home.

She was enjoying herself immensely. And she was enchanted by the story of all the children and by her first sight of them. She was almost envious of Mrs. Harrison and was admiring of Mr. Cornwell.

"I do think it a splendid job you are doing, sir," she said to him now. "But what gave you the idea? Or was it his lord-ship's?''

He looked at her and smiled. He was quite as willing as the marquess and the other guests to take her seriously, she thought in some surprise. He had a pleasant face. It was not at all handsome, but it was good-natured. It was the kind of face that would inspire trust in troubled children, she thought. Just as his rather solid frame would inspire respect and a sense of security.

"It was a joint brainchild, actually, ma'am," he said. "We dreamed up the idea one night, thought at the time that we must both have taken leave of our senses, and are even more convinced of the fact two and a half years later." He chuckled. "I have never been happier in my life."

"How wonderful it must be," she said somewhat wistfully, "to be able to devote one's life to children."

"Are you sure you wish to come gathering greenery, ma'am?" he asked. "It is a longish walk to the trees and there is bound to be a great deal of noise and foolery. I cannot assure you in all confidence either that the language will all be suitable for a lady's ears."

"I would not miss it for worlds," Amy said. "This is what Christmas is all about, sir—children and decorations and trudges in the snow. And company."

He actually winked at her as he set his empty glass down. "Never say I did not warn you, ma'am," he said.

Amy felt herself turn pink, reminded herself that she was thirty-six years old, and told herself not to be silly.

"I would imagine," the marquess said to Judith, "that by the time these children have finished gathering and decorating there will be more greenery inside the house than out. And a great deal more noise and chaos. I hope you will not mind. I was a little afraid last year that my aunts might have an apoplectic fit apiece. But they smiled and nodded and were enchanted—and horrified the boys by kissing all the girls. The boys thought that they would surely be next. Fortunately, my aunts had more sense of decorum."

Judith laughed, finding the situation and his humor amusing despite herself.

"I should have told you about the children," he said. His eyes were looking very directly into hers, a hint of a smile in them again. "But I was afraid that you would cry off if you knew. It was shameful of me, was it not?"

Judith felt a twinge of alarm. If she had not known him eight years before and again in the past few weeks, she might well be gaining a totally different impression of him than the true one, she thought. He seemed quite human suddenly. More than human. And there was a warmth in his look.

Yet there was something else too, something quite intangible and unexplainable.

"I have a feeling," she said, "that Rupert and Kate are going to be talking with nostalgia about this Christmas for a long time to come."

"I hope so," he said. "And their mother too."

She was saved from having to reply, though she felt shivers all along the length of her spine, by the appearance of the butler at the door to announce that Mrs. Harrison, Mr. Rockford, and the children were ready to leave.

"We had better not keep them waiting a single moment then, Max," Mr. Cornwell said. "If the children are ready to leave, that means right now at this very moment if not five minutes ago."

Christmas had been a lonely time when he was a child and a boy. His father had sometimes had house guests and had frequently invited neighbors to various entertainments, but he had never felt the necessity of seeing to it that there were other children to play with his son.

Now he loved Christmas and loved to surround himself with people who might be lonely if he paid no attention to them—and with children. His and Spence's decision to open children's homes in the village had been an inspired if a somewhat mad one.

He had done this before—gone out with the children and Spence and Mrs. Harrison to gather the decorations for the house. And it had always been a merry occasion. But there had never before been the added festive detail of snow.

And there had never been Judith Easton on his arm. She had taken it with some hesitation when they had stepped out of the house. But there had been no excuse not to do so. The boys and Spence and Rockford were pulling the heavy sleds.

Rupert was walking along with two older boys, Daniel and Joe, and gazing up at them somewhat worshipfully. Kate was holding Mrs. Harrison's hand—at least she was until Daniel stopped, made some comment about the nipper's boots, and hoisted her up onto his thin shoulder. Kate made no protest but sat with quiet contentment on her new perch. Judith drew in a deep breath and then chuckled.

Amy was walking between the two newest girls, sisters, talking cheerfully to them before taking them both by the hand. No, Judith Easton had no excuse for not taking his arm.

"They have been with Mrs. Harrison for only four or five months," Lord Denbigh said, nodding in the direction of the two little girls with Amy. "The mother was stabbed by a lover and both girls were dependent upon gin as a large part of their diet. Their first two months here were very difficult for Mrs. Harrison and a nightmare for them. They are still quieter than the other children, but they are coming around. If you had seen them four months ago, Judith, you would not believe the difference in them now."

"Poor little girls," she said, gazing ahead at them. "They must have known more suffering in their few years than most people can expect in a lifetime. Imagine all the countless thousands who never know even such a reasonably happy ending as this one. I hate driving into London past the poorer quarters. Though that is a very cowardly attitude. The poverty and the suffering exist whether I can block them from my consciousness or not."

She was unbelievably beautiful, he thought, looking down at her. Far more so than she had been eight years before. He could not look at her without feeling the churning of old desires. Touching her was enough to catch at his breathing.

There was a sense of unreality about the moment. He was walking with her, talking with her on his own land—with Judith. And he was to have her with him over Christmas, for a full week. And while his main purpose had nothing to do with the peace and joy of the season, he had decided to allow himself some pleasure from her presence too. For despite his basic dislike of her, his opinion of her character, and his intention of breaking her heart as she had broken his, she was also the most desirable woman he had ever known.

He desired her. He wanted her. And since it did not at all contradict his purpose to do so, he would do nothing to quell the feeling.

"I believe that the mistake many people make," he said, "is looking at the whole vast problem of poverty and social inequality and feeling helpless and guilty. For there is nothing the average man or woman can do to solve a universal social problem. But all of us can do something on a very small scale. There are thousands of children in England suffering untold hardships at this very moment. But twenty children who would have swelled those numbers by only an infinitesimal amount are well fed and well loved, have their futures secured, and are at the moment having a boisterous good time."

The unfortunate Toby was having his face rubbed in the snow again by four screeching girls.

"That lad," the marquess said, "is going to have to learn something about diplomacy. Or something about running fast."

"Why did you do it?" she asked, looking up at him, frowning. "Just because your friend needed the financial backing?"

"Partly, I suppose," he said. "And partly because I was a lonely child."

"Were you?" Her frown had deepened.

"An only child," he said. "It was a terrible fate. Perhaps it was not my parents' fault since my mother died when I was an infant. But I have always vowed that when I married I would have either no children at all or half a dozen."

Her flush was noticeable even against the rosiness that the cold was whipping into her cheeks. *Those children might have been yours too,* he told her very deliberately with his eyes. *Ours.*

"It would be dreadful to have no children," she said. "Mine have been the light of my life for several years."

"Even before your husband died?" he asked her quietly.

Her eyes wavered from his and fell for a moment to his lips.

"Was it all worth it, Judith?" he asked her. "Were you happy?"

She looked ahead of her again. He heard her swallow. "It was my choice," she said at last. "I chose my course and I remained committed to it."

"Yes," he said, "I believe you did. It is a pity sometimes, is it not, that it takes two to make a good marriage."

Her arm had stiffened on his. Perhaps he had gone too far, he thought. Perhaps he was moving too fast. Perhaps he should not have started calling her by her given name, though she had made no open objection to his doing so. Perhaps he should not have started yet caressing her with his eyes. And perhaps he should not have made any reference to the past or to her marriage, which was, after all, none of his business.

However, he was saved from the present situation when a soft, wet snowball collided with the back of his hat, tipping it forward over his brow, and he turned sharply to detect the culprit. One moment later he was darting after seven-year-old Benjamin, whose flesh had been so deeply ingrained with soot two years before when he had dropped down the wrong chimney in the marquess's town house to land in the study hearth when his lordship was occupying the room that it had been impossible to know even what color his hair was.

"Attack an enemy from behind, would you, Ben?" Lord Denbigh roared, grabbing the child about the middle. "There is only one fitting punishment for that: to be strung up by the heels and forced to contemplate the world upside down."

He dangled the shrieking and giggling child by the ankles while all the other children cheered and jeered and advised his lordship to drop Ben head first into the nearest snow drift.

Ben was hoisted onto the marquess's shoulders for the remaining distance to the trees. Judith had joined Mrs. Harrison.

Mr. Rockford volunteered to take the largest sled and the three largest boys to find and load a suitable Yule log. Kate, who was still on Daniel's shoulder, and Rupert went with them. Mrs. Harrison took some of the girls to find mistletoe. Mr. Cornwell took several boys and a few of the girls to gather holly. He needed people who would not squeal too loudly at pricking their fingers once or twice, he said.

"That excludes you, Val," he said cheerfully and winked at the girl.

"Violet, Lily, and I will come too," Amy said. "Holly has always been my very favorite decoration. There could not possibly by a Christmas without holly."

"Pine boughs for the rest of us, then," the marquess said. "Toby and Ben, haul a sled apiece, if you please. Mrs. Easton, if you would care to stay here, we should not be long. The snow is very deep among the trees."

"And miss the fun?" she said, smiling at him. "Never."

And they waded off through the deeper snow toward a grove of pine trees. Half an hour later their sleds were laden and their arms too, and they were at leisure to look about them for signs of the other groups.

Judith gasped suddenly. "Fire!" she cried. "Something is on fire. Rupert! Kate!" There was panic in her voice. She started forward.

The marquess laid a firm hand on her arm and chuckled. "A cozy fire inside a gamekeeper's cottage," he said. "The children all know about it and visit it as often as they may. It is Rockford's group at a guess. I don't believe either Mrs. Harrison or Cornwell would allow the children to indulge themselves when there is work to be done. But one group is enjoying some warmth and some indolence."

Two young boys in their group whooped with delight and made off through the deep snow in the direction of the line of smoke.

"Kate and Rupert among them," she said, relaxing beneath his grip. "They are with Mr. Rockford's group."

"They will all be punished," he said. "They will miss the fight and be as furious as a pack of devils."

"Fight?" Judith asked.

"Snowball fight," he said. "We cannot expect all work and no play from such a large number of children, now can we? A good fight is what everyone needs as a reward before we start back to the house.''

"Oh, dear," she said.

But everyone else, emerging from the trees at about the same time, greeted the idea with wild enthusiasm.

"Men and girls against ladies and boys," the marquess announced. "Five minutes to prepare and then battle in earnest."

He grinned as the two teams lined up a suitable distance apart and began feverish preparations. The boys on the other side were building impressive ramparts and snow banks, which would be largely useless as they would all be unable to resist coming out in front of them to fight when the action started anyway. His girls were busy making a reserve supply of snowballs.

The missing party, newly warmed from their rest at the gamekeeper's cottage, arrived before the five minutes were at an end and joined in the preparations with enthusiasm.

"Time up!" the marquess yelled when the five minutes were over, and the air rained snowballs. There were squeals and yells and bellows and giggles, and sure enough, his girls had the early advantage as the boys abandoned their fortifications and were forced to make their weapons while defending themselves against continuous attack.

Miss Easton, he saw, flanked by two of the larger boys, who were certainly as large as she, was engaged in a duel with Spence. Mrs. Harrison was defending herself against attack from a group of her girls. Rockford, laughing and clearly enjoying himself, was allowing a group of little boys, including Rupert, to score unanswered hits on his person.

And then a large snowball shattered directly against the marquess's face.

"Oh, no," Judith Easton yelled as his eyes locked on her. She was laughing helplessly. "I have lamentably poor aim. I was throwing at that little boy who just hit me." She pointed at Trevor.

He bent and scooped up a large handful of snow, not taking his eyes from her despite the fact that two more snowballs hit him, one on the shoulder and one on the knee. He molded his snowball very deliberately.

"You would not," she called to him as he strode toward her, and she stooped down to scoop snow harmlessly in his direction and then turned to dart behind the snow hills thrown up by her boys.

He followed her there. She was still laughing. And looking damned beautiful, he thought. He would not allow himself for the moment to think anything else. He was enjoying himself.

"Don't, please," she said, setting her hands palm out in front of her. She could not stop laughing. "Please don't."

He reached out with one booted foot, caught her smartly behind the ankles, jerked forward, and sent her sprawling back into the snow bank. Beyond the bank there was a great deal of noise and a great barrage of snowballs still flying in both directions.

"How clumsy of you," he said, stretching down his free hand for one of hers. "Do allow me to help you up, ma'am."

"Oh, most unfair," she said. "I am going to be caked with snow."

"In future," he said, drawing her to her feet when she set her hand in his, "you must be careful about allowing your feet to skid on the snow." He drew her all the way against him and held her there with one arm about her. "You could easily break a leg, you know."

The laughter was dying from her face, only inches from his. A great awareness was taking its place in her eyes. He could feel his heart beating in his throat and in his ears. He moved his head an inch closer to hers, his eyes straying down to her mouth. Her lips were parted, he saw.

The temptation was great. Almost overpowering. One taste while everyone's attention was distracted and they were partially shielded anyway by the snow bank. One taste, though it was far too early for such familiarity. But he had a plan to follow. A plan that called for greater patience and caution.

"Revenge can be very sweet sometimes," he told her in a low voice, keeping his eyes on her mouth as he brought his hand from behind her and pressed his snowball very firmly against her face.

"Argh!" she said, sputtering snow.

He laughed and turned away. "Time up!" he yelled. "I have penetrated the enemy defenses, as you can all see, and declare the men and girls to be the winners."

Shrieks of delight from the girls and high-pitched insults hurled at the boys in place of snow. Loud protests and blood-curdling threats from the boys.

"Back to the house," the marquess said. "If we cannot have luncheon and rehearse for the Christmas pageant soon enough, there will be no time for skating on the lake afterward."

Skating! The word was like a magic wand to set everyone scurrying in the direction of home. Most of the children had skated the year before during a cold spell and remembered their bruises and their triumphs with an eagerness to have them renewed.

"I can skate like the wind," Rupert Easton told the marquess, falling into step beside him and reaching up a hand to be held, forgetting for the moment that he was six years old and a big boy.

"Then I will have to see proof this afternoon," Lord Denbigh said, taking the hand in his. Judith, he could see, was walking with Rockford. He, inevitably, was doing all the talking.

The marquess was still regretting that he had not after all kissed her before making use of his snowball.

8

Gathering the Christmas greenery had not taken as long as expected. There was still time when they returned to the house to decorate the drawing room and the ballroom, though the marquess did suggest that perhaps the children would welcome a rest before beginning work again.

"Of course," he added to Mr. Cornwell, who was taking a bundle of holly very carefully from Amy's arms, "I might have saved my breath as you obviously have not taught the meaning of the word *rest* in that school of yours yet, Spence. What do you teach, anyway?"

Judith hoped fervently that the outing would have tired Kate even if not Rupert. She hoped that at least her daughter would be willing to be taken back to the nursery. But Kate had attached herself to Daniel, and Daniel had promised that he would lift her onto his shoulders so that she could hang some of the greenery over the mantel and perhaps over some of the pictures.

"Though I think you'd 'ave to sprout arms ten feet long to reach the pictures, nipper," he added. "P'raps I'll stand on a chair."

Judith closed her eyes briefly.

She longed to escape, but there was no excuse to do so. Lord and Lady Clancy and Sir William and Lady Tushingham had also appeared to help, and even the marquess's aunts had come downstairs from their rooms to exclaim at the enormous piles of holly and mistletoe and pine boughs and at the size of the Yule log.

Mr. Cornwell, Amy, Mr. Rockford, and the Tushinghams would help supervise the decorating of the drawing room, it was decided. The rest of the adults would move on to the ballroom.

She longed to escape, Judith thought, and yet there was

that old seductive excitement about the sights and smells of Christmas in the house. The smell of the pine boughs was already teasing her nostrils. At Ammanlea the servants had always done the decorating. At her home they had always done it themselves. It was good to be back to those days, and good to see so many children happy and excited and working with a will.

She shook off the mental image of Daniel standing on a delicate chair in the drawing room with Kate on his shoulders reaching up to a picture. One of the adults would doubtless see to it that no unnecessary risks were taken.

Several large boxes had been set in the middle of the ballroom and soon the children were into them, unpacking bells and ribbons and bows and stars—several large, shining stars.

"To hang from the chandeliers," the marquess explained. "No, Toby, it would be far too dangerous. I would hate to see you with a broken head for Christmas. I shall do it myself."

And Judith, gingerly separating piles of holly into individual sprigs so that the children could rush about the room placing them in suitable and unsuitable spots, also watched the marquess remove his coat and roll up his shirt sleeves to the elbows. She watched him climb a tall ladder held by Lord Clancy and two of the biggest boys in order to attach the stars to the chandeliers.

She held her breath.

And then looked away sharply to resume her task and suck briefly on one pricked finger. She did not want this to be happening, she thought fiercely. She did not want this feeling of Christmas, this growing feeling of warmth and elation, to be associated in any way with him.

But how could she help herself? Ever since her arrival the afternoon before, and especially this morning, she had been fighting the realization that perhaps he was not at all as she had always thought him to be. She remembered her impressions of him eight years before, impressions gathered over a two-month period. He had seemed cold, morose, harsh, silent. She had been afraid of him. And there had been nothing in London this time to change that impression.

Oh, there had been, of course. There had been his civility to Amy, his kindness to her children and even to her. But her fear of him had not lessened. She had suspected his motives, had assumed that somehow it was all being done to punish her, since he knew that the worst he could do to her was inflict his company on her and ingratiate himself with her family.

But here? Could she really cling to her old impressions here? He was mingling with twenty children from the lowest classes, teasing them, playing with them, making them as happy as any children anywhere at Christmas time. And it could not even be said that it was just a financial commitment to him, that he provided the money while Mr. Cornwell and Mrs. Harrison did all the work and all the caring. That would not be true. He so clearly loved all the children and enjoyed spending time with them.

She recalled the contempt she had felt for him in London when he had remarked on one occasion that he had a fondness for children. He had not lied—that was becoming increasingly obvious. Rupert had tripped along at his side all the way back to the house, his hand in the marquess's, talking without ceasing.

"There," she said to Violet, smiling, "that is the last of it."

Mrs. Harrison and two of the girls were just coming in with armloads of ivy, she saw.

She did not want this to be happening. Lord Denbigh, still in his shirt sleeves, was standing in the middle of the ballroom, his hand on Benjamin's shoulder, pointing across the room at something. Ben went racing away.

He was not at all thin, Judith thought. His waist and hips were slender, but his shoulders and upper arms were well muscled beneath the shirt and his thighs too. She caught the direction of her thoughts and swallowed.

He had waited almost eight years for a second chance with her, he had told her in London. And this morning he had asked her if it had all been worth it, if she had been happy. And he had held her against him—she turned weak again at the knees with the memory—and had almost kissed her.

And the shameful thing was that she had wanted it in a horrified, fascinated sort of way. She would have done nothing to stop it. She had a curiosity to know what his mouth would feel like on hers.

She shuddered.

"I must confess," Lady Clancy said, coming to stand beside her and gazing about at the ballroom, which had suddenly become a room full of Christmas, "that Clement and I were not at all sure that we were doing the right thing in accepting our invitation. But I am already beginning to enjoy myself more than I have done for years. Max and Mr. Cornwell and Mrs. Harrison have done wonders with those children, have they not?"

The decorating having largely been completed, the children were having noisy good fun, mostly with a few sprigs of mobile mistletoe. There was a loud burst of merriment from the far side of the room, accompanied by catcalls and loudly hurled insults, when Val soundly slapped Joe's face after he had stolen a kiss.

"Keep yer 'ands to yerself," she said before letting loose with rather more colorful language.

"But I got mistletoe," Joe protested. "It's allowed."

"I don't care if you got a certificate all decorated up wiv gold lettering from the Archbishop of Canterbury," Val said. "Keep yer 'ands to yerself or I'll chop 'em off at the wrists."

The other boys all gave an exaggerated gasp of horror.

"It is Christmas," the marquess said, "and mistletoe does excuse a great deal of familiarity, but a gentleman is a gentleman for all that, Joe. A simple 'May I?' 'would solve the problem. No lady would be so ragmannered as to refuse."

"Yeh, Val," someone yelled, and there was another loud outburst of laughter.

"Max is taking them all skating this afternoon?" Lady Clancy said to Judith. "I do believe I may go out myself. I used to fancy myself a skater."

"I never could stay upright," Judith said. "I gave up even trying years ago."

"Well you know," Lady Clancy said, "the secret is to keep your weight over your skates. So many people pull back out of fear and then, of course, lose their balance."

There was still a great deal of laughter from the children, especially from one group of them behind Judith and Lady Clancy, but they continued to converse with each other and did not look to see what was happening.

" 'Ere, guv," someone yelled. There were smothered giggles from some girls.

"I can still feel some of my bruises," Judith said. The marquess was striding toward them. She could feel the familiar breathlessness and tried to continue the conversation, her face expressionless, her voice cool.

But she turned her head with sudden suspicion as he drew closer. One tall boy, grinning wickedly, was standing directly behind her, a sprig of mistletoe waving above her head. But it was too late to duck out of the way. Lord Denbigh, she saw, was standing directly in front of her.

"May I?" he asked.

What could she do? Give in to a fit of the vapors and swoon at his feet? Say no? With all the children and the adults too either smiling at her or convulsed with merriment? She nodded almost imperceptibly.

And then his hands came to rest lightly on either side of her waist and as she drew breath his lips touched her own.

Briefly. Only for the merest moment. But she felt as if she had been struck by a lightning bolt. Sensation sizzled through her. And she felt as if it would be quite impossible to expel the air she had just drawn into her lungs.

"Aw, guv," the boy who was standing behind her said, and she became aware at the same moment of jeering voices about the ballroom, "carn't yer do better than that?"

"Certainly," the marquess said, and Judith stared into his heavy-lidded eyes and felt that she would surely die. "I merely raised my head because I remembered that I had forgotten to wish Mrs. Easton a happy Christmas."

Somewhere, youthful voices were cheering. Lady Clancy was chuckling close by. Someone behind her whooped and whistled. Judith's fingertips came to rest against a muscled chest, warm beneath the silk of his shirt, and she fought desperately to detach her mind from what was happening.

It was not an indecorous kiss under the circumstances. She told herself that. He touched her only at the waist, holding her body a few inches from his own. And his mouth was light on hers. His mouth. Not his lips. He had parted them slightly over hers so that she was aware of warmth and softness and moistness.

Andrew had never kissed her so, she told herself, deliberately keeping up the flow of an interior monologue. There had been only an increased pressure to show his heightened passion. After the first year he had rarely kissed her at all.

She had never been kissed just so.

It lasted only a few seconds. Ten at the longest, she guessed. An eternity. The world had turned right about. The stars had turned, the universe. She was being indescribably foolish.

"Happy Christmas, my lord," she said coolly.

"You see, Joe?" Lord Denbigh said, turning his head and raising his voice. "No slaps, and the lady even wished me the compliments of the season. That is the way to do it, my lad."

He released her waist finally and turned away to organize a tidy-up.

"Little rascals," Lady Clancy said with a laugh. "Max is a better sport than I would have expected. And you, too, my dear. I must say that both Clement and I were disappointed when you married Mr. Easton instead of Max. He was always a favorite with us, shy though he was—and still is to a certain degree. He disappeared for a whole year after your marriage. No one seemed to know where he was. He went walking in the Lake District and Scotland, apparently— all alone. But that is old history and I do not wish to embarrass you. I am glad that you have been able to bury your differences. I wonder if luncheon is ready. It must be very late already."

"Yes," Judith said. "I imagine all these children must be ravenous. They have done a good day's work already."

*   *   *

After luncheon, Mrs. Harrison and Mr. Cornwell took the children into the drawing room for a rehearsal of their pageant. Amy had been invited to go with them. She took Rupert with her while Judith took Kate upstairs to the nursery for a sleep.

All the children had parts, Mrs. Harrison explained to Amy. There were no scripts.

"Most of our children cannot read well yet," she explained. "We have merely told them the story and allowed them to improvise their lines—sometimes with hair-raising results, though I have great faith that they will all perform beautifully on Christmas evening and be perfect angels."

"Would you like to be a shepherd, lad?" Mr. Cornwell asked Rupert, laying a hand on his shoulder. "We can always use more shepherds."

Amy smiled gratefully at Mr. Cornwell as Rupert raced off to join a small group of boys.

"You do not by any chance have some skill at playing the pianoforte, ma'am, do you?" he asked her. "Mrs. Harrison declares that she is all thumbs, but I am afraid that even my thumbs would be useless. Our angel choir cannot possibly sing without accompaniment. They would go so flat that we would have to go belowstairs to find them."

Amy laughed and flushed. "I do," she said, "and would gladly relieve Mrs. Harrison if she wishes it."

"If she wishes it?" He took her by the arm. "Eve, come here. Christmas has come early for you."

Amy was soon seated on the pianoforte bench surrounded by the angel choir.

"Cor," one of them said, "you got a luverly voice, missus."

"Thank you," she said. "Maureen, is it? And so do all of you if you will just not be afraid to sing out. Sing from down here." She patted her stomach.

Mr. Cornwell came and stood behind the bench when the full rehearsal started. He chuckled.

"Can we keep you, ma'am?" he asked. "What would you ask as a salary? That sounded almost like music."

"This is such fun," Amy declared a moment before

clapping a hand over her mouth as the innkeeper's wife beat the innkeeper over the head for suggesting that they turn Mary and Joseph away.

"Not the head, if you please, Peg," Mr. Cornwell said firmly. "The shoulder maybe? And not too hard. Remember that you are just acting." He added in a lower voice, for Amy's ears only, "The angel did not wait for the glory of the Lord to shine around about the shepherds during our first rehearsal. She kicked them awake."

Amy stifled her mirth.

And she remembered suddenly a dark tent on the River Thames and the prediction about children. Lots of children. And about a comfortable gentleman of middle years whom she would soon meet.

But how foolish, she thought, giving herself a mental shake. How very foolish. Mr. Cornwell would surely run a million miles if he could just read her mind. Poor Mr. Cornwell.

And her father would have forty fits if she ever decided to fix her choice on a gentleman who worked for his living caring for and educating a houseful of ragamuffins from the London slums.

It sounded like rather a blissful life to Amy.

Silly! she told herself.

The marquess joined his aunts and Sir William in a game of cards in one of the smaller salons.

Soon enough it would be time to skate. The children, Lord Denbigh thought, would not allow him to forget that promise despite the fact that they had had a busy day and faced the walk home at the end of it.

There was a large box of skates he would have taken out to the lake. No one who needed a pair would find himself without, though he remembered from the previous year that many of the children preferred to slide around on the ice with their boots. He had already had a portion of the lake cleared of snow.

"What a delightful child little Kate Easton is," Aunt Edith said.

"And very prettily behaved," Aunt Freida added.

The marquess and Sir William concentrated on their cards.

"Maxwell, dear," Aunt Edith said, "Frieda and I were wondering—it was so long ago that neither of us can be sure—but it seems to us, if we are remembering correctly, that is . . . Of course, dear, we never went up to town and our brother did not keep us informed as much as perhaps he might. Though of course, he was a busy man. But we were wondering, dear . . ."

"Yes," the marquess said. He had grown accustomed to his aunts during several visits in the past few years. "You are quite right, Aunt Edith. And you too, Aunt Frieda. Mrs. Easton and I were betrothed for almost two months eight years ago."

"We thought so, Maxwell," Aunt Frieda said. "How sad for you, dear, that she married Mr. Easton instead. And how sad for her to have lost him at so young an age. He must have had auburn hair, I believe. The children both have auburn hair, but Mrs. Easton's is fair."

"Yes," Lord Denbigh said, "he had auburn hair."

"How very kind of you, Maxwell, dear, to invite her and her children to Denbigh Park for Christmas," Aunt Edith said. "Some men might have borne a grudge, since she is the one who ended the betrothal if we heard the right of the story. And I daresay we did as it would not have been at all the thing for you to have done so, would it?"

The marquess pointedly returned his attention to the game of cards. He had been in danger of forgetting during the morning. But he had a vivid image now of Easton as he had been—handsome, laughing, charming, a great favorite with the ladies, and with another class of females too.

Lord Denbigh had never suspected that a romance was growing between Easton and Judith, though he had seen them together more than once and Easton had almost always danced with her at balls. He had not seen the writing on the wall, the marquess thought, poor innocent fool that he had been.

And he remembered again as he and Aunt Edith lost the hand quite ignominiously, entirely through his fault, how he had tortured himself after she had run away with Easton with images of the two of them together, of the two of them intimate together. He had walked and walked during that year, constantly trying to outstrip his thoughts and imaginings.

And then the news almost as soon as he finally returned to town that she was with child.

He had been in danger of forgetting during the morning. He had forgotten when he kissed her in the ballroom. He had forgotten everything except his fierce hunger for her and his awareness that he was kissing her for the first time and that she was warm and soft and fragrant and utterly feminine.

Well, he remembered now. He would not forget again. And he was not sorry that young Simon had maneuvered him into kissing her, for there had been a look in her eyes and a slight trembling in her lips. She was not indifferent to him. It was not by any means an impossible task he had set for himself.

"Ah," Aunt Edith said with satisfaction as they won the hand, "that is better, Maxwell dear. I thought a while ago that you had quite lost your touch."

"And I hoped the same thing," Sir William said with a hearty laugh. "One more hand to decide the winner, Denbigh?"

"Judith," Amy said, letting herself into her sister-in-law's dressing room after knocking, "do you think this bonnet becoming? Would my green one look better?"

Judith looked up in surprise. Amy had worn her brown fur-trimmed bonnet through most of the winter without once asking anyone's opinion.

"It will be a great deal warmer than your green one," she said. "How was the rehearsal?"

Amy came right into the room and laughed. "Quite hilarious," she said. "Those children flare up at the slightest provocation, Judith. Val, who plays the part of Mary, is the fiercest of all. She thumped poor Joseph in the stomach when he was not paying attention to some of Mrs. Harrison's instructions. And yet there is a warmth about their presentation that will be quite affecting, I believe. Mr. Cornwell says they have come a long way since they started three weeks ago."

Judith smiled at her sister-in-law's enthusiasm.

"Rupert is a shepherd," Amy said. "Mr. Cornwell suggested it and Mrs. Harrison said it would be all right."

"Oh dear," Judith said, "I hope he was not making a nuisance of himself."

Amy laughed. "Mr. Cornwell said that there are so many shepherds anyway that one more will be neither here nor there."

Mr. Cornwell. Judith looked at the bright spots of color in her sister-in-law's cheeks.

"Are you ready?" Amy asked eagerly. "I would hate to find that everyone has left without us."

But everyone had not, of course. They were all gathered in a noisy group in the great hall.

"Where's that nipper?" someone demanded loudly, and Kate chuckled and left Judith's side to be borne away on Daniel's shoulder.

The lake was only a few hundred yards to the west of the house, not a long walk. Judith walked there with Mr. Rockford and watched with interest as Amy took Mr. Cornwell's arm and chattered brightly to him. She did not even look unduly short in his company. Her head reached to his chin.

Amy had never had a beau. Judith's heart ached suddenly. She hoped that her sister-in-law was not about to conceive a hopeless and quite ineligible passion.

"Mama." Rupert rushed at her as soon as she reached the lake, a pair of skates clutched in his hands. "Help me put them on. I want to show you how I can skate. I can skate like the wind. Papa said, remember?"

Andrew had done so little with his children. But it was good, Judith thought, that her son remembered at least one thing and one occasion when his father had been kind to him and shown him some affection. He must have loved Rupert, she thought. He had been ecstatic with pride at his birth. He had been far less so at Kate's. He had wanted another son.

"Yes, I remember," she said. "And Papa knew what he was talking about. He was a splendid skater himself. But it has been a long time, Rupert. You must not be surprised if you need to find your skating legs before you can compete with the wind again."

She was down on one knee in the snow lacing the skates over Rupert's boots. People all about her were doing the same thing, though some of the children were already on the ice without skates, sliding and sprawling and laughing. Daniel, she saw with some amusement, was strapping a small pair of skates onto Kate's feet and leading her by the hand to the edge of the lake. He was not himself wearing skates.

"I think your daughter has a champion," the Marquess of Denbigh said from behind her. "You cannot know how fortunate she is to have won his protection. All the other children live in mortal terror of his fists."

"Oh dear," Judith said.

"Watch me, Mama," Rupert called as he reached the edge of the ice and prepared to step onto it. "Watch me, sir."

"I am watching," Judith called. "Oh dear," she said again as her son landed flat on his back even before his second skate had touched the ice.

"Give him an hour," the marquess said. "He will improve. And he does not have far to fall. That is the advantage of skating when one is a child. You are not skating?"

"No," she said. "I came to watch. I never could get a feel for skating. My feet always would move at twice the speed of the rest of my body."

"Ah yes," he said. "Painful."

He left her without another word and skated onto the ice. He did so quite effortlessly, Judith noted with some admiration and envy. And he took Rupert by the hand and one of the little girls and patiently slowed his pace to accommodate their wobbling ankles and stiff legs.

Amy and Mr. Cornwell, she saw, had organized a line of children, all holding hands, Amy between two of them and Mr. Cornwell between two others. The children were moving gingerly forward. Judith could hear Amy's laughter. Skating was something she had always been good at.

Some of the boys and a few of the girls were darting recklessly about on their skates. Others were still skidding about on their boots. Lady Clancy was gliding gracefully about the perimeter of the skating area with Mr. Rockford.

9

It was a lovely sight, Judith thought, waving at a beaming Kate and glancing at Rupert, who was so intent on frowning at his feet that he did not see her. It was so rare in England and so precious. Snow was still clustered on the branches of some of the more sheltered trees and was banked high about the area that had been cleared for the skating. Scarves and hats and mittens were bright against the white and the gray. And then there were the shrieks of merriment coming from the ice.

Rubert was skating alone finally, his arms outstretched. His pace was slow but he was beaming with triumph and risked one glance at the bank to make sure that she was watching him. She smiled and waved.

And then she was aware of Lord Denbigh stepping off the ice. She thought for one moment that he was coming to speak with her, but he stopped at the box of skates and rummaged among its contents. And then he really did come toward her, a pair of skates in one hand.

"These should fit you," he said. "Let me help you on with them."

"I don't skate," she said. "I told you that."

"I understand," he said. "You cannot skate alone, or at least you think you cannot. You will not be skating alone. You will be with me and I will undertake not to let you fall." He was down on one knee, one hand outstretched, waiting for her to lift a foot.

"No," she said indignantly. "I cannot, and I do not wish to."

"Afraid, Judith?" he asked, looking up into her face.

"Oh," she said, and she could hear the slight shaking in her voice, "I wish you would not."

"Call you Judith?" he said. "I would prefer it to Mrs.

117

Easton. Quite frankly, I do not wish to be reminded of that name. Will you call me Max? Then we will be equal.''

"No," she said, "it would not be seemly. Besides, I do not want to."

She realized suddenly that she must have lifted one foot. A skate was already strapped to it and he was waiting for her to lift the other foot.

"Set your hand on my shoulder," he said, "so that you will not lose your balance."

"I wish I knew," she said as she obeyed, "why you are doing all this."

He said nothing until he had finished his task. Then he straightened up and looked down at her. "But you do know," he said. "I told you in London—at the foot of the stairs in your own home."

She frowned. "But why would you want a second chance with me, as you put it?" she said. "You did not care the first time, did you? It was an arranged match."

She flushed. She had not intended to make such an unguarded reference to the past.

"On your part perhaps," he said. "Take my arm, Judith. When we reach the ice, I am going to set my arm about your waist. Put your own up about my shoulders. And don't even think of falling. You are not going to do so."

For the first minute or so he might as well have carried her, Judith thought with a great deal of embarrassment. Her skates certainly felt quite beyond her own control. Amy went by with Mr. Cornwell and waved at her, and Rupert called to her to watch him. No one seemed to be paying any particular attention to her, she realized finally, with some relief, though she did not believe she had ever felt so foolish in her life.

But someone was taking notice of her. The Marquess of Denbigh was laughing and when she looked up it was to find his face alight with amusement. She had never noticed until that moment what very white and even teeth he had.

"I am too tall for you," he said, bringing them to a halt.

"You are quite unbalanced by the position of your arm. Let us try something different."

He kept his one arm firmly about her waist while he took her nearer hand in his free one. And she did indeed find it easier to maintain her balance.

"Oh," she said without thinking, "this is fun." And she heard herself laughing.

"I have the utmost confidence in you," he said. "I daresay that by this time next year, provided we have at least two months of cold weather both this year and next and you practice diligently every day, you will almost be able to skate alone."

"Oh," she said, laughing again. "I don't believe that was a compliment, was it? How lowering."

"Relax," he said. "You are tensing again. You cannot skate when you are tense."

"Oh," she said, looking up at him. And the laughter died. She was aware suddenly of his closeness, of his one arm tight about her, the upper part of it pressed against her shoulder.

He was staring back down at her, the amusement gone from his face too. His eyes were intent, steely gray beneath drooped lids. It was the look that had always terrified her when she was a girl. A look that she had not at all understood at the time, though she believed that she understood it very well now.

"You are not sorry you came, Judith?" he asked. "I did trick you into coming. You realized that. You would not have come if I had asked you alone, would you?"

"No," she said.

"And are you still sorry?" he asked. "Would you return home tonight if you could?"

She swallowed and looked sharply away from him. "The children are having a wonderful time," she said. "And so is Amy."

"You know," he said, "that that is not what I am asking you, Judith."

"I don't know," she said, and she looked back up into his eyes again. "I don't know. There is something about you I do not trust."

"Is there?" he asked. "Or is it something about yourself? Do you not trust yourself to keep on believing that you did the right thing eight years ago?"

She drew in a sharp breath. "I must believe that," she said fiercely. "There are Rupert and Kate."

"Yes," he said. "You are right there, Judith. There are your children. But that was then. This is now. It is not the same thing at all. We are both older."

"Yes," she said.

And she wondered if he was right. Was it herself she did not trust? But it was not that. There was something about him. There was still that something.

But perhaps she was wrong. Surely she must be wrong. He had come very close to declaring an affection for her, to demonstrating to her that he was indeed trying to fix his interest with her.

Was it possible? Was it possible that after all this time and all the humiliation she had dealt him he was considering renewing his offer for her?

The idea was absurd when put into words in her mind.

And yet there were his looks and his words.

But then there was that something else too.

"Can we go to see the dogs, guv?" someone yelled across the ice.

"Oh, yes, can we?" There was a chorus of voices.

"I fear the house is about to be invaded by the canine kingdom," the marquess said. "I had all the dogs confined to the stables out of respect to my guests. But these children know very well that several of the animals normally live in the house. I hope no one has a fit of the vapors when they take up residence again. Will you?"

"We have dogs at home," she said.

"Ah, yes," he said. "You mentioned that once before." He raised his voice. "Off to the stables, then. But no biting the dogs, mind."

There was a burst of raucous laughter as the children scrambled off the ice and tore impatiently at skate straps.

"I get Rambler," Daniel announced loudly. "Come on, nipper. Up you come."

Judith watched her daughter being borne away toward the stables.

"Your grooms will have forty fits apiece, Max," Mr. Cornwell said. "I had better go after them. Would you like to come, Miss Easton?"

"I shall be along too," the marquess said. He looked down at Judith. "But I cannot leave you stranded in the middle of the ice, can I? Do you wish to see the dogs too?"

She was being given a chance to shorten this encounter with him? A chance to return to the house alone or with Mr. Rockford and Lady Clancy?

She put up her chin. "Yes," she said, "I would."

Christmas Eve. It was snowing again, the flakes drifting lazily down without the aid of wind. There was enough to freshen up what had already fallen, Lord Clancy announced after a morning walk, but not enough to bury the house to the eaves.

Miss Edith Hannibal was afraid that the carriages would not be able to take them to church that evening.

"And it never quite seems to be Christmas without church," she said. "Indeed, I cannot remember a year when we did not go to church. Was there ever such a time, Frieda? But of course there was the year Mama was so sick. Indeed, she died the day after Christmas. We did not go to church that year, but then it did not seem at all like Christmas that year anyway."

The marquess assured his aunts that most of them would enjoy the walk since the church was only a mile away. There were two sleighs to convey those who would prefer to ride.

No one was quite as busy as on the day before. Except the servants, that was. By midmorning, tantalizing smells were already escaping from belowstairs and those people who were still in the house were invited down to the kitchen to stir the Christmas pudding in its large bowl.

Judith clasped her hands over Kate's and they stirred together, both laughing. Rupert took a turn alone.

Amy had left the house soon after breakfast, declining the

marquess's offer to call out one of the sleighs, choosing to walk to the village instead.

"I have offered to play the pianoforte for the angel choir," she had told Judith the night before. "Mrs. Harrison plays only indifferently and was most grateful for my offer. And Mr. Cornwell says that the children will cheer when they know I am willing to join their caroling party. They are always delighted to have someone among them who can hold a tune, he says." She laughed merrily. "We will be going all about the village as soon as darkness falls, coming to the house here last. It all sounds quite perfectly splendid."

Mr. Cornwell had also been talking with Amy about his future plans for the homes. And Amy had apparently suggested to him that in future it might be a good idea to have a home in which there were both boys and girls.

"It will be more like a real family, I told him," Amy said. "There would be problems, of course, which Mr. Cornwell was quick to point out to me, but it would be a lovely idea, would it not, Judith? What it would need, of course, is a married couple to oversee it. A couple whose own children are grown up, perhaps, or who have been unfortunate enough never to have had children of their own. Then it would be a splendid experience for them too."

Amy was very obviously enjoying herself. The lure of a great house on the eve of Christmas could not hold her from a day spent in the village with her new friends.

Lord Clancy and Sir William retired to the billiard room after luncheon. The ladies sat in a salon with their needle-point and embroidery while Mr. Rockford entertained them with stories of a recent visit to Paris and a not so recent one to Wales. The marquess's aunts, seated one each side of the fire, soon nodded off to sleep, lulled by the heat and the particular drowsiness that afternoon brings—and perhaps by the droning voice of the lone gentleman in the room too.

Judith was upstairs in the nursery, reading a story to Rupert and hoping that Kate would have a sleep since she was likely to have a late night. Rupert sat still at her feet and listened, playing with the ears of the collie stretched out before him as he did so, though all morning he had been restless and had demanded a dozen times at the very least to know when the children would be arriving to stay.

The Marquess of Denbigh had some errands to run, he had announced at luncheon. He always delivered a basket of food to all the cottagers on his estate each Christmas Eve and always put a personal gift of a few gold coins inside each. This year the task of delivering the baskets was complicated by the snow, but it could be done nevertheless. He would not delegate the task to his servants, knowing that his people set great store by his visits. Besides, he would deprive himself of some pleasure if he neglected to go.

He set out in one of the sleighs, delivering baskets to the closest of the cottages first. It was not a fast job. He did not refuse a single invitation to step inside the cottage to take refreshments. He grinned to himself as he turned the horses' heads for home again and another load of Christmas offerings. There was always the danger on the afternoon of Christmas Eve that he would become too drunk to attend church in the evening. Everywhere he went he was offered either ale or cider, and always a generous mugful because he was the marquess and must be suitably impressed.

Two footmen carefully loaded the sleigh for his second run. But he hesitated before taking his place again, and glanced with indecision at the house. It would not really do, he thought. He was enjoying his afternoon, enjoying the smiles on the faces of his cottagers and their somewhat flustered conversation. He was enjoying the widening eyes of all the children as he handed each a coin.

He should not spoil the atmosphere of Christmas. He should not bring darkness to his mood.

He frowned, something fluttering at the edge of his memory. And then he remembered the fortune-teller out on the ice of the River Thames. He remembered her telling him that there was darkness in him as well as a great deal of light and that Christmas might save him from being swamped by the darkness. He shrugged. He had never given heed to such nonsense. But he remembered that afternoon with some pleasure.

And he found himself running up the steps to the house,

peering into the salon, and then taking the stairs two at a time to the nursery floor. He knocked at the door and let himself in.

She was sitting in a rocking chair by the window, wearing the simple blue wool dress that she had been wearing that morning. Her daughter was asleep in her arms, one small hand spread on her bosom. Her son was on his stomach on the floor at her feet, his legs bent at the knees, his feet waving back and forth. He was tickling the collie's stomach.

The marquess felt a stab of some indefinable longing. It was such a very quiet, contented domestic scene.

Rupert jumped to his feet and ran toward the marquess. The collie tore after him, barking at this promise of a new game. "Are they here?" the boy asked.

Lord Denbigh rumpled his hair. "I heard your mama tell you earlier that they would be coming for the caroling this evening and then walking to church with us," he said. "Does the day seem quite interminable? How would you like a sleigh ride?"

"Ye-es!" Rupert jumped up and down. "Super! May I, Mama?"

"The invitation is for your mama too," the marquess said. "Would you like some fresh air, ma'am? I am delivering baskets to my cottagers."

Her face brightened. "Are you?" she said. "Oh, I always used to enjoy doing that at home with Mama and Papa. It was always the beginning of Christmas, the start of that wonderful feeling that only Christmas can bring."

"The little one has just fallen asleep?" he asked.

"Yes," she said, getting carefully to her feet. "I shall put her to bed."

And there. He had done it. He had ruined his afternoon, brought darkness into it. Except that he would not think of the ultimate revenge, he decided as he offered his arm to lead her down the stairs and out to the waiting sleigh. He would not think about how such encounters as this would all be used to contribute gradually to the final denouement.

He would pretend that he had no other purpose than to

enjoy her company. He had very little time left in which to do so. He had been without her for almost eight years. He would be without her for the rest of his life. Surely he could allow himself a few days in which to feast his eyes on her beauty. Besides, all time spent with her would contribute to his ultimate purpose.

She was wearing a fur hat rather than a bonnet, one that completely covered her hair and her ears. She tucked her hands inside a matching muff. Her face, he noticed, did not owe its beauty to her hair. It was a classically beautiful face in its own right.

They sat side by side in the sleigh, Rupert squashed between them, surrounded by cloth-covered baskets. The collie had been left curled at the foot of Kate's bed.

"Mm," Rupert said. "They smell good."

"At least we will not starve if we get stuck in a snow bank," the marquess said, and the boy giggled.

They did not talk a great deal. But the air felt fresher with her sitting beside him, and the crunching of the horse's hooves on the snow and the jingling of the harness bells and the squeaking of the sleigh runners were more intimate and more festive sounds.

"This is the most beautiful weather there could possibly be," she said, lifting her face to the high broken clouds above and drawing in a deep breath. "It makes of the world a fairy-tale place."

And Lord Denbigh knew that she shared his mood.

They paid eight visits in all and were invited inside each of the eight cottages. Lord Denbigh found himself living out an unplanned fantasy. What if she had not broken off their engagement? They would have been married now for eight years. They would be paying these calls together as man and wife, the ease of years of acquaintance and intimacy between them. And they would be going home together afterward to their guests and their children and a shared Christmas. And when it was all over they would stand together on the steps of Denbigh and wave good-bye to their departing guests. And they would be alone together again, with their family. Perhaps she would be with child again.

Mrs. Richards had delivered her fourth child less than two weeks before. The child was awake and fussing, though Mrs. Richards insisted that they come inside for refreshments. The baby had been fed already, she assured them.

"Oh, may I?" Judith asked, smiling at Mrs. Richards and leaning over the baby's crude cradle.

Mrs. Richards was flustered, but she assured Mrs. Easton that the baby had had a clean nappy only a few minutes before.

And Judith lifted the child from the cradle and held it gently to her shoulder. The fussing stopped and the baby wriggled its head into a comfortable position and sucked loudly on a fist. Judith closed her eyes, smiling, and rubbed a cheek against the soft down on the baby's head.

"Oh," she said, "one forgets so quickly how tiny newborn babies are. How I envy you."

Lord Denbigh turned his head away sharply and addressed a remark to Mr. Richards. He felt as if he had a leaden weight in his stomach. For some reason he felt almost as if he were about to cry. Steady, he told himself. Steady. He should not have let down his guard for even a moment. Had he not learned his lesson long ago?

"Was that the last one, sir?" Rupert asked when they emerged from the Richardses' cottage and took their places in the sleigh again. "Are we going home now? Will the carolers be coming soon?"

The marquess laughed. "Not for several hours yet," he said. "But I tell you what we will do, with your mother's permission, of course. We are close to the village, and your aunt is with Mrs. Harrison and Mr. Cornwell and the children. Doubtless they have all sung carols until they are blue in the face. We will take you there and leave you in your aunt's charge. How does that sound?"

Rupert shouted out a hurrah.

"Is that all right with you, ma'am?" the marquess asked. "This lad could well drive you to insanity within the next few hours if we do not rid ourselves of him."

Judith laughed. "They will probably make you sing, Rupert," she warned.

"I can sing," Rupert said indignantly.

Five minutes later he was admitted to the house where all the children and adults were gathered and swallowed up into the noise and cheerful chaos.

"Amazingly," Mr. Cornwell told them, "we have had not a single casualty all day even though Mary tried to box the ears of all the kings for setting down their gifts closer to Joseph than to her. The heavenly host are beginning to sound almost like a choir with Miss Easton to provide the accompaniment and to sing along to keep them in tune. And sometime within the next few hours we will have to decide how twelve volunteers are to carry five lanterns—a minor problem. I can confidently predict, Mrs. Easton, that we will be able to deliver your son to you this evening all in one piece."

And so, Lord Denbigh discovered, quite without planning to be, he was alone with Judith Easton, a mile-long drive between them and home. He drove his team in silence, and decided on the spur of the moment to take a long route home. He turned along a little-used lane that led uphill until it was above a grove of trees and looking down on the house from behind. He had always loved the view from up there. He eased his horses to a halt.

"I used to come up here a great deal as a boy," he said, "and imagine that I was lord of all I surveyed."

"And now you are," she said.

"And now I am."

The silence between them was companionable. Strangely so, considering what had happened between them in the past, considering his reason for having her at Denbigh Park, and considering the fact that she did not trust him—she had told him so the day before.

"You are very different from what I have always thought you to be," she said quietly.

"Am I?" He turned to look at her.

"You care," she said. "All your house guests are people who would have spent a lonely Christmas without your invitation, are they not? And you are generous to your people. I expected that you would wait outside each cottage until someone came outside to take a basket from your hands. But you visited and made conversation. And there are the children in the village. You have far more than just a financial commitment to them.''

"Perhaps it is all selfishness after all," he said. "I have found that I can secure my own happiness by trying to bring some to other people. Perhaps I am not so very different from what you thought, Judith."

She frowned. "You used to be different," she said. "You used to be cold, unfeeling. But then, of course, our betrothal was forced on you. Perhaps I was unfair to judge you just on that short acquaintance."

Cold? Unfeeling? Had she not known? Had she not realized? Cold? He remembered how he had used to toss and turn in his bed, living for the next time he would see her, wondering if he would have the opportunity to touch her, perhaps to kiss her hand. Unfeeling? He remembered the pain of his love for her even before she left him and his fear that he would not be able to give her all she desired from life.

A forced betrothal? He had gone to his father the morning after his first meeting with her and begged to have the marriage with her arranged as soon as possible. Although he had been apprehensive at the prospect of allowing his father to choose his bride, he had forgotten his misgivings as soon as he had met her. The betrothal, the wedding could not be soon enough for him.

Poor naive fool that he had been. Twenty-six years old and entrusting his heart, his dreams, all his future hopes to a young girl he did not even know. A young girl who had preferred charm and flirtation and the apparent glamor of a near elopement. A young girl who had broken his heart without one thought to his feelings—because she had believed him cold and unfeeling. Had she ever tried to see beyond his shyness? Had she ever tried to get to know him?

And now she sat calmly beside him telling him that that was the way he had been. She still did not understand.

But she would. *Oh, yes, my lady,* he told her silently and bitterly, *you will know what it feels like.*

10

The Marquess of Denbigh turned sideways, rested one arm on the back of the seat behind her, and slid his free hand inside her muff to rest on top of her hand.

"Perhaps," he said. "It is always difficult to know what goes on in another's mind. I thought you were content with our betrothal, Judith, but apparently you wanted something different. Well, you had it—for a while. And you have your children."

She was looking down at her muff. Her hand was warm and still beneath his own.

"Yes," she said.

There was a silence between them again, not so comfortable as before. There was an awareness, a tension between them. Her hand stirred. He looked at her, his face hardening.

"Did you love him?" he asked.

"Yes." She answered him without hesitation.

"Always?" he asked. "To the end?"

"He was my husband," she said, "and the father of my children."

"In other words," he said, "it was loyalty, not love after the honeymoon was over. Did you not know about him, Judith, before you married him?"

He thought she would not answer. She stared downward for a long time. "I was eighteen," she said. "I was still young enough to believe that one person can change another through the power of love. He was very handsome and very charming. And very persuasive. Did you know why he married me?"

He had often wondered, since though she had been beautiful and well-born, she had not been particularly wealthy. He had wondered why Easton had saddled himself with a wife when his subsequent actions had seemed to prove that it was not for love.

"He loved you, I suppose," he said.

"You did not know," she said. "I thought these things quickly became general knowledge in the gentlemen's clubs."

He felt a pulse beat in his throat. Had Easton raped her?

"Tell me," he said.

She turned to look at him and smiled ruefully before looking away down the hill. "It was a wager," she said. "It seemed that there were enough gentlemen willing to wager a great deal of money on the belief that Andrew could not snatch me away from a wealthy viscount and heir to the Marquess of Denbigh."

The pulse was hammering against his temples.

"He told me," she said, "after we had been married for about a year. He thought it a huge joke. He thought the story would amuse me."

There was one thing the marquess wished fervently. He wished that Easton were still alive so that he could kill him.

"I thought you would have known," she said.

"No."

He withdrew his hand from her muff and turned in his seat. He picked up the horses' ribbons and gave them the signal to start down the slope that would bring them around the east side of the house. He did it all mechanically, without thought. Her words were pounding in his head.

He thought of a shy and beautiful eighteen-year-old, fresh from the schoolroom, fresh from the country, pitted against the practiced charms of a handsome and accomplished flirt and rake. She had been married because of a wager. He had suffered those months and even years of agony because of a wager.

"Your daughter must be awake by now," he said as the sleigh drew to a halt before the front doors. "Bring her downstairs for tea, Judith, will you? My aunts dote on her, if you had not noticed."

"Yes, I had," she said. "And I will bring her down. Thank you."

He watched her ascend the stairs to the house and disappear into the warmth of the great hall before taking the sleigh and the horses to the stable block.

Did this change everything? he wondered. Did this mean that she had been as much of a victim as he? But she was still guilty of not having said anything to him. She had still behaved dishonorably, running away without a word or even a note. But she had been eighteen years old and in the clutches of an unprincipled rake.

He needed to think, he knew. But he had no time to think. He would be expected indoors for tea. Besides, he did not want to think.

If there was one place in hell hotter than any other, he thought viciously as he strode back to the house, he hoped that it was occupied by Andrew Easton. It was not a Christmas wish or even a Christian one, but he wished it anyway.

The caroling had always been one of Amy's favorite parts of Christmas. This year it was even more special with almost all of the singers being children. They went from house to house, singing lustily and not always quite on key. Several of the children pushed close to her when it came time to sing.

"You got a lovely voice, mum," Joe told her. "The rest of us sounds like rusty nails."

"Speak for yerself," Val yelled at him.

Amy laughed and felt warmed and wanted and very happy. Mr. Cornwell always stood behind her shoulder, sharing the music with her.

At each house they were offered refreshments, always welcome after the cold walk. Where some of the children put all the cakes they took Amy could not fathom. For none had bulging pockets.

"There will be a few stomachaches tomorrow or the next day," Mr. Cornwell said when she mentioned her concern to him. "But it is Christmas."

Some of the smaller children showed signs of weariness before they had finished making their calls. Amy, feeling

a slight dragging at her cloak, found little Henry clinging
to her.

"Are you tired, sweetheart?" she asked him, and when
he nodded she picked him up and carried him. How wonderful, wonderful, she thought as he nestled his head on her
shoulder. She knew what the psalmist had meant when he
had written of a cup running over. But Henry was no
featherweight.

"Here," Mr. Cornwell said, appearing beside her, "let
me take him, ma'am. Henry, is it? He is our youngest."
He lifted the child gently into his own arms. "We cannot
have you out of breath when we arrive at Denbigh Park, now,
can we? You sing better than any angel I have ever heard."

Amy laughed. "And how many angels have you heard,
Mr. Cornwell?" she asked.

"In the last little while?" He grinned at her. "None,
actually, ma'am, except you. And my friends call me Spencer
or Spence. I consider you my friend."

"Spencer," Amy said, and flushed. She had never called
any man by his given name except her brothers. "Then you
must call me Amy."

"Amy," he said, smiling. "A little name for a little lady.
You live all the time with Mrs. Easton?"

Yes, Amy thought, as Peg ran up beside her and took her
hand, my cup runneth over.

It was almost ten o'clock when the carolers finally arrived
at Denbigh Park, bringing a draft of cold air with them
through the front doors and a great deal of noise and
merriment. Cheeks and noses were red and eyes were
shining. Stomachs were full. Five of the smallest children
clutched the lanterns and hoisted them high when it came
time to sing, though they were largely for effect; the hall
was well lit. The smallest child of all was asleep against Mr.
Cornwell's shoulder.

The marquess and his guests came down from the drawing
room to listen to the carols, quite content to have their own
singsong to Miss Frieda Hannibal's accompaniment interrupted. Kate, her cheeks bright with color, her eyes wide

with the lateness of the hour, clung to Judith's neck and waved across a sea of heads at Daniel.

Mr. Cornwell had a hand on Amy's shoulder and watched the music she held in her hands.

The carolers made up in volume and enthusiasm what they lacked in musical talent, Judith thought after they had sung ''Hark the Herald Angels Sing'' as if they were summoning all listeners to the nearest tavern and ''Lully Lulla Thou Little Tiny Child'' as if they intended their rendition to be heard in Bethlehem.

It did not matter that the choir was unskilled. It did not matter at all. For there they all were, crowded into the great hall of Denbigh Park, a roaring log fire burning at either side of it, sharing with one another and their listeners all the joy of Christmas.

There was nothing quite like the magic of those few days, Judith thought. And every year it was the same. Even during those years with Andrew's family, though she had not enjoyed them on the whole, there had always been some of the magic.

Or perhaps magic was the wrong word. Holiness was perhaps a better one. Love. Joy. Well-being. Goodwill. All the old clichés. Clichés did not matter at Christmastime. They were simply true.

Everyone was smiling. Mr. Rockford, whose conversation was never of the most interesting because he did not know when to stop once he had started, had one of the marquess's aunts on each arm and was beaming goodwill as were they. Sir William and Lady Tushingham, who had regaled them at dinner with stories of their nephews' and nieces' accomplishments and triumphs, were flanked by Lord and Lady Clancy and looked rather as if they were about to burst with geniality.

The Marquess of Denbigh was standing with folded arms, his feet set apart, smiling benignly at all the children. Just a week before, Judith thought, she would not have thought him capable of such an expression.

And Amy was smiling up over her shoulder at Mr. Cornwell, the singing at an end and the hubbub of excited children's voices being in the process of building to a new crescendo. And he was pointing upward to a limp spray of mistletoe that some wag had suspended from the gallery above and lowering his head to give her a smacking kiss on the lips.

Judith, watching his beaming face and Amy's glowing expression, felt as if warmth was creeping upward from her toes to envelope her. If anyone on this earth deserved happiness, she thought, it was Amy. And there would be nothing at all wrong with that match. Nothing.

"Mama!" Rupert was patting her leg and talking quite as loudly and excitedly as any of the children. "Did you hear me? I got to carry the lantern for part of the way. And I am going to walk to church with Ben and Stephen. They said I may."

" 'Ow's my nipper?" Daniel was demanding loudly, and Kate wriggled to be set down from her mother's arms.

There were more refreshments and a great deal more noise in the half hour that remained before it was time to go to church. The marquess's aunts and Sir William and Lady Tushingham would ride to church in the sleighs, it had been decided. Lord and Lady Clancy would walk, though the marquess offered to have one of the sleighs return for a second trip.

Three of the smaller children, including Henry, gave in to the lateness of the hour and the long excitement of the day and the novelty of having the big house to sleep in and agreed to stay with Mrs. Webber and be put to bed. Kate, after several huge yawns, was persuaded to stay with them.

And so they set out into the crisp night air, the distant sound of the church bells ringing out their glad tidings of the birth of a baby in Bethlehem and the coming into the world of a savior.

"It is so easy to forget," Judith said, finding herself walking beside the marquess and taking his offered arm. "There is so much to do and so much to enjoy that sometimes we forget what the season is all about."

"Yes," he said. "Going to church on Christmas Eve is rather like walking into the peace at the heart of it all, is it not? But we will be reminded again tomorrow. The children will be performing their pageant between dinner and the start of the ball.''

''Yes,'' she said, smiling.

She liked him. She admitted the amazing truth to herself at last—not only that she liked him but that he was a likable person. And she wondered if he had always been so or if he had changed in eight years. If he had always been like this, she thought, then . . .

She stopped her thoughts. She did not want to be sad on Christmas Eve. She did not want to look back in regret on all that she might have missed. Besides, there were Rupert and Kate. Her years with Andrew had not been all bad. She had not wasted those years of her life. There were her children.

The sounds of the church bells pealing out their invitation grew louder as they stepped onto the village street. People were flocking to church, many of them on foot, some by sleigh.

The Marquess of Denbigh smiled to himself. The singing at the village church was not usually noted for its volume or enthusiasm. And yet tonight, with the familiar Christmas hymns, the whole congregation seemed infected by the spirited singing of the children. And the rector, no longer rendering a virtual solo, as he was usually forced to do, lifted up his rich baritone voice and led his people in welcoming a newborn child into the world once more.

There was no time like Christmas, the marquess thought, to make one feel at peace with the world. He could not for the moment think of one enemy whom he could not forgive or one enmity that was worth holding onto. The one spot of darkness on his soul he pushed from his mind. It was unbecoming to the occasion. And he was filled with that unrealistic dream that infects all of the Christian world at that particular season of the year that love was enough, that all the problems of the world and of humanity would be solved if only the spirit of Christmas could persist throughout the year.

He smiled inwardly again. He knew that it was a foolish dream, but he allowed himself to be borne along by it nevertheless.

Judith shared his pew to the right, his aunts and Rockford to his left. His other guests sat in the pew behind, the children behind them again. His neighbors packed the rest of the church. It was a good feeling of well-being. He turned his eyes to the right as the congregation sat for the sermon and watched Judith clasp her hands loosely in her lap.

And he indulged in his other dream for a moment before turning his attention to what the rector was saying. She was his wife and had been for several years. Their children were at home in the nursery or sitting behind them with the other children. They were celebrating Christmas together.

He knew that there was something about her, about his relationship to her and his plans for her, that he needed to think through. There were perhaps some adjustments to make in light of new evidence. But not at present. Later he would think.

Judith, sitting beside him, was trying to remember a Christmas when she had felt happier. There had been the Christmases of her childhood and girlhood, of course. They had always been happy times. But since then? Surely the first year or two after her marriage had brought pleasant Christmases. Certainly Ammanlea had always been full of family members and children. There had been all the ingredients for joy.

But she remembered that first Christmas, when she had still been in love with Andrew. He and his brothers and male cousins had spent the afternoon and evening of Christmas Eve going from house to house wassailing and using the occasion as an excuse to get themselves thoroughly foxed. Andrew had fallen asleep several times during church while she had prodded him with her elbow with increasing embarrassment. And all the next day at home they had continued to drink.

And that had been the pattern for all the Christmases of her marriage and for the first of her widowhood.

It was little wonder, she thought, that she was feeling so

happy this year. So unexpectedly happy. She had been horrified when Lord Denbigh had trapped her into coming to Denbigh Park. She had still been convinced that he was a harsh and unfeeling man and that he had issued the invitation only to punish her for humiliating him eight years before.

She had never dreamed that she could come to like him, and more than that, to admire him. She had never dreamed that she would stop fighting the strong physical attraction she felt for him.

She had stopped fighting, she realized. She had stopped that afternoon, if not before. She could still feel the warmth of his hand on hers beneath her muff—the hand that was now spread on one of his thighs. She glanced at it. It was a slim, long-fingered hand, which nevertheless looked strong.

It was strange to realize that for a two-month period eight years before she had been betrothed to him. They had been within one month of their wedding when she had run off with Andrew. What would marrige to him have been like? she wondered. Performing those intimacies of marriage with him. Bearing his children. Sharing a home with him in the familiarity of everyday living.

She shivered and turned her attention to the rector.

Halfway through the lengthy sermon there was a slight rustling from the pews where the children sat. A few moments later Rupert wriggled his way between his mother and the marquess, yawned widely, and tried to find a comfortable spot for his head against her arm. She smiled down at him and marveled at how well all the other children were behaving. It was a long and a late service after a busy day.

Rupert's head fell forward and Judith lifted it gently back against her arm. Her son looked up at her with sleepy eyes. He should have stayed at the house with Kate, she thought. But of course he would have been mortally offended had she suggested any such thing.

And then the marquess's arm came about the boy's shoulders, drawing him away from her, and his other slid beneath Rupert's knees and he lifted him onto his lap and drew his head against his chest. Rupert was asleep almost instantly, his auburn curls bright against the dark green of Lord Denbigh's coat.

Andrew's child, Judith thought. Her husband's child cradled in the arms of the man she had jilted and never faced with either explanation or apology. The man who might have been her husband, the father of her children. She felt an almost overwhelming longing to move closer and to close her eyes and rest her head against his shoulder.

She was falling in love with him, she realized with sudden shock. No, perhaps it was already too late. She had fallen in love with him. With the Marquess of Denbigh. It was incredible. But it was true.

There was no longer any thought in her mind of the suspicions that had troubled her in London and again here at Denbigh.

"The dear little boy," Miss Edith Hannibal said to the marquess as the congregation spilled out of the church after the service and exchanged cheerful Christmas greetings while the church bells pealed again. "He is fast asleep."

The marquess was carrying Rupert, the child's head resting heavily on his shoulder.

"You must tive him to me," Miss Hannibal said. "I shall take him home in the sleigh, Mrs. Easton, and his nurse will have him tucked up in bed in no time at all."

"Thank you, ma'am," Judith said, smiling.

"And I shall take that little one on my lap," Miss Frieda Hannibal said. "It was a very long service for children, was it not, Mr. Cornwell? But they behaved quite beautifully. They could teach a lesson to several of the children of our parish, who are allowed to fidget and whisper aloud in church. Edith and I find it most distracting."

"Thank you, ma'am," Mr. Cornwell said, and he waited for the marquess's aunt to seat herself in the sleigh before laying in her lap the little girl who was sleeping in his arms. "This is Lily, ma'am. If she should wake up, you may assure her that her sister is quite safe with Mrs. Harrison and will be home in no time at all. Lily becomes agitated when separated from her sister.''

"Then we must squeeze her sister in between us," Miss Edith Hannibal said. "There is plenty of room, I do assure you, Mr. Cornwell. Come along, dear."

Violet climbed gratefully into the sleigh.

In the meantime, Sir William and Lady Tushingham had singled out two little boys whose eyes were large with fatigue and who, Lady Tushingham declared, reminded her very much of two of her dear nephews, now twenty-two and twenty-four years old, and had taken them on their laps in the other sleigh.

Mrs. Harrison arranged the remaining children into pairs and led the way home. There was loud excitement over the fact that they were to spend the night and all the next day and night at Denbigh Park.

"It's the feather pillows wot tickles me," Toby told a younger child. "Your 'ead sinks right through 'em to the bed."

"Last year we all 'ad gifts," Val said. "But I daresay the guv spent all 'is money last year."

"I remember the mince pies," Daniel said. "I ate 'leven."

"Ten," Joe said. "I counted. It was ten."

"It was 'leven, I betcha," Danial said, bristling. "You want to make somethin' out of it, Joe?"

"It was ten," Joe said.

"Someone is going to be hanging by ten toes over the nearest snowbank in a moment," Mr. Cornwell called sternly.

"I tell you what," Mr. Rockford said, walking among the children and sweeping up into his arms one little boy who was yawning loudly. "Tomorrow whenever you eat a mince pie, Daniel, you let me know and I will keep count. We will see if you can stuff ten or eleven into yourself."

"Twelve," Daniel said loudly. "I 'ave to beat last year's count, sir."

"His lordship's cook may well be in tears," Mr. Rockford said. "No mince pies left by the end of Christmas morning.

Yes, lad, rest your head on my shoulder if you wish. Now I could tell you a story about mince pies that would have your hair standing on end . . .''

Amy took Mr. Cornwell's offered arm and walked behind the children with him.

"You must be tired, Amy," he said. "You have had a busy day and have done more walking than anyone else."

"Yes, I am," she said. "But I do not believe I have ever lived through a happier day, Spencer."

"Really?" he said. "You do not find it intolerable to be surrounded by children all day long, listening to their silliness and exasperated by their petty quarrels?"

"But I think of what their lives were like and what they would be like without your efforts and those of his lordship and Mrs. Harrison," she said, "and I could hug them all until their bones break."

"Impossible!" He chuckled. "You are just a little bird, Amy. You would not have the strength to crack a single bone."

"I have always hated even thinking of the poor," she said. "Their plight has always seemed so hopeless, the problem too vast. And I could cry even now when I think of all the thousands of children who might be with us here but are not. But there are twenty very happy children here, Spencer, and that is better than nothing."

"You like children," he said, patting her hand. "I have watched you today talking with them. That is sometimes the most neglected part of our job. There is always so much to do and so much talking to be done to them as a group. I do not always find as much time as I would like to talk with them individually."

"They have such fascinating stories to tell," she said.

He looked down at her. "And all of them quite unfit for a lady's ears, I have no doubt," he said. "I should not have encouraged you to spend a day with us."

"A lady's ears are altogether underused," she said, provoking another chuckle from him. "Perhaps we should be told more of these stories by our governesses or at school and spend a little less time dancing or sketching or learning how to converse in polite society.''

''My dear Amy,'' he said, patting her hand again, ''we will be making a radical out of you and scandalizing your family.''

''Is caring about children being radical?'' she asked.

''When the children are from the slums of London, yes,'' he said.

''Well then,'' she said briskly, ''I must be a radical.''

''All in one tiny little package,'' he said. ''But of course,'' he added, grinning at her when she looked up at him, ''diamonds are small too and pearls and rubies and other precious gems.''

''Flatterer!'' she said. She looked back over her shoulder suddenly. ''Where are Judith and Lord Denbigh?''

''Lagging a significant distance behind,'' he said. ''I have been in the habit of thinking that Max is as confirmed a bachelor as I have always been. It seems I have been wrong. It is intriguing, though, that Mrs. Easton is the lady who was once betrothed to him. Most intriguing.''

''Judith will not have it that he is trying to fix his interest with her,'' Amy said. ''But it is as plain as the nose on her face, and has been since we were in London. I am glad you have noticed it too. I was sure I was not imagining things.''

''And what will you do if she remarries?'' he asked.

She was silent for a while. ''I have my parents' home to go back to,'' she said.

''You do not sound enthusiastic about the prospect,'' he said.

''I will think of it when the time comes,'' she said.

''A wise thought,'' he said, curling his fingers about hers as they rested on his arm.

11

It did not feel particularly cold. There was no wind and the sky was clear and star-studded. They strolled rather than walked, by tacit consent letting everyone else outstrip them before they were even halfway home.

"Aunt Edith and Mrs. Webber will see to it that your son is put to bed," he said. "He will probably not even wake up."

"They very rarely have late nights," she said, "and the past two days have been unusually active and exciting ones for them."

They strolled on in silence.

"It is Christmas Day," she said. "It always feels quite different from any other day, does it not?"

"Yes." He breathed in deeply. "Even when one cannot smell the goose and the mince pies and the pudding. Happy Christmas, Judith."

"Happy Christmas, my lord," she said.

"Still not Max?" he asked.

She said nothing.

He was close to reaching his goal, he thought. He could sense it. She would not call him by his given name, perhaps, but there was none of the stiffness of manner, the anger even, that he had felt in her in London. She had accepted his escort to and from church without question, and he had not had to use any effort of will to force her to slow her steps on the return walk. The others had disappeared already around a distant bend in the tree-lined driveway.

Perhaps he would not even need the full week. There was triumph in the thought. She had resisted him eight years before, but then of course he had been a great deal more shy and inexperienced with women in those days. She would not resist him now. His revenge, he sensed, could be quite total and very sweet.

Sweet? Would it be? Satisfying, perhaps. But sweet? His triumph was tempered by the fact that he had just come from church on Christmas Eve and been filled with the holiness and joy of the season. He had wished the rector and all his neighbors a happy Christmas. He had just wished Judith a happy Christmas.

He wished suddenly that it were not Christmas. And he wished that his thoughts had not been confused by what he had heard that afternoon. He was so close to putting right a wrong that had haunted him for eight years. So close to getting even.

And another thought kept intruding. If he was so close to reaching his goal, then surely it would be possible to use his triumph in another way. It would be possible to secure a lifetime of happiness for himself.

For he had made a discovery that afternoon—or rather he had admitted something that had been nagging at his consciousness for some time, perhaps ever since he had set eyes on her at Nora's soirée: He was still in love with her. The love that he had converted to hatred so long ago was still love at its core.

And yet the hatred was still there too. And the hurt. And the inability to trust again. He had trusted utterly before and been hurt almost beyond bearing. He would be a fool to trust her again—the same woman. He would be a fool.

Around the next bend in the driveway the house would come into sight.

Through all the years of her gradually deteriorating marriage, Judith thought, only one conviction had sustained her. Sometimes it had been almost unbearable to have Andrew at home, frequently drunk, often abusive, though he had never struck her. And yet it had been equally unbearable to be without him for weeks or months at a time, knowing that he was living a life of debauchery, that he would be coming back to her after being with she knew not how many other women.

Only one thought had consoled her. If she had not married

Andrew, she had thought, she would have been forced to marry the Viscount Evendon, later the Marquess of Denbigh. And that would have been a thousand times worse.

She walked beside him along the driveway to his house, their boots crunching the snow beneath them, their breath clouds of vapor ahead of them, and held to his arm. And she was aware of him with every ounce of her being. And aware of the fact that they were alone, that they had allowed everyone else to get so far ahead that they were out of sight and earshot already.

If she had not been so naive at the age of eighteen, she thought, and had not misunderstood her physical reaction to him; if there had not been that stupid wager and Andrew had not turned his practiced charm on her; if several things had been different, would she have fallen in love with the viscount then? Or would she at least have accepted the marriage that her parents had arranged, prepared to like her husband and to grow to love him?

They were foolish questions. Things had happened as they had and there was no point in indulging in what-ifs.

His footsteps lagged even further as they approached the bend in the driveway and hers followed suit. She could feel the blood pulsing through her whole body, even her hands.

She turned to him when he stopped walking and fixed her eyes on the top button of his greatcoat as his gloved hands cupped her face. She lifted her hands and rested her palms against his chest. And she lifted her eyes to his and then closed them as his mouth came down to cover hers.

He was kissing her as he had the day before beneath the mistletoe, his lips slightly parted, the pressure light. And the wonder of it filled her. He was the man she had feared for so many years. She tried to remember the impression she had always had of his face until recent days—narrow, harsh-featured, the eyes steel-gray, the lips thin. It was he who was kissing her, she told herself.

The moan she heard must have come from her, she realized, startled. And then one of his arms came about her shoulders and the other about her waist, and he drew her against him. She sucked in her breath.

He must not overdo it, he told himself. He must not move too fast, must not frighten her. He must be patient, take it gradually. He wanted total victory, not a partial one. His motives might be confused, but he knew that he wanted victory.

And yet she tasted so sweet. And so warm. He set his arms about her and drew her against him and fought to keep his control. She was soft and yielding and shapely even through the thicknesses of his greatcoat and her cloak.

He had waited so long. So very long. An eternity. And here she was at last in his arms. He could not force his mind past the wonder of it. She was in his arms after an eternity of emptiness.

He lifted his head and looked down into her eyes in the darkness. They looked directly back into his and he read nothing there but acceptance and surrender. He was not going too far. She wanted this too. And in the faint light of the moon and stars through the branches of the trees she looked more beautiful than ever.

"Judith," he said.

"Yes," she whispered.

He did not know what his hands were doing until he looked down to see them undoing the buttons on her cloak. He left only the top one closed. And then he was undoing the buttons of his greatcoat, opening it, opening her cloak, and drawing her against him, wrapping his coat about the two of them.

And he brought his mouth down to hers again, open, demanding response, pushing at her lips with his tongue, exploring the warm soft flesh behind them when they trembled apart, demanding more, and sliding his tongue deep inside when she opened her mouth.

He wanted her. God, he wanted her. He loved her. He slid one hand down her back, drew her hard against him, chafed at the barrier of clothing between them, wanted to be inside her.

He wanted her. He had always wanted her. And he had waited so long. Judith.

"Judith."

She had never felt physical desire before. She realized that now. She had been in love before, had had stars in her eyes, had been eager for the intimacy of marriage, had tolerated it while she had been in love. But she had never felt desire.

Never this bone-weakening need to be possessed. Never this aching desire to give herself. Her hands must have unbuttoned his evening coat and waistcoat, she thought dimly. They were at his back, beneath both, against the heat of his silk shirt.

She heard her name as his mouth moved from hers to her throat. He was holding her to him so that she could be in no doubt that his desire matched her own.

"Yes," she said. "Yes."

And then the side of her face was against the folds of his neckcloth, one of his hands holding it there, his fingers threaded in her hair. Where was her bonnet? she wondered vaguely. His other arm was about her waist and he was rocking her against him. She could hear the thumping of his heart. And she could feel him drawing deep and even breaths, imposing calm on himself. She closed her eyes and allowed herself to relax.

God, he thought, it was not easy. It was not easy to love the woman one hated. He held her, his eyes closed, and rested one cheek against the top of her head.

Judith. Perhaps he should not blame her. Not after what he had learned that afternoon. She had been very young, just a green girl in the hands of a rake intent on winning a wager. Perhaps he should forget, let go of all the hatred that had been in him so long that it was almost a part of him.

But how would he ever be able to trust her again? Even at the age of eighteen she should have behaved better than she had. She should not have sent her father. She should have told him herself. He did not believe he could ever forgive her for that even if he could excuse her for the rest.

"You should know better than to walk alone with a man on a dark driveway at night," he said.

"Yes." Her voice was low. She did not sound worried or sorry.

"You never know what might happen to you," he said.

"No."

"Judith." He rubbed his cheek against her hair. "Call me by name. Just once. Please?"

"Max," she said softly. She lifted her head and smiled up at him a little uncertainly.

He set his hands at her waist and took a step back from her. He bent down and picked up her bonnet from the driveway, shook the snow from it, and handed it to her. And he buttoned up his greatcoat and drew his gloves from his pockets—he could not remember removing them or putting them there.

"I have been wanting to do that for a long time," he said.

She finished doing up her cloak and looked up at him. "I have wanted it too," she said. A smile touched her lips. "Max."

He leaned down and kissed her softly on the lips once more. "My aunts will be imagining that we have been caught and devoured by wolves if we do not appear soon," he said, and he held out a hand for hers.

A minute later they had rounded the bend in the driveway and were in sight of the house. They both chuckled at the surprising sight of a few of the older children with Spencer Cornwell, and Amy too, engaged in a fierce snowball fight close to the front doors.

Late nights seemed to make no difference to children on Christmas morning. There was always far too much excitement ahead to allow them to sleep until a decent hour.

Judith tried to pretend that she was dreaming and burrowed her head beneath the blankets and pillows. But the chill little body that wormed its way beneath the covers next to her and laid cold feet against her thighs and encircled her neck with little arms was too persistent a dream. And the larger body that launched itself on top of her refused to be ignored.

"Wake up, Mama!" Rupert demanded.

"Are you awake, Mama?" Kate asked, kissing Judith's cheek.

She did not want to be awake. Having lain awake through much of the night reliving the evening, marveling at the wonder of it, dreaming about the consequences of it, she had finally fallen asleep very late. And she had been having dreams that she wanted to cling to, dreams of strong arms about her and a warm mouth open over hers.

"I am now," she said with a sigh, and turned to wrap one arm about each child and pull them into a close hug. "What day is it? I have forgotten."

She laughed as they both answered her question, one in each ear. Of course it was. How could it be any day other than Christmas Day? There was a special feel about the day, as she had said on the way home from church the night before, something that made it different from any other day of the year.

"Oh, so it is," she said. "How silly of me to forget. What shall we do now? Go back to sleep for a while? Or shall we wash and dress and go in search of breakfast?"

She chuckled again at the chorus of protests that greeted her. Even Kate at the age of three knew very well that that was not the routine for Christmas morning.

"Presents first, Mama," Kate said, kissing her on the cheek again and looking at her with wide, pleading eyes.

"Please," Rupert added.

"Presents?" Judith frowned. "Ah, yes, presents. Now let me see, I believe there are a few here somewhere."

Rupert bounced on the bed.

"I tell you what," Judith said. "You two run along and wake Aunt Amy—gently, please—and bring her here while I see if I can find any presents."

"Silly Mama," Kate said, scrambling down from the bed. "You know where the presents are."

Judith reached out to ruffle her hair.

In truth, she thought—and felt guilty at the thought—she would have liked nothing better than to rush through washing and dressing and brushing and all the other tasks that would have to be completed before she could go downstairs to breakfast. She wanted to see him again.

She pushed her feet into a pair of slippers and drew on a dressing gown over her nightgown, then went in pursuit of the pile of parcels that were hidden at the botom of a wardrobe in her dressing room.

She still felt as if she were in something of a daze. She was a woman of twenty-six years, a widow, the mother of two children. And yet she was wildly, exuberantly, head over ears in love. Far more so, she thought with another stab of guilt, than she had ever been with Andrew.

And yet the object of her feelings was none other than the man she had jilted in order to marry Andrew. The man she had feared and disliked at the time and during all the years since until just a few days ago. Not even as long. Even as recently as two days before she had been wary of him, suspicious of his motives. There had been something about him that had made her uneasy.

She smiled to herself as she carried the parcels through to the bedroom and piled them beside the bed. It was herself she had been wary of. It had seemed just too strange to be true that she was attracted to him, that she was growing to like him and admire him, and that she was falling in love with him.

Amy had been right all along, she thought. He had been trying to fix his interest with her from the start. That was why he had arranged all those meetings and outings with her in London, and that was why he had invited her to Denbigh Park for Christmas.

He was in love with her too. If she had had any doubt, then it had been swept away the night before when he had kissed her. And afterward he had led her home, her hand in his, until they had come up to the others, and then liberally pounded her with snowballs as they joined in the battle that the others had started. He had laughed the whole time.

She loved to hear him laugh, to see his harsh features softened and made handsome.

When would he declare himself? she wondered. Today? It seemed likely. It was Christmas Day. And would she accept? She had two children whose security and happiness she must put first in her life. But he knew all about her children and was fond of them, she was sure. And they liked him and his home.

Was it possible that after all she was to be his wife? Eight years after she should have married him?

Her thoughts were interrupted by the return of the children, bringing Amy along with them.

"Ooh!" Kate said as she caught sight of the brightly wrapped gifts.

Rupert ran across the room and dived headlong onto the bed.

"How kind of you to invite me in," Amy said. "I have not been a part of a family gift opening for years."

Judith stared at her sister-in-law. Oh, yes, that must be true, she thought. It had always been the custom at Ammanlea for each family group to open gifts privately. But Amy had belonged to no family group. How cruel they had all been never to think of that.

"But you are an essential part of our family," Judith said. "We could not possibly begin without you."

There was a special glow about Amy, Judith thought as she handed the first parcel to Kate. And she was not convinced that Christmas morning and the gift opening could account for all of it. Amy and Mr. Cornwell had given up the snowball fight before everyone else the night before and had stood together on the steps of the house, watching the battle and laughing. His arm had been loosely about her shoulders.

Judith wondered if her sister-in-law was feeling as she was feeling that morning.

Was he at breakfast already? she wondered. Would he have left before they arrived there?

The morning was taken up almost entirely with gift giving. First the children were presented with their gifts in the morning room—books from Mrs. Harrison, balls from Mr. Cornwell, and watches from the marquess. The marquess's aunts too had something each for them: hand-knitted caps for the boys and mittens for the girls. The other guests all gave them some coins each so that Daniel declared loudly that they were all rich enough to join the ranks of the nobs.

Kate pulled at Rupert's hand until he went from the room and upstairs with her to drag down the box of Christmas bows they had made in London but not used after all. She gave

one to each of the children. The two that remained she gave
to the Misses Hannibal, each of whom insisted on hugging
and kissing her.

"Come an' sit 'ere, nipper," Daniel said to her, "an' I'll
let yer listen to my watch ticking."

The marquess smiled. If Kate were growing up in the same
neighborhood as Daniel, she would have a powerful protector
against all harm. The boy would probably grow into her
devoted servant.

Lord Denbigh had small gifts to distribute to each of his
guests after the children's excitement had begun to subside
a little. He had given his aunts more precious gifts in private
earlier that morning.

And after that there were the servants to call in and present
with their gifts and Christmas bonuses and to serve with tea
and dainties left in the kitchen by the cook and brought up
by him and Nora and Judith and Miss Easton. That part of
the day's ceremony had always used to be an unbearably embarrassing one for the servants as they had attempted to make
conversation with their employers. Since the coming of the
children, however, that had all changed.

Lily and Violet, awed to silence by their own gifts, sat
on either side of Annie, one of the scullery maids, as she
unwrapped hers and she smiled at them and appeared to feel
quite at home even though she was in his lordship's morning
room with his lordship present, standing in the middle of
the room with a large silver tray in his hands.

The gift-opening was always, the marquess thought, one
of the loveliest parts of Christmas. But then, every part of
Christmas seemed the loveliest as it happened.

She was looking exceptionally lovely that morning, he
thought, his eyes straying to Judith. She was wearing a simple
wool dress of deep rose pink. Wool was flattering to a slender
figure, he decided, his eyes passing over her. Slender, but
very shapely too. He remembered again the feel of her in
his arms the night before, when he had pushed back her cloak
and drawn her inside his greatcoat and she had opened his
evening coat and his waistcoat and put herself against the
silk of his shirt.

Slender and shapely, warm, yielding, arched against him, making no resistance even when he had brought the lower half of her body intimately against him.

"Listen." It was Lily, looking shyly up at him, her watch held up toward him. Her eyes, gin-drugged but a few months before, were wide with Christmas.

He stooped down, put his ear obediently to the watch and listened for a few seconds. "It ticks as loudly as your heart," he said. "You must not forget to wind it up each night."

"Never," she whispered fervently. "Thank you."

He smiled and kissed her cheek. "Your smile is thanks enough, Lily," he said.

She turned abruptly away, suddenly anxious because she had left Violet's side for a moment.

He glanced to Judith again and caught her eye. She half smiled at him and returned her attention to his housekeeper, with whom she was conversing. It was hard to know what she was feeling. She looked remote, serene, as she had always looked when they were betrothed. Perhaps she was deliberately hiding her feelings?

As she had done then?

And what had those feelings been then? She had jilted him in order to marry a rake. She must have had no feelings for him at all. Or else her feelings must have been negative ones. Perhaps she had actively disliked him.

And now? She had responded to him with hunger the night before. But that might mean nothing. She had been a widow for longer than a year. Perhaps she was just ripe for a man's attentions. Any man's.

It was impossible to know. But her behavior this morning was warning enough of one thing. He might be in love with her again—or still in love with her—but he must never trust her again, never allow himself to hope for a future with her. For even if she was responding to his lovemaking now and would perhaps accept an offer of marriage from him, he would not be sure that it was not just loneliness for any man that drove her to accept. He would find out only after they were married, when it was too late.

She had broken his heart once. He was not going to allow

it to happen again. He did not think he would be able to survive its happening again.

But for all that, he hoped that he was more to her than just any man. If he was to break her heart as she had broken his, and cause her even one fraction of the pain he had suffered, then it was important that she at least fancy herself in love with him.

Last night he had been sure. This morning he was uncertain again. But then he supposed he would always feel unsure of himself with Judith Easton.

"No, no," he said to his flustered cook. "I shall return the tea tray to the kitchen."

The children had eaten most of the food from the trays even though they had had a large breakfast. Judith took the three trays in a pile and followed the marquess with the tea tray from the room and down the back stairs to the kitchen.

She looked up at him as they set their trays down on the wide kitchen table. "The lace handkerchief is beautiful," she said. "I am sorry that I do not have a gift for you."

"Your presence here in my house is gift enough," he said and watched her cheeks glow with color. He laid the backs of two fingers against her jaw.

She smiled at him and he was sure again. There was a certain look in her eyes, an open and an unguarded look.

"Save some dances for me tonight," he said. "The opening set and at least one waltz?"

"Yes," she said.

There was no time to say anything else. The servants were coming back down the stairs.

But he was sure of her again and ready to move on to the final stages of his revenge, and he was wishing once more that it was not Christmas. He wanted to be happy, yet it was impossible to feel quite happy when plotting the misery of another human being. Even if it was right and just to do so. Even if she deserved it. Even if he owed it to himself to get even.

He wished he was not still in love with her. And he wished she had not told him what she had the afternoon before to shake his resolve and make him wonder if she had been quite as much to blame as he had always thought. He wished he could stop thinking. He wished that humans were not always plagued by thoughts. And by conscience.

He wished it was possible simply to love her. Simply to trust her.

12

The Marquess of Denbigh dismissed his valet and glanced once more at his image in the full-length pier glass in his dressing room. Yes, he decided, he looked quite presentable enough to greet his neighbors and to host his Christmas ball. He felt as if he should look somewhat like a scarecrow.

His guests had found various amusements during the afternoon. His aunts had slept and gossiped with Lady Tushingham in one of the salons, Nora and Clement had gone out walking, taking three of the girls with them, Rockford had gone skating with some of the boys, Sir William had retired to the billiard room with Spence and a few more of the boys, Mrs. Harrison had taken several other children out to a distant hill to sled, Judith and Miss Easton had played games in the nursery with several of the younger children.

Everyone had seemed accounted for until, passing through the hall to join the billiard players, he had received a message from one of the grooms that some of the dogs who were not allowed in the house had been set loose and were causing something of a commotion in the stableyard. There he had discovered four guilty urchins who had been trying to make a dog sled until all six of the dogs had burst from their harness, flatly refusing to cooperate, and scattered to the four corners of the earth.

The marquess grinned at the memory. And sobered again at the memory of Ben, who had cowered and thrown both arms defensively over his head when he had seen the marquess approaching. It was hard to persuade the children to shake off old habits and expectations. He had once held Ben in his arms, soot and all, and promised him that never again would be he flogged for any wrongdoing, real or imagined.

He had taken all four boys out of the stableyard while his

grooms gathered up stray dogs, and engaged them all in a wrestling match in the snow. Ben had soon been giggling helplessly.

They had eaten their Christmas dinner early and stuffed themselves with goose and all the good foods that went along with it. And they had all declared that they had not left even one spare corner for the pudding but had eaten it anyway.

The children's party had come next, a riot of games in the ballroom, which all his guests had attended though there was dinner to recover from and a ball to get ready for. He grinned afresh at memories of Aunt Frieda blindfolded in a game of blindman's buff and quite unable to catch anyone while the children had shrieked with laughter about her.

Rockford had caught Aunt Edith beneath a sprig of mistletoe and pleased her enormously by giving her a smacking kiss. Spence had kissed Miss Easton a little less smackingly and a little more lingeringly later beneath the same sprig. Lord Denbigh wondered if a romance was blossoming in that direction.

Judith had joined in one of the relay races and had raced the length of the ballroom and back, her skirt held above very trim ankles, her face glowing with the fun of it. His heart had somersaulted.

And now it was almost time for the outside guests to arrive, earlier than usual so that they could watch the children's pageant before the ball began and the children were herded off to bed.

It was no wonder he was feeling like a scarecrow, the marquess thought, turning to leave the room so that he could be sure of being downstairs before the first arrival.

No one had played a single hand of cards all day. And except for the wine at dinner, she had not noticed anyone drinking any alcohol. What a difference from Christmas at Ammanlea, Judith thought, taking a chair in the marquess's ballroom, nodding to neighbors she had noticed at church the night before, and waiting for the pageant to begin.

This Christmas had been wonderful. If there were not one more moment of it to come, it would be the best Christmas she had ever known. But there was more to come. There was the pageant that the children had worked so hard to prepare and Rupert's excitement at being a shepherd.

"I am the one who cannot wake up, Mama," he had explained to her in some excitement. "I miss what the angel says and have to be told by Stephen and dragged off to Bethlehem. I have to yawn the whole time until I see the baby."

Judith smiled at the memory of Rupert practicing his yawns.

"It is hard to yawn, Mama," he had said, "when you are not tired."

"I am sure you will do quite splendidly when the time comes," she had assured him.

Kate climbed onto her lap and stared expectantly at the empty stage area.

And there was the ball to come. The dancing. She had always loved dancing. And he had asked her to save the opening set and at least one waltz for him.

There was a growing glow of excitement in her. There had been little time all day to exchange more than the occasional glance and word with him. But his looks had been warm, full of an awareness of what had happened between them the evening before. During the ball they would touch again and talk again. Perhaps he would find the chance to take her aside and declare his feelings.

He loved her. She knew he did. She could see it in his eyes whenever she looked into them. He loved her as she loved him.

She wanted him to kiss her again as he had kissed her the night before. She wanted him to hold her. She wanted to hold him. She wanted more than those kisses. She wanted everything. Her cheeks grew warm at the thought.

"There is Aunt Amy," Kate said, pointing across the ballroom to where Amy was taking her place at the pianoforte.

Conversation about them was dying away as attention turned expectantly to the empty half of the ballroom. Judith smiled and rubbed a cheek against Kate's curls and caught the marquess's eye across the room.

* * *

Amy sat down on the bench behind the pianoforte and looked about the ballroom at all the splendidly dressed ladies and gentlemen who had come for his lordship's ball. And she made sure that her music was in proper order on the music rest. She set her hands in her lap and waited for Mary and Joseph to trudge through the ballroom doors on their weary way to Bethlehem.

She had always loved Christmas because of church and the caroling and the decorating and because it always brought her nieces and nephews to a house that was usually quiet and lonely. And she had always liked to have her brothers and their wives close to her again, reminding her that she was part of a family. But she had never experienced a Christmas as wonderful as this one.

There was Lord Denbigh and the courteous, kindly manner in which he tried to see to it that all his guests were comfortable and entertained. And his interest in Judith, which would surely blossom into a splendid match for her sister-in-law, who deserved more happiness than she could have known with Andrew. And there were the other guests, all amiable, even the unfortunately tedious Mr. Rockford, and willing to accept her as an equal.

And there were the children. All the wonderful children with their exuberance and mischief, their fun and their wrangling, their sad and funny stories from their past, and their capacity to bring joy into any adult's heart.

And the snow and the food and the decorating and skating and snowball fights and . . . oh, and everything.

And Spencer. Amy could feel her heart thumping faster. She had never had a gentleman friend. Never anyone to call her by name and to talk with her and laugh with her and throw snowballs at her and set a careless arm about her shoulders. No one had ever kissed her beneath the mistletoe except her brothers.

Spencer had kissed her twice under the mistletoe and once without. He had kissed her outside the ballroom doors a few minutes before. The children had been ready in their dressing room, though a few of them had still been dashing about in near hysteria. Mrs. Harrison had told Amy that she might take her place and they would try not to keep her waiting longer than half an hour or so—those last words spoken with a harassed look tossed at the ceiling.

Spencer had accompanied her from the dressing room and through the great hall to the ballroom doors, one arm about her shoulders.

"You are a real sport, Amy," he had said. "I do not know what we would have done without you."

"It is not over yet," she had said. "Perhaps I will suffer from a massive dose of stage fright and suddenly find myself with ten thumbs."

He had bent his head and kissed her firmly on the lips. "You could not let us down if you tried, Amy," he had said. "There is far too much love in you for the children. And far too much common sense too."

He had opened the ballroom door for her and winked at her as she passed through.

Friendly kisses all? she wondered, lifting a hand to touch her lips. Or had there been more to them? A real affection, perhaps. Her eyes grew dreamy. She wished . . . Oh, she wished she were fifteen years younger and six inches taller and beautiful. Or pretty at least. She wished . . .

The ballroom door opened again and Amy could see two frightened faces beyond it with Spencer beaming down at them. Mary and Joseph were approaching Bethlehem.

Mary and Joseph were approaching Bethlehem. She was tired and brave and cross and not always careful in her choice of words. And he was strong and tender and reassuring— and could not resist returning one insult rather sharply. They were a loving and weary and very human couple.

The innkeeper, harassed by an unusually packed house and bad-tempered and demanding guests, would have turned away the couple from faraway Galilee without a qualm of conscience, but his wife fiercely defended the right of a woman just about to give birth to be given some place other than the street. Hands on hips, she browbeat the poor man until she suggested the stable, his voice heavy with sarcasm.

And then she drove him out with a broom to clean a manger ready for the baby.

The Bible story, though beautifully written, the Marquess of Denbigh thought, somehow took the humanity out of the players. His ragamuffins from the slums of London put the humanity right back in and made a strangely touching, almost a moving, experience out of it.

The wise men called one another all kinds of idiot as they argued over which route would take them in the direction of the star, but all of them gave the impression that they would have followed it through quicksand if that was the way it pointed. The shepherds, except for the one who remained snoring and whistling on the ground, cursed the air blue in their terror at the appearance of the unknown but soon dropped their jaws in wonder and awe. The angel told them to shut up and pay attention. The choir sang like angels only slightly off-key.

And then Mary in the stable was bending protectively over the manger, warning the shepherds to stay back because she did not want them passing any sickness on to her baby. And she shushed one of the kings, who spoke too loudly for her liking. And she beamed down at the manger and reached down with a tickling finger just as if it were a real baby lying there and not just a doll from the nursery.

Joseph folded his arms, frowned about at the whole gathering, including the angel, and tried to look tough. Anyone who had it in his mind to harm the baby was obviously going to have to go through him first.

Rupert Easton was certainly never going to be able to earn a living as an actor, the marquess thought with amusement, watching the boy yawn and stretch with exaggerated gestures until he gasped at sight of the baby and fell to his knees.

The marquess glanced across the room at Judith. She was leaning forward in her chair, one arm about her daughter, smiling broadly and watching her son intently. He would be prepared to wager that there were tears in her eyes.

And indeed, he thought, there were probably several eyes in the room that were not quite dry. For all the occasional irreverence of their language, these children were bringing alive a story so familiar that sometimes it lost its wonder. Into a very human world, a world full of darkness and imperfection and violence, a savior was being born. And despite everything, despite all the human darkness of the world, he was being welcomed and loved and protected—and worshiped.

There was a sudden and unexpected ache in Lord Denbigh's heart. And a reminder of something that had eluded his conscious mind for the moment. So much darknesss. And so much light. Especially at Christmas. Light to dispel the darkness. A single candle to put the darkness to flight. A Christmas candle.

Unless the darkness fought against it too stubbornly and snuffed it forever.

He joined in the loud and appreciative applause that greeted the ending of the pageant, and found that he had to blink his own eyes several times.

She was late for the ball. It had taken a long time to quiet Rupert's excitement after the success of the pageant. All of the children had been made much of by the assembled adults before being finally herded off to the dining room for refreshments before bed. All of them had been in a mood to swing from the chandeliers, as Mr. Cornwell had put it.

Long after Kate had been tucked into bed, Judith had sat in the nursery with Rupert on her lap, reading a story to him, assuring him that yes indeed, she had heard him snoring, and that yes, certainly his yawns had been very convincing, and finally singing lullabies to him just as if he were an infant again, her fingers running through his soft auburn curls.

She wondered if Mrs. Harrison and Mr. Cornwell were having a similarly hard time getting the other children settled down. And gracious, they had twenty to cope with, not just one. She suspected that Amy was helping them, too, and probably Mrs. Webber.

Her son was growing up already, she thought as she got to her feet eventually and carried him to his bed. He was getting heavy. She looked down at his sleeping face with love and a little regret. She wished she could have kept him as a baby for a little longer. She thought of Mrs. Richards' new-born and of how it had felt in her arms. She wished she could have another child. Kate was three years old already.

A dark-haired baby . . . Would he ask her that night? she wondered. Had she refined too much on a kiss? They had after all been walking alone along a dark driveway. They would have had to be almost inhuman not to have given in to the temptation of the moment. Perhaps he had no intention of making her an offer. Perhaps he did not love her.

But he did. She had seen it in his eyes, those keen heavy-lidded eyes that had used to disturb her, frighten her. She had seen it in his eyes. He did love her.

She was late. The dancing had already started when she reached the ballroom. But she was not the last, she saw, looking about her. Mr. Cornwell, Mrs. Harrison, and Amy had still not come down. The marquess was dancing with an older lady. He was dressed with all the formality of a London ball, and was all gold and white, his silk knee breeches, embroidered waistcoat, and brocaded evening coat all varying shades of gold, his stockings and linen of gleaming white.

Had she ever thought that he was not a handsome man? she wondered. She could hear her heart pounding in her ears.

"I thought you had deserted me completely when you did not appear for our dance," he said with a smile, coming to her as soon as the set ended. "Did you finally get your children to sleep?"

"Yes," she said. "Rupert was very excited."

"I suppose," he said, "that deciding to have them perform their pageant just before bedtime was not a great idea. I have too little experience with children, I am afraid."

"But they have taken a wonderful feeling to bed with them," she said. "They did very well and were well praised for it."

"One thing I have learned about children in the past two years," he said. "They will respond to one word of praise faster than to ten of criticism. They need to feel good about themselves, as we all do. Good comes out of love and evil out of hatred. And here I am mouthing platitudes. Come and dance with me.''

She smiled and remembered the very stiff and formal and unsmiling gentleman to whom she had been betrothed for two months a long time ago. And the harsh, morose gentleman whom she had met again in London just a few weeks before. She looked up at the man who had just said with easy informality, ''Come and dance with me.''

It was a very intricate country dance, which she remembered only with difficulty and great concentration. Some people who attempted it did not know it at all. There was a great deal of laughter in the room as couples or individuals occasionally went spinning off in quite the wrong direction. Both the marquess and Judith were laughing as he spun her down the set after they had been separated for some of the patterns.

''There you are again at last,'' he said. ''Did you promise to save a waltz for me, Judith? If not, promise now.''

''I promise,'' she said, and they were separated again. She was dancing with a very large gentleman who was wheezing rather alarmingly from his exertions.

It was quite the most wonderful ball she had ever attended, she decided, looking about her at the twirling dancers and the berry-laden holly and up to the stars that twisted and glinted with the lights of dozens of candles above them in the chandeliers. By London standards it would not have been described as a great squeeze by any stretch of the imagination, but still to her it was wonderful beyond words.

She was back with Lord Denbigh again. ''What a wonderful ball this is,'' she told him.

''You are not trying to flatter the host are you, Mrs. Easton?'' he asked her.

''Yes, I am,'' she said. ''I also mean it.''

He smiled at her before they parted company yet again. She would have been looking forward to their waltz with some impatience if she had not also wanted to live through and savor every moment of the evening.

* * *

"I have never seen them so excited or so puffed up with their own worth," Mr. Cornwell said.

"They had every right to be," Mrs. Harrison said. "They did quite splendidly even if in the final performance they disregarded or forgot every suggestion we had made to them about their use of the English language. My only consolation is that half the audience probably had never even heard some of the words before. Perhaps they assumed they were Latin or Greek."

Amy laughed. "I could have hugged every one of them," she said.

"I believe you did," Mr. Cornwell said.

The three of them were standing in the doorway of the ballroom, watching the vigorous country dance that had already been in progress by the time they arrived. Mrs. Harrison was being beckoned by the marquess's aunts and made her way to the empty chair beside them.

"Well, dear," Mr. Cornwell said, "Christmas is almost over."

Amy looked sharply up at him. "Yes," she said. "But it has been wonderful, and the glow of it will carry us all forward for some time to come."

"I sometimes worry about my boys," he said with a sigh. "And about the girls too. Shall we stroll? It seems that this set is not nearly finished yet." She set her arm through his and they began to stroll out into the great hall. "I worry about what will happen to them when we finally have to let them out into the world to fend for themselves."

"But you will not let that happen until they have been well prepared for some employment, will you?" she said. "And I believe that his lordship will help them find positions."

"Yes," he said. "But will they forget everything else they have learned? Love and sharing and respect and courtesy toward others and belief in themselves and everything else?"

Amy chuckled. "I do believe, Spencer," she said, "that you are sounding like any father anywhere. You are busy giving your charges wings but are afraid to let them fly. If they are loved, they will love. And they will carry with them everything else you have taught them and shown them and been to them."

everything else you have taught them and shown them and been to them."

He patted her hand. "You are a beautiful little person, Amy Easton," he said. "Where have you been hiding all my life?"

She laughed. "That is the first time I have ever been called beautiful," she said. "My family hid me at home. They were afraid I would be hurt if I went out into the world. They clipped my wings, you see."

"Was it smallpox?" he asked her.

She nodded. "Only me," she said. "It afflicted no one else in the family. For which I can only be thankful, of course."

"If they had only allowed you from home," he said, "you would have been called beautiful many times, Amy. Your beauty fairly bursts out from inside you."

"Oh," she said.

He worked his arm free of hers and set it about her shoulders. "And the exterior is not unpleasing either," he said. "Have you allowed a few pockmarks to influence your image of yourself?"

"Oh," she said, "I stopped even thinking about my appearance years ago. We have to accept ourselves as we are, do we not, or live with eternal misery."

"I wish . . ." he said, and stopped. He smiled at her. "I wish I had met you ten years ago, Amy, and had a fortune as large as Max's."

She swallowed. "I have never believed that wealth necessarily brings happiness," she told him. "And age makes no difference to anything." She looked up at him, liking and affection and hope in her eyes.

He stopped and drew her loosely into his arms. "Ah, Amy," he said, resting his cheek against the top of her head, "these are foolish ramblings. Forgive me. It has been a lovely Christmas, has it not?"

"Yes." There was an aching pain stabbing downward from her throat to her chest. And an inability to say more because she was a woman and because she had no experience whatsoever with such situations. "It has been the loveliest."

She drew her head back to smile at him and he lowered his to kiss her warmly on the lips.

"Come," he said, "I had better take you back to the ballroom while you still have some shreds of your reputation left. Will you dance the next set with me?"

"I have never danced in public," she said.

He frowned at her. "Clipped your wings?" he said. "Did they cut them off completely, Amy?"

She smiled.

"But in private?" he asked. "You danced in private?"

She nodded.

"Then we will see and hear no one else in the ballroom," he said. "You will dance for me—in private. Will you?"

"I would like to try," she said.

He drew her arm through his again and curled his fingers about her hand.

13

His Aunt Frieda was flustered and tittering, protesting to Mr. Rockford that she had never seen the waltz performed and indeed had not even danced at an assembly for more years than she cared to remember.

Mr. Rockford was insistent and Aunt Edith nodding and simpering. Judith was close by and enjoying the moment.

"It is a very easy dance to learn, ma'am," she said. "All you have to do is move to counts of three and allow the gentleman to lead you."

Aunt Frieda threw up her hands, tittered again, and looked alarmed. The Marquess of Denbigh grinned as he walked up to the group.

"My dance, Judith?" he said, extending a hand to her. "Why do you not watch us for a minute, Aunt Freida?"

"Oh, yes," his aunt said gratefully as Judith placed a hand in his. "That would be best, Maxwell."

"And I am quite sure," Aunt Edith said, "that Maxwell and Mrs. Easton will waltz quite splendidly, Frieda, since they have both recently been in town and the waltz is all the crack there."

Judith was smiling up at him as he led her onto the floor and set one hand on her waist. "It was rather rash of Mr. Rockford to ask your aunt," she said. "She will probably have a fit of the vapors when she sees what a very improper dance it is."

"I believe my aunts are made of sterner stuff," he said. "And improper, Judith? Merely because one faces the same partner for the whole dance and can carry on a decent conversation?"

She continued to smile as the music began.

Both of his aunts were watching them intently. He was

very aware of that and kept his steps simple. And he held her at arm's length, her spine arched back slightly from the waist, her hand light on his shoulder.

Improper? Hardly. There was distance between them. He touched her only at the waist, her other hand clasped in his. And yet there was something intimate about the waltz. There was something created within the circle of bodies and arms, some awareness, some tension. Not always, it was true. But with some partners. With Judith it was an intimate dance.

He kept his distance, kept his steps simple, kept conversing lightly with her. His aunts were still watching them, though Rockford was talking to Aunt Frieda and bowing.

It had been an intimate dance in London at the Mumford ball. Almost unbearably intimate. And tense. He had deliberately fostered the tension on that occasion, keeping his eyes fixed on her face the whole time, neglecting to converse with her. He had hated her at that time. Hatred and the desire for revenge had outweighed the renewed attraction he had felt toward her.

And now? But he did not want to spoil the evening or Christmas by thinking and analyzing.

"You were quite right," she said. "Your aunt is ready to try."

They both watched Aunt Frieda take her first dance steps in years.

"I would almost be prepared to say that a romance is in the making," the marquess said, grinning, "if Aunt Frieda were not at the very least twenty years older than her partner. I believe Rockford has taken a liking to my aunts because they are always willing to listen to his stories—even if they do frequently fall asleep before he has finished."

"I think he is enjoying Christmas," she said. "You have made at least one of your lonely persons happy."

"Lonely persons?" He looked at her with raised eyebrows.

"Lady Clancy's name for your guests," she said.

"Lonely persons." He smiled and shook his head. "You too, Judith?"

Her smile faded slightly. She searched his eyes. "Why did you invite me?"

He twirled her about a corner of the ballroom now that there was no longer the necessity of keeping his steps simple. "You do not know?" he asked her.

"Because we would have spent Christmas alone in town without your invitation?" she said.

"Four of you?" he said. "Alone? It could have been a very cozy Christmas."

"Yes," she said. He held her eyes as he whirled her to the music. "I thought you were bringing me here to punish me."

"To punish?" he said.

She nodded. "You knew I was uncomfortable with you in London," she said. "You knew that I did not wish to be in your company. I thought you had devised this as the ultimate punishment. A week in your country home at Christmastime."

He smiled at her. "But you have changed your opinion?"

She continued to search his eyes. And then she nodded slightly again. "It is a Christmas that has been made wonderful by your kindness to many people," she said. "I do not believe you could spoil it all by bringing one person here out of hatred. I misjudged you in London. Perhaps I have always misjudged you. I am sorry."

Her eyes wavered to his mouth and then returned to his. And he gazed back at her. So beautiful. So slender and warm. And so very, very beautiful. And he held his mind blank. He had to do so, for he knew that a fierce war would rage in his mind if he but opened up his thoughts. His desire for her, his love for her at war with his determination to complete what he had begun. And it was so close to completion. It could be completed within a few minutes if he so chose.

"You are making me uncomfortable," she said. Her cheeks were flushed. "Why are you looking at me like that?"

"Because I can think of no other way of looking at you," he said.

They were close to the doors leading out into the great hall. He waltzed her toward them and through them and continued to dance with her on the tiles. He looked keenly at each of the two footmen standing there, and they both hurried away as if they had remembered pressing business elsewhere.

"My only alternative," he said, "is not to look at you at all." He set the hand he held flat over his heart and held it there with his own. He tightened his arm about her waist, drawing her against him until she slid her own hand from his shoulder up about his neck and rested her forehead against his shoulder.

He continued to waltz with her, her body moving in perfect time with his own. He rested one cheek against the smooth hair at her temple.

"I have guests I must return to when this set is at an end," he murmured into her ear after a few minutes had passed. "There is no time for what we both wish to do, Judith."

She raised her head and looked up at him, shocked. And yet there was knowledge in her eyes too, and the admission that he was right, that what was between them was no idle or innocent flirtation.

"Tomorrow," he said. "Arrange to have the afternoon free. Will you?"

She gazed into his eyes for a long time and he could see the conflict of emotions in hers. "Yes," she said at last.

He stopped dancing, closed the distance between their mouths, and kissed her. She responded instantly, molding her body to his, opening her mouth even without persuasion, moaning as he licked hungrily at her lips.

"Max," she said when he moved his mouth to her chin and down to her throat.

But he had not forgotten where they were: in the middle of the great hall, the doors to the ballroom open beyond it.

"Tomorrow," he said, straightening up, cupping one hand lightly against her cheek. "Tomorrow we will settle everything between us, Judith." He was not even sure himself what he meant by those words. He held his thoughts blank. He did not want to know.

"Yes," she said, and she raised a hand to cover his.

He kissed her softly on the lips once more.

First the merest suggestion of light on the eastern horizon. Then a gradual lifting of the blackness of the world to gray. A brighter line of light turning from white to pale gold to brighter gold, to pink, to orange-gold. And then all the glory of the dawn sky before the sun came up.

Judith watched it all from the windowseat in her room, where she sat warmly wrapped in a blanket from the bed, her knees drawn up against her, her arms tight about them.

It looked as if it was going to be a glorious day. Cold but glorious. Even as she watched she saw him—Max—emerging from the stable block on horseback, a large bundle tied behind his saddle. He rode beneath her window, picking his way carefully, not pressing any speed on his horse because of the snow. Why was he up so early after such a late night?

But it was midwinter. She had no idea what time it was, but it was probably not as early as the coming of dawn made it seem. He was up for some morning fresh air and exercise. She wished she were with him.

She looked back into the room. It was a pretty and a cozy room despite the fact that the fire had died down long ago and the air was chill. It looked familiar already, even after just a few days. It looked like home.

Would it be home? she wondered. Would Denbigh Park be her home? After this afternoon she supposed she would know the answer to her question. She knew it now. But it seemed just too wonderful to be true. Could she really be finding such happiness so soon after the ending of a bad marriage, in which she had expected to be trapped for the rest of her life? And with Max of all people?

It was hard to believe in such happiness. And so, even though she was almost certain of it and would be certain before this day was over, she was anxious, too. What if she had misinterpreted all the signs?

She had expected to have her answer on Christmas Day. She had fully expected it at the ball, when he had waltzed with her, when he had danced her out into the great hall.

She had expected him to declare his love for her, to make his offer for her. It had been all there in his eyes and in his mouth when he had kissed her.

Instead, he had said something that had taken her by surprise. "There is no time for what we both wish to do, Judith," he had said.

She had been shocked. For what they both wished to do? Make love? He wanted to make love to her? But of course it was there in his face. And it was what she wanted too. It had not taken her many moments to admit that to herself.

If she had been in any doubt of his meaning, there had been his next words. He wanted her to be free for the whole of tomorrow afternoon. For the whole of *this* afternoon. Why? So that he might ask her to marry him? A few minutes would suffice for that. A whole afternoon?

He was going to make love to her. Her breath caught in her throat and she set her head back against the wood paneling behind her. That very day. He was going to make love to her. And she had not noticed any resistance in herself, though she had been awake for more than an hour already and had lain awake for an hour after the ball before sleeping. She was going to allow it. She was going to allow him to take a husband's privilege with her. But not as a passive experience, she knew. She was going to make love to him too. They were going to make love to each other.

"Tomorrow we will settle everything between us, Judith," he had said.

She closed her eyes. They would make love and he would ask her to marry him and she would say yes. And they would live happily ever after. Except that it would not be as simple as that, of course. She knew from experience that it would not. Every day for the rest of their lives they would have to work hard on their marriage. But it would be worth it.

Oh, it would be worth it.

Judith shivered and pulled the blanket more closely about her. Was she being a fool? Why had he not declared himself the night before? He might have done so and still asked her to be free for him this afternoon. They might have made love as a betrothed couple.

She thought for one moment of the uneasiness she had felt before coming to Denbigh Park and for a day or so after arriving. The feeling that there was something a little frightening about him. Perhaps . . . but no. She had seen into his eyes. His eyes could not lie. Oh, his eyes could perhaps, but not what was behind his eyes. And she had seen what was behind them.

How many hours until the afternoon? she wondered. How many interminable hours?

Christmas was over, she realized suddenly.

The children were up early. They breakfasted as fast as they could and scurried from the room in order to cram into the morning hours a whole day's worth of entertainment. They were to return to the village after luncheon. They skated and sledded and made snowmen and chased and played with the dogs. Some of them took their new balls into the ballroom and got under the feet of the servants who were clearing up after the night's ball. A few of the younger ones went to the nursery to play with Kate and ride the rocking horse.

"You must be longing for the sanity that the next few hours are going to restore to you, Max," Mr. Cornwell said, having abandoned his charges to the care of other willing adults for half an hour. He was sitting in his friend's library, one leg hooked casually over the arm of the chair on which he sat.

The marquess handed him a glass of brandy. "It will be quiet," he said. "My guests may find it unbearably so. The children have been general favorites, I believe."

Mr. Cornwell twirled the brandy in his glass and sipped on it. "We could not quite have foreseen all this two years ago, could we?" he said. "I must confess, Max, that I really did not expect to succeed. Did you?"

The marquess slumped into the chair opposite his friend's. "Yes," he said. "I expected that we would successfully set up homes, Spence. We were both too determined to allow the scheme to fail utterly, I think. What I did wonder about was whether the homes would become almost like other foundling homes with time—impersonal places where the children's basic physical needs would be cared for but nothing else. I wondered if the life would really suit you.''

"I cannot imagine one that would suit me more," Mr. Cornwell said.

The marquess smiled. "You are like an experienced and indulgent father, Spence," he said. "You do not sometimes feel the need for a wife to make the illusion of family life more of a reality?"

His friend looked at him warily and lowered his glass. "Good Lord," he said. "What a strange question to ask, Max. I am almost forty years old."

The marquess shrugged. "I thought perhaps Miss Easton . . .'' he said.

Mr. Cornwell set his glass down and got to his feet. "Miss Easton is a lady, Max," he said.

"And you are a gentleman," Lord Denbigh said.

Mr. Cornwell scratched his head. "And father to ten lads who are anything but," he said. "Use your head, Max. I would not give up my boys, and even if I did, I would have almost nothing to offer a lady. It is true that I have enough blunt that you do not have to pay me a salary, but that is because my needs are modest. I would not dream of inflicting my situation on Amy."

"A pity," the marquess said. "I like the lady."

"And so do I," Mr. Cornwell said fervently. "Good Lord, Max."

The marquess smiled. "Sit down and relax while you have the chance," he said. "And finish your brandy. She is going to walk back to the village with you after luncheon?"

"Violet and Lily have asked her," Mr. Cornwell said, "and half a dozen other children too. We are all going to have tea together at the girls' house to celebrate the success of the pageant."

"Ah," the marquess said, "then young Easton will want to go too."

Mr. Cornwell chuckled. "It is quite a challenge to have to find a wholly new part in a play at the very last moment," he said. "And I hated to have the boy be a shepherd and just stand about quite mute. I am afraid he almost stole the scene. I fully expected our angel to tell him to pipe down when he was snoring so loudly. Yes, he will be coming to tea, of course.''

"His sister will feel left out," the marquess said.

"Oh, she can come too," Mr. Cornwell said. "One extra child here or there really does not make much difference. And her aunt will be there to watch her. Young Daniel will be pleased. I think she reminds him of a little sister he left behind—which reminds me, Max. We might try to mount a search for her and include her with our next batch. Amy thinks it would be a good idea to have a home with boys and girls together and perhaps a married couple to care for them. What do you think?''

"An admirable idea," the marquess said, looking keenly at his friend.

The morning seemed interminable. He should not have risen so early, he supposed. But he had been unable to sleep. He had got up before dawn and taken blankets out to the gamekeeper's cottage in the woods, though there were bedcovers already there. And he had spent half an hour there gathering firewood, preparing a fire so that all that needed to be done was to light it.

He wondered if she would come with him there. He had made his intentions very clear to her the night before. He had left her in no doubt. He had seen the shock in her eyes, a virtuous lady being so openly propositioned by a gentleman who was not even her betrothed. But he had seen the desire too, the temptation, and the acceptance. And she had said yes.

That had been last night, of course. During the night and now in the cold light of day she might well have changed her mind. And she knew very well what was going to happen between them if she came with him.

He had wanted her to know that. He did not want either her or his own conscience to be able to tell him afterward that it had been rape. She knew that if she came with him that afternoon he was going to take her. The only thing she did not know was his motive.

But then, did he?

She had her chance. Her chance to avoid his revenge

despite the care with which he had set it up. He would get even with her if he could. But he could never force anything on her. He could not ravish her.

If she was the virtuous lady she appeared to be, he thought, watching the brandy swirling slowly in his glass, his jaw hardening, then she would find some excuse for not accompanying him that afternoon. She would save herself. And if she did so, if she refused to come, then he would let her go at the end of the week. Perhaps she would feel regret. Perhaps she already expected a declaration from him. Perhaps she would be disappointed—severely so maybe. It would be a sort of revenge. Not as satisfactory as he had originally planned, but good enough.

Truth to tell, he was becoming somewhat sickened by the whole thing. He wished her husband had not died or that he had never heard of it. He wished he had not heard that she was in London or that he had ignored the knowledge. He wished to God that he had never seen her again.

"Perhaps her mother will want to come with her," Mr. Cornwell said.

The marquess looked up blankly. "Judith?" he said. "She has promised to come walking with me."

Mr. Cornwell raised his eyebrows and pursed his lips. "Has she, now?" he said. "In that case, Max, I shall have to assure the lady that the girls' house will be quite full enough with twenty-two children and three adults."

"Thank you," the marquess said. "I would appreciate that, Spence."

"I am not surprised, of course," Mr. Cornwell said. "It would have been pretty obvious to a blind man in the past couple of days. Your aunts have been nodding and looking very smug behind your back."

Lord Denbigh got abruptly to his feet and set his half-empty glass on the tray. He put the stopper back in the decanter. "It is not quite what you think, Spence," he said. "We had better go and see if any of my servants or dogs have been worried to death yet."

His friend chuckled and set an empty glass down beside his.

* * *

"You are quite sure you want to go?" Judith was stooped down tying the strings of Kate's hood beneath her chin.

Two large dark eyes looked back up at her and the child nodded.

"You want to be with the other children?" Judith smiled.

"Daniel is going to carry me on his shoulder," Kate said.

"You like Daniel?" Judith asked.

Kate nodded again.

"And you do not mind if Mama does not come with you?"

Kate put her arms about her mother's neck and kissed her cheek. "I'll tell you about it when I come home," she said.

"Well," Judith said, "Aunt Amy will be with you." She need not feel guilty, she thought, or as if she were neglecting her children. Rupert had already raced from the room and downstairs. And Mrs. Harrison, Mr. Cornwell, and Amy had all asked—separately—if Kate might be taken along too so that she would not be the only child left alone.

"Of course you must not feel obliged to come," Amy had said when Judith had expressed her concern. "Goodness, Judith, do you not believe that I will guard the children with my life? Besides . . ." she had added, but she had looked uncomfortable and had not finished the sentence.

Besides, she wished for some time alone with Mr. Cornwell? Amy had not been looking very happy all morning. Or rather, she had been looking too determinedly happy. Judith had seen her looking so once or twice when her father and her brothers had persuaded her to forgo some expected outing that might take her into too close a communication with strangers.

Had things not gone well for Amy at last night's ball? Judith wondered. Amy had been so very excited at the prospect of attending a ball. And she had danced several sets, two of them with Mr. Cornwell.

But there had been no announcement or private confidence during the evening—or this morning. Had Amy too been expecting, or hoping for, a declaration and not received it?

Kate reached up a hand to take hers and they left the

nursery almost to collide with Amy, who was coming to meet them.

"Are you ready, Kate?" she asked. "Oh, and all nice and warmly dressed. Are you going to hold Aunt Amy's hand?"

"Ride on Daniel's shoulder," Kate said.

"Ah, of course," Amy said. "Daniel." She smiled brightly at Judith.

There was noisy chaos in the great hall. Mr. Rockford was solemnly shaking hands with all the children while the Misses Hannibal were kissing them. Two balls had escaped from their owners' hands. Someone was demanding to know what time it was since he had forgotten to wind his watch. A chorus of voices answered him. Mrs. Harrison and Mr. Cornwell were organizing the children into twos for the walk to the village. The marquess was standing cheerfully in the middle of it all.

"All right," Mr. Cornwell said in the voice that always drew everyone's attention, "before we quick march, what do you have to say to his lordship?"

"Thank you," twenty voices chorused. "Guv," someone added.

"Hip hip," Mr. Cornwell said unwisely.

"Hooray!" everyone shrieked, and caps and mittens and balls flew upward and then rained down on the great hall.

"Hip hip."

"Hooray."

"Hip hip."

"Hooray."

The marquess grinned as everyone broke ranks to retrieve lost possessions.

"We may be out of here before nightfall, Max," Mr. Cornwell shouted over the hubbub.

"I shall send the carriage for you and the children, ma'am," the marquess said to Amy.

"Oh, please do not," she said to him earnestly. "We will enjoy the walk."

"As you will," he said, glancing from her to Mr. Cornwell and back again.

And then they were on their way, more or less in twos

and more or less at a brisk march. Kate and one of the smallest boys rode sedately on other children's shoulders. Mr. Rockford had already gone in search of Sir William in the billiard room. The Misses Hannibal assured each other that they must not catch a chill from the opened front doors and retreated to a warm salon.

The hall was suddenly very quiet.

"You will come walking with me, Judith?" the marquess asked.

Walking? She looked up into his eyes. "That would be pleasant, my lord," she said, noticing how foolish her formality sounded after the night before.

"Go and dress warmly, then," he said. "I shall meet you down here in—ten minutes' time?"

"Yes," she said.

He looked stiff and cold, his face harsh, his eyes hooded. Almost as he had always used to look, she thought, with a quickening of her breath and a sudden strange stabbing of alarm. But then he smiled, and he was Max again.

She smiled in return and turned to hurry from the great hall to the staircase.

14

There was a chilly wind blowing so that even though the sky was clear and the sun shining, it was less pleasant outside than it had been for the past two days. She held the hood of her cloak together beneath her chin and clung to his arm.

She had thought that he must have changed his mind or that perhaps she had misunderstood all the time. Perhaps he really had just wanted to spend an afternoon with her. But she knew soon after they had left the house just where he was taking her. And she was not sure whether to be glad or sorry.

"You are cold?" he asked her, and he unlinked his arm from hers, set it about her shoulders, and drew her firmly against his side. They walked on through the snow. "Soon you will be warm."

It was a promise that made her knees feel weak. She rested her head against his shoulder since that seemed the most sensible place to set it.

"Max," she said at last when they had trudged through the snow for a while in silence, retracing their steps of a few days before, when they had come with the children to gather the greenery for decorating the house, "where are we going?" She was talking for the sake of talking.

"You know where," he said, stopping and turning her to face him. "You did understand me last night, Judith? You do not wish to go back?"

There was something. His voice was low. He was looking down at her lips. She could feel the warmth of him through his greatcoat. But there was something intangible. Her own conscience? Could she be quite so coolly doing what she was doing?

She shook her head and he brushed his lips briefly over hers before they walked on.

She had made no protest at all. Only the question whose answer she must have known. And only the slightly troubled look when he had given her the chance, even at that late moment, to go back, to be free of him. He held her protectively against his side, feeling her slenderness through the thickness of their clothing.

But she had shaken her head and looked at him with such a look of—nakedness in her eyes that he almost wished that he could turn back himself or direct their steps somewhere else and pretend that all along his intention had only been to walk out with her. There had been desire in her eyes, as he had intended. And there had been that other in her eyes too—as he had also intended. Except that seeing it there he had been terrified. Terrified of his power over another human being. The same power as she had exerted over him eight years before.

To be used as cruelly.

"Max," she said, and her voice was breathless even though they had not been walking fast or into the teeth of the wind. They were turning to take the path through the trees that Rockford and the bigger boys had taken a few days before, the one he had taken that morning. "Are you going to make love to me?"

"What do you think?" he asked.

"I think you are." Her voice was shaking.

"Do you want to go back?" he asked.

"No."

He wanted to. He wanted to turn and run and run and never stop running.

She would not have been at all surprised if her legs had buckled under her. They felt not quite like her own legs, but like wooden ones she was unaccustomed to. There was something wrong about what was happening, something sordid, something calculated. Except that his arm was about her and her head was on his shoulder. And she loved him more than she had ever thought it possible to love. And she wanted to give him something to make up for what she had done to him all those years ago. She wanted to give him herself.

And it was good that the giving would come before his offer, she thought. It would be a free and unconditional gift. The cottage was in sight, a real cottage, though very small. Not the rude hut she had expected. It was in a little clearing by itself.

There was not a great deal of light inside the cottage. The two windows were very small, and the clearing was surrounded by trees. He lit a candle with the tinderbox on the mantel and set it on the small table. And then he stooped down to hold a light to the fire he had set that morning.

"Keep your cloak on," he said, straightening up and turning to her. She was standing quite still just inside the door. He watched her eyes stray to the newly made up bed in one corner of the room. She licked her lips. "This is a small room. It will be warm in here in no time at all."

"Yes," she said, and raised her eyes to his. They were full of that nakedness again. There were no defenses behind her eyes. She was totally at his mercy. And he was intending to show her none. "Max."

There was something about his eyes, something about the set of his jaw. Was he having second thoughts? Was he feeling that he had gone quite wrongly about this whole business of courtship? She was having no such misgivings. Since the door had closed behind them a couple of minutes before, she had put behind her all her doubts and all her guilt. She was where she wanted to be and with the man she wanted to be with and she would think no more. She reached up a hand and set it lightly against his cheek.

He took the hand in his and turned his head to kiss her palm. When he looked back to her, something had lifted behind his eyes and they smiled at each other.

"This is where I want to be," she whispered to him.

"Is it?" he asked. "It should not be, Judith. You should turn and run through that door and keep on running and not look back."

He was giving her her last chance. He begged her with his eyes to take it. He should reach behind her, he thought, and open the door and push her out and bar the door behind her. He turned his head to kiss her palm again.

"I am where I want to be," she said again, and her free hand was on his shoulder and she was his for the taking.

"Judith." He bent his head half toward her and stopped. Her eyes and her lips were smiling at him, but the eyes were growing dreamy.

He was afraid. She could see the uncertainty in his eyes, the pleading for something. Reassurance? Was he afraid of bringing ruin on her? Afraid that she would weep afterward and blame him?

"Max," she said, and she closed the distance between their lips until hers touched his. "I love you."

And then she gasped and clung to him with both hands as he made a sound that was more like a growl than anything else and wrapped her about with arms like iron bands and kissed her with an almost savage hunger.

He could not draw her close enough. He wanted her against him, inside his own body, part of him. He had wanted her for so long. Always. He had always wanted her. And he had always wanted to hear those words. Always. All his life. In her voice. Spoken to him. He wanted her. Now. Sooner than now.

There was heat against his back. He was shielding her from the warmth of the fire. He turned her in his arms, not taking his mouth from hers, fumbled with the strings of her hood, tore at the buttons of her cloak, threw it from her, gathered her against him again, and thrust his tongue into her mouth.

But he did not want her like this. He did not want to take her. He did not want to master her. He wanted to love her. He wanted her to love him. He had waited so long. So very long. His arms gentled. His mouth moved to brush her cheek, to kiss her below the ear.

"Judith," he said into her ear, "I have waited so long for this."

"Yes," she said, and her hands began to work at the buttons on his greatcoat and she was lifting it away from his shoulders and sliding it down his arms. It fell to the floor. "Are you warm enough?" She was undoing the buttons of his coat.

"Am I warm enough!" He tightened his arms about her,

imprisoning her hands against his chest, and laughed down at her. "Have you ever asked a more foolish question in your life, Judith?"

She laughed back at him, the sound low and seductive and carefree. "Probably not," she said. "But you know what I meant."

"Let's take our time, shall we?" he asked her, brushing his lips across hers. "We have all afternoon. Let me kiss you silly before we undress each other. Will you?"

She laughed again. "Kiss me silly!" she said. "I like the sound of it. Let me kiss you silly too."

She did not need to. Just holding her like this, the heat from the fire warm on his arms about her, her face turned up to his, laughing, made him want to shout with joy. He wanted to pick her up and spin her about and about until they both collapsed from dizziness. But the room was very small. And as like as not they would collapse onto the fire.

He laughed down at her. "Proceed then," he said. "No quarter given or asked?"

"Never," she said, and she put her arms up about his neck and lifted her mouth for his kiss.

The tone of the afternoon had changed. The sexual tension, the total concentration on the physical deed that was to be performed between them, had been replaced by something else. Judith did not even try to put that something into words in her mind, but she felt it and responded to it. There was warmth, affection, love between them.

She smoothed her fingers through his hair as they kissed each other lightly, warmly, exploring almost lazily with lips and tongues and teeth and withdrew from each other occasionally just to smile and murmur words that they would never afterward remember. Passion was there, held in check for the moment, to build to fierceness and even frenzy later, but for the time there was the warmth of love.

His hair, she discovered, was thick and soft to the touch. His lips, which she had always described to herself as thin, were warm and firm and very masculine. And his eyes— those steel-gray eyes with the heavy lids—held her enslaved. Bedroom eyes.

"Bedroom eyes," she murmured to him and watched those eyes soften into an amused smile.

"A between-the-sheets body," he said against her mouth, and they both chuckled before he deepened the kiss.

He had withdrawn all the pins from her hair, slowly, one at a time, dropping them carelessly to the floor about her. She shook her hair when he had pulled free the last one and he ran his fingers through it—full-bodied silky hair the color of ripe corn.

His hands explored her lightly, unhurriedly, through the wool of her dress. Breasts as full and as firm as they looked, hard-tipped for him, a small waist, shapely hips, flat stomach, firm buttocks. And warm, all warm and delicious and inviting from the proximity of the fire.

He could not remember a time when he had felt happier.

"Judith," he murmured to her, lifting his head to look down into dreamy eyes and at a mouth that looked thoroughly kissed.

"Max."

"Profound conversation," he said, rubbing his nose across hers.

"Yes."

"I think the room is warm enough," he said, and he found the buttons at the back of her dress and began to undo them.

"Yes."

Her eyes wandered over his face as he continued his task and then drew the dress over her shoulders and down her arms with the straps of her chemise. She closed her eyes when he had her naked to the waist and held her a little away from him so that he could look at her. He lowered his head to kiss one shoulder and one breast.

Beautiful. More than beautiful. Need began to burn in him.

He slid his fingers down inside all her clothing so that his palms were flat against her back, and he lowered it all over hips and buttocks until it fell to her feet. And she kicked free of the clinging fabrics and boots and stockings.

She marveled at the fact that she was not for a moment embarrassed even though there was a bright fire behind her and a candle burning on the table and daylight peering in at the windows, and even though he was looking at her and touching her and kissing her. And even though he was fully clothed. She had always been embarrassed with Andrew when he had raised her nightgown, even when she had still loved him. But the thought of her husband did not form itself fully in her mind.

She was undressing him. He stood still and watched her, her eyes lowered to the task of undoing buttons. He had never had a woman undress him before. It was a far more erotic experience than having a valet do it. The thought made him smile. She looked up and saw it.

"Are you trying to put my valet out of a job?" he asked.

She smiled and shook her head and he kissed her deeply, tasting the heat of her mouth with his tongue, allowing passion to build in him.

"Coward," he whispered to her. She had stopped with the removal of his coat and waistcoat. He reached up and removed his neckcloth and undid the top button of his shirt. But her hands pushed his aside and continued the task.

Dark hair curled on his chest, and it was a well-muscled chest despite his lean physique. She leaned forward, her face against his chest, her eyes closed, and breathed in the smell of him. Cologne, sweat, pure maleness. A throbbing low in her womb was threatening the steadiness of her legs again.

Her feet were cold, bare against the packed earth of the floor. She raised the left one to warm against the right.

"Cold feet?" he asked.

She lifted her head and smiled fully at him. "Yes and no," she said. "Mainly no." And she watched the laughter gather in his eyes again as he leaned down and swung her up into his arms.

The bed was soft and comfortable against her back. Surprisingly so. He had put a down-filled cover beneath the sheet, she realized. She watched him pull his shirt free of his waistband and remove it entirely. And she watched as he pulled off his Hessian boots and undid the buttons at his waist.

He watched her the whole time, watching him, unashamed, uncovered, waiting for him. He watched her glance at him as he removed his pantaloons, and swallow.

The bed had never been meant to hold two. But soon enough they would take up no more space than one. He lay carefully on his side beside her, propped on one elbow.

"Feet warmer?" he asked her.

She set one against his leg. It was cold.

"I have a cold woman in bed with me?" he asked, lowering his head, pecking at her lips.

"No," she said. "The woman is warm enough from the ankles up."

"Is she?"

"Yes." There was a catch in her voice. He deepened the kiss. And he feathered one hand over her breast, his thumb circling the tip before touching it, brushing over it. He felt her draw in breath.

The slow languorous time of love was past. The heat of passion was back, but with it an intimacy that went beyond the mere physical. She could feel it in his hands, in his mouth, his body. And it was with the love at the core of her, not just with her hands and her mouth, that she touched him.

She let her hands roam over him, touching leanness and hardness and muscle. And warmth and dampness and desire. She explored him and touched him as she had never dreamed of touching Andrew. And she wanted him. She wanted him with a fierce ache. She wanted him at the core of her. She wanted to give and receive everything. All that there was.

"Max."

It was an ache that he was building to an almost unbearable tension. He was touching her where she had never been touched with a hand, with fingers, stroking, parting, feathering, tickling. Pushing inside. Deeper inside. She felt her muscles clench around him.

"Max."

"I want to be there," he said. His voice was low against her ear.

"Yes."

"Do you want me, Judith?"

Foolish words. Her body and her voice were crying out for him. "Yes."

"There?"

"Yes."

"Here?"

His weight was on her, his blessed weight, bearing her down into the softness of the bed, and her thighs were being opened against the hardness of his legs, and he was there, pressing where his fingers had been, holding, waiting.

"Yes."

He was watching her, her eyes tightly closed, her face tense. Beautiful. And he savored the moment. The moment for which he had waited all his life. This was not something he would do in quick frenzy. He was going to love her as he had dreamed countless times of doing it. In a moment he would be inside her and she would be his. And he would be hers. She opened her eyes.

"Like this," he said. "Like this, Judith." And he held her eyes with his as he entered her, feeling himself gradually sheathed in heat and moistness and contracting muscles.

"Yes," she said. Her voice was almost a sob.

He had to lower his head and close his eyes for a moment so that he would not lose control.

It had always been a purely physical thing. Not quite unpleasant except toward the end when she disliked and despised Andrew. But not quite pleasant either. Something a little embarrassing, a little distasteful. A duty. Something she had always wanted to be over and done with quickly. She had never, even in the early days of her marriage, really enjoyed the sexual act.

There could be nothing more physical than what was happening to her now. An act performed slowly and in nakedness. Heat. Depth. Wetness. The sound of wetness. A slow deep rhythm.

And yet there could be nothing more beautiful on this earth. His body. Hers. Himself. Herself. Their love meeting and entwining and expressing itself inside her. Both of them

inside her, exchanging love, exchanging selves in the slow
rhythm of the early stages of the love act. One body. The
phrase suddenly made perfect sense to her.

"Max?"

"Mmm." He lowered his head to hers, kissed her warmly.

"Max, it hurts."

"Does it?" He continued to kiss her, felt her hips move
against his, felt the stirrings of climax in her, and speeded
his rhythm.

He could not wait much longer. He wanted the closeness,
the intimacy, never to end. He wanted never to let her go,
never to allow her to be free of him. But the physical act
must end. It was time for the ultimate giving and receiving.
He wanted to feel her final surrender, the final opening to
him, the final pushing beyond the barrier of her tension. And
he wanted to give himself, his seed, his future to his woman.

And she was coming to him, lifting to him, tensing against
him, whimpering, and then opening and stilling with the
wonder and shock of her surrender, and shuddering and
reaching for him and crying out his name.

And his seed sprang in her and he held her to him, feeling
all his strength, all his tension drain out of him and into the
woman he had loved all his life, for all eternity. He heard
the sound of her name.

When she woke up, she was lying on her side pressed
warmly against him, her head on his shoulder, his arm about
her, the blankets up around them both. She could not
remember ever feeling quite so comfortable.

The room was warm, the fire crackling in the hearth. He
had got up some time after their first loving and built it up
again before returning to the bed to love her again.

She could not see the room because she had her back to
it. But she could picture it in her mind, small and snug. An
idyllic cottage in the woods. She wished they could spend
the rest of their lives there, and smiled at the thought. The
two of them and Rupert and Kate all together in the one-
roomed cottage for the rest of their lives. And perhaps . . .
well, she had made the calculations last night. She had known

even before leaving the house with him that this was quite
the most dangerous part of her month. And he had loved
her twice.

The two of them and Rupert and Kate and a black-haired
baby. She smiled again at the absurdity of her own thoughts
and tipped her head to look up at him. He was awake and
gazing back at her, his face quite serious.

"What are you thinking?" She raised a hand and laid the
backs of her fingers against his jaw.

He shook his head slightly.

"I was thinking about our living here in this cottage for
the rest of our lives," she said. "Silly, is it not?"

"Yes," he said.

"How long have we slept?" she asked. "It is still daylight
outside, but we will have to be going back soon, won't we?"

"Yes," he said.

"Mmm." She sighed. "I wish we did not have to. Don't
you?"

"We have to," he said. He was still not smiling.

"Max." She rubbed her face against his chest, kissed him
there, and tipped her head back again. "I love you."

He looked back at her and said nothing.

She rested her fingertips against his cheek and gazed into
his eyes. There was something there, something far back in
them. "What is it?"

"I am embarrassed," he said.

"Embarrassed?" She laughed, but he did not smile. She
sobered again.

"I thought you understood," he said. "You did understand, did you not, Judith? That this is just a Christmas
flirtation?"

Her hand stilled against his cheek. She frowned slightly.
"No," she said. "No, Max. Don't do this. It is not funny.
Don't look at me like that."

"It was understood from the start, was it not?" he said.
"You are a widow and young and it is Christmas. I
thought . . . but perhaps I did not make myself clear."

"Max." She withdrew her hand from his cheek and
pounded the edge of her fist once against his chest. "Don't

be silly. Do you think to frighten me only so that you can laugh at me? Do you think to make me doubt what this has been? Don't be silly. And don't spoil it. Tell me you love me. Tell me.''

He set the back of one hand over his eyes. "Judith," he said. "I am so sorry. I had no idea that your feelings were involved. I had no idea. I thought you felt as I did.''

She lay very still, looking into his face, though his eyes were still covered by the back of his hand. And it was as if a giant hand had lifted the cottage up and off its foundations and they had been exposed to all the chill of a winter's day and the cutting force of the wind. She felt cold to the very heart.

And she knew—she had known from his first word though she had fought against the knowledge—that he was not teasing, that he would not the next moment reach out to pull her to him and laugh away her fears. She knew that she had been right about him from the start. She knew that she had been made his victim, that she had made herself his victim.

For it was not a Christmas flirtation. And it was certainly not Christmas love. It was vengeance from hell and had nothing to do with Christmas at all. She understood it all at last in a blinding flash.

He had not changed. He had never changed. And she had been right about him eight years before. He was cold to the very core. She had shamed him publicly and she had had to be punished. She had been punished.

She got up quietly from the bed and dressed silently and quickly. She found as many hairpins as she could on the floor and pinned up her hair without benefit of mirror or comb. She drew on her boots and her cloak and pulled up the hood over her head. She tightened the strings beneath her chin.

And she left the cottage without once glancing at the bed. She closed the door quietly behind her and began the long trudge back to the house through the snow.

He lay still, his hand over his eyes, until he heard the door close behind her.

He had had no idea as he had lain awake, holding her to

him, waiting in dread for the moment when she would stir and look up at him, exactly what he would say to her when the moment for talking came. He had had no idea which side of his warring nature would finally win.

He had listened to himself almost as if he were standing beside the bed observing himself. Observing both of them. "I love you," she had said, and the words had come straight from the depths of her being. Her body pressed to his had uttered the same words. And her eyes had told him the truth of them. She loved him.

Triumph. Total victory beyond his best expectations. Revenge complete. She would suffer from rejection and humiliation as he had suffered. She would suffer from unrequited love as he had suffered. She would suffer from an uncontrollable hatred as he had suffered.

She would know darkness. Darkness that fought and fought against the light and threatened always to put it out.

He turned his head sharply and looked at the candle on the table. It was out although it had not completely burned down. A single candle snuffed. The fire was dying down and dusk was beginning to settle beyond the windows.

He set both hands over his face. After a few minutes he rolled over onto his stomach and buried his face and hands in the pillows.

15

It was the day after Christmas. Not at all the time to think of work. Several of the villagers called at the homes as soon as they knew that the children had returned, bringing food offerings and stories of Christmas, and bringing with them ears to be filled with the children's own accounts of the holiday.

She was not to think that they lived normally in such chaos and in such decadent luxury, Mr. Cornwell told Amy with a smile. The following day they would be back to work, the boys spending the morning with the rector having a Bible lesson, the girls stitching with Mrs. Harrison.

"And you must not believe that my boys will run straight to perdition while I walk home with you," he told her. "There are plenty of adults to keep a friendly eye on them, and a few who will keep a firm hand on them if necessary."

"It is very kind of you," Amy said. "But I did not intend to give you an extra two-mile walk."

He patted his rather round middle. "After the rich foods of the past two or three days," he said, "I think perhaps I should have a two-mile walk every hour, Amy."

She laughed. The children walked ahead of them, Kate holding Rupert's hand and looking up occasionally to show interest in the long story he appeared to be telling her.

"Lovely children," Mr. Cornwell said. "Nicely behaved. It is a pity they lost their father so young."

"Yes," she said. "They look very like my brother. He was a handsome man."

"But Mrs. Easton is young," he said. "Doubtless they will have another Papa soon. Will you mind?"

"No," she said. "I love Judith as if she were my real sister."

"You will still live with her when she remarries?" he asked. "Have you made a final decision?"

"No." She spoke quite firmly. "But not with Judith. That would not be fair."

"But not with your family again," he said. He patted her hand as it rested on his arm. "They overprotected you, Amy."

"I am afraid they did," she said. "Since I have been away from them, I have found people to be very kind. I am not treated like some sort of monster after all."

He clucked his tongue. "Did you expect to be?" he asked. "Did you really expect to be?"

She smiled. "All three of my brothers are unusually handsome men," she said. "I believe all my family acted out of the wish to protect me. I suppose I came to believe that some terrible disaster would befall me if I left the nest. I am glad that Judith persuaded me to do so."

"But you may go back to them?" he asked.

"I don't know," she said. "I have made no definite plans for the future."

They were halfway along the driveway already. Soon they would be at the house. The next day his boys and he would be back at work again and unlikely to come near Denbigh Park. And she would have no further excuse to visit them. Time passed so quickly, she thought, and remembered a time not so long in the past when she had believed just the opposite.

"I wish . . . " he said, and stopped. "I wish you would meet some gentleman you could be fond of, Amy. Someone with a comfortable home and fortune. Someone with whom you could spend your remaining years in contentment."

Her throat ached as if she had just run for a mile without stopping. "I once dreamed of it," she said, "of a home and children of my own and a modest place in society. I no longer care much for the home and it is too late for the children. But I would still like to belong somewhere, to feel wanted and needed. To feel useful. But I count my blessings every day of my life."

"Ah," he said. "To feel useful. I can understand that need,

Amy. It is the way I felt before Max and I dreamed up our plan for our children's homes.''

"Yes," she said, "and you found your dream. How I envy you.''

They had reached the house. Rupert and Amy turned to look at them and Mr. Cornwell waved them on toward the doors.

"Run inside and get warm," he said.

"Will you come in and warm yourself before returning?" she asked.

"No." He patted her hand. "If I do that, Max will insist on calling out a sleigh or a carriage, as like as not and I will not get the exercise I need.''

"Thank you for walking with me," she said as he took her hand in both of his and held it. "It has been a wonderful Christmas, has it not? The best I can ever remember.''

"And for me too," he said, raising her hand to his lips. "You will be here for a few more days, Amy? Perhaps I will see you again before you leave. If I do not, have a safe journey home. I shall always hope that you find what you deserve in life. I'll never forget you.''

She bit her lip. "Or I you," she said. And in a rush, "You are the first friend I have ever had outside the family.''

"Am I?" He smiled at her. "Then I am deeply honored. And I shall hope always to be your friend. Perhaps if your sister-in-law and Max . . .'' He smiled and shrugged. "Then perhaps we would meet again.''

She nodded.

"Amy," he said softly, "it would not work. Believe me, it would not. You are a lady and brought up to the life of a lady.''

An empty, empty, empty life, she thought, concentrating on their clasped hands. She nodded.

"I think maybe I should not come here in the next few days," he said.

She nodded again.

"Good-bye, then, my dear," he said after a pause. "For the first time in more than two years I wish things could be a little different, but they cannot.''

She looked up into his face. "I wish it too," she said. "I wish other people did not always *always* know what is best for me. Is it my size, I wonder? Is it because I look so much like a child to be protected?" She withdrew her hand from his. "Good-bye, Spencer. Thank you for these few days. I cannot tell you all they have meant to me."

And she turned about and was gone up the steps and into the house before he could even return his arms to his sides. He stood for a long time frowning after her.

The Marquess of Denbigh was standing in the great hall when the two children came inside alone. He raised his eyebrows and looked at them.

"We just came home from the village," Rupert explained to him. "Aunt Amy is outside with Mr. Cornwell. Mr. and Mrs. Rundle came visiting and Mr. Rundle said he once met my papa. He said that papa liked to watch all the mills outside town, but Mrs. Rundle would not let him tell me about them. I think it was because ladies do not like to watch mills. Do they?"

"It is not considered a genteel sport for ladies," the marquess said, noticing that the little girl looked tired. She clung to her brother's hand and gazed upward at him with those dark eyes, which were going to fell a large number of young bucks when she was fifteen or sixteen years older. He smiled at her. "They do not derive much enjoyment from watching noses get bloodied. Don't ask me why."

The little girl had detached herself from her brother's side and was standing in front of the marquess, her arms raised. He picked her up and she set her arms about his neck and rested her cheek against his.

"Tired?" he asked.

She yawned loudly.

"Do you want me to carry you up to the nursery?" he asked.

She nodded. "Daniel lost his ball," she told him.

"Did he?"

"But he found it again."

"I am glad to hear that," he said.

"They all play cricket in the summer," Rupert said. He was trotting up the stairs at the marquess's side. "Cricket is a super game. I am going to play on the first eleven when I got to Eton, just like my papa did. Uncle Maurice told me."

"So did I," the marquess said, ruffling the boy's hair. "It is a noble ambition."

"Did you?" Rupert said, looking up at his host with renewed respect. "But I would like to play with the boys here. They all say that Joe is the best bowler. Perhaps if we come back in the summer I will be allowed to play with them. I will be almost seven by the summer."

The boy's hand was in his, Lord Denbigh noticed.

"I want to play with the dogs when we come back," Kate said.

The marquess allowed Rupert to open the nursery door since he did not have a free hand himself. Judith turned from the window at the far side of the room as they entered. She had obviously been awaiting the return of her children. Her face looked as if it had been carved out of marble.

"Mama." Her son raced toward her. "There was a gentleman at the house in the village who used to know Papa. He said I look just like him. He said he would have known me anywhere."

She rested a hand on his curls.

The marquess bent down to set Kate's feet on the floor. But she squeezed his neck tightly before scurrying across to her mother with some other pressing piece of news and kissed his cheek.

Judith was bending down to listen to her daughter's prattling as he turned to leave the room.

Christmas was not quite over, it seemed. The decorations still made the house look festive, and there were still all the rich foods of the season at dinner. And it appeared that the marquess's aunts had busied themselves during the afternoon organizing a concert for the evening.

"Everyone is to do something, Maxwell," Aunt Edith told him when they were all at table. "Miss Easton was not here, of course, when we made the plans. She was in the village

with the dear children. But I am sure she will favor us with
a selection on the pianoforte.'' She smiled at Amy. ''And
you and Mrs. Easton were out walking.'' Her smile, echoed
by Aunt Frieda and Lady Tushingham, was almost a
smirk.

''I shall read 'The Rape of the Lock,' '' Lord Denbigh said.
''It always shocks the ladies.''

''But I am sure it cannot be quite improper despite its title
if you are willing to read it aloud with ladies present, dear
Maxwell,'' Aunt Frieda said.

Judith supposed she would sing. Amy would be willing
to play for her. She had deliberately seated herself beside
Mr. Rockford at dinner, knowing that a few carefully selected
questions would keep him talking the whole time. She
excused herself as soon as Lady Clancy got to her feet to
signal the ladies to leave the gentlemen to their port,
promising to return to the drawing room in time for the
concert.

Kate and Rupert were both fast asleep, she found when
she looked in at the nursery. She went to her own room.
Her heart plummeted when there was a tap on the door almost
immediately and Amy came inside. She so desperately
wanted some time alone. But she needed to talk with her
sister-in-law too.

''Amy,'' she said, ''I have been meaning to tell you that
we must . . .''

But Amy did not wait to hear what she had to say.
''Judith,'' she said, her voice agitated, ''is it possible that
we can leave here tomorrow? Or that I can, perhaps? Is it
possible that you can come with someone else later or else
that you will not wish to leave at all?''

Judith had been wondering how her sister-in-law would
react to having to leave Denbigh Park a few days earlier than
they had planned. She frowned and watched aghast as Amy
burst into tears and hurried across the room to gaze out of
the window onto the dark world beyond.

''Amy?'' she said. ''What is it?''

''Oh, nothing.'' Amy blew her nose. ''Just homesickness.

This was not such a good idea after all, Judith. I have never been away from home at Christmas.''

"Mr. Cornwell?'' Judith asked softly.

Amy blew her nose again. "What a foolish, pathetic creature I am,'' she said. "I am thirty-six years old and from home for the first time in my life, and I fall stupidly in love with almost the first gentleman I meet.''

"And he with you, if my eyes have not deceived me,'' Judith said. "He seems very fond of you, Amy. Did something happen this afternoon?''

"Only good-bye,'' Amy said. "And the assurance that 'it' would never work—whatever 'it' is. I am a lady, you see, and have been brought up to the life of a lady.''

"Have you ever told him,'' Judith asked, "how lonely that life was, Amy, and how sheltered from the world you have always been? And have you ever told him how you surrounded yourself with the children and happiness whenever all your family came to visit?''

Amy did not answer. She sniffed and Judith knew that she was crying again.

"Oh, Amy.'' Judith crossed the room and set firm hands on her sister-in-law's thin shoulders. "We live in a cruel world. We women have to wait for the men to make all the moves, don't we? And if they decide not to do something, there is almost nothing we can do about it.''

"Perhaps he does not even want me,'' Amy said. "Why should he? Look at me, Judith. And I am too old to be starting to bear children—or almost too old anyway. He must have guessed my feelings. It must have been embarrassing to him. I am fortunate that he is a kind man.''

Judith clucked her tongue impatiently. "These things can be sensed, Amy,'' she said. "If you have felt that he cares for you, then you are probably right.''

Amy straightened her shoulders and blew her nose once more. "I cannot bear to stay here even one more day,'' she said. "Will you mind if I leave, Judith? Will Lord Denbigh be offended, do you think?''

"My things are already packed in the dressing room,''

Judith said. "I have already sent word that the carriage is to be got ready for the morning."

Amy turned and looked up at her with reddened eyes. Judith's smile was a little twisted.

"It seems that it was something of a mistake for both of us," she said. "I just wish it were possible to leave tonight, Amy. No!" She held up her hands sharply as her sister-in-law took a step toward her. "Please don't say anything, or ask any questions. Not yet. My control can be very easily broken and there is this wretched concert to be lived through. Perhaps on the journey home I will tell you all about it."

"But has he not made you an offer?" Amy asked. "I thought . . . It seemed so obvious that . . ."

"No," Judith said. "It was just a Christmas flirtation, Amy, nothing more."

"Oh, no." Amy frowned. "It was definitely more than that, Judith. He . . ."

"I think we should go down to join the ladies," Judith said. "Shall we?"

Amy sighed. "It was all so perfect until this afternoon, was it not?" she said. "In time, Judith, we will remember that and judge it after all to have been one of the best Christmases ever, perhaps *the* best."

"Yes," Judith said. "Perhaps in time."

There was much sleeplessness in Denbigh Park that night. Amy stood at her window long after everyone had gone to bed, staring sightlessly out, thinking of Judith's words. It was something that could be sensed, Judith had said from an experience of life that was more extensive than Amy's. If Amy thought he had cared, then he probably had.

He had cared. She was sure of it. He had wished things could be different. He had wished he were ten years younger and wealthy. He had wished she could find someone who would make her comfortable for the rest of her life.

He cared.

Life was cruel, Judith had said. Women had to wait around for men to speak, and if the man never spoke, then the woman remained disappointed. Unfulfilled. Unhappy. Life a dreary waste.

Tomorrow she would go away with Judith. And she would never see him again, or all those children. In time, Judith would marry again. It was inevitable even if for some strange reason she did not marry Lord Denbigh. And then she, Amy, would go home again. And that would be the end of life until the time, some unknown number of years in the future, when she breathed her last.

Because she was a woman. Because he was a gentleman and did not believe his way of life suitable for a lady. And because she was a woman and unable to speak up against him.

She was thirty-six years old. Perhaps she would live for thirty or forty more years. Years of dreariness and uselessness and humiliation—because she was a woman and unable to speak her piece.

It was a stupid reason. Because she was a woman!

Well, she thought finally, and the thought sent her to bed at last, if she allowed such a stupid reason to spoil the rest of her life, perhaps she deserved the future that was yawning ahead of her.

She was going to persuade Judith to put off calling the carriage until noon. If she did not lose her courage with the light of day, she was going to use the morning to speak her piece. If she did not lose her courage . . .

She scrambled into bed.

Judith lay in bed staring up into the darkness. She could still feel the physical effects of that afternoon's happenings. Her breasts were still tender. There was still an ache where they had coupled. And if she closed her eyes, she could still feel him. And smell him.

She did not close her eyes.

The anger, the hatred that had sustained her during the walk home that afternoon, during that brief and unexpected meeting with him in the nursery, and during the interminable evening of cheerful Christmas entertainment, had faded. She was no longer either angry or filled with hatred. She was empty, blessedly free of any violent feelings.

And she began to live again through the events of eight
years before. The very correct, very harsh-looking man who
had been her betrothed, who had escorted her to the various
ton events of the Season, conversing with her stiffly, never
touching more than her hand. Her own frightening awareness
of him, which she had naively interpreted as revulsion. And
Andrew, handsome, charming, smiling, easy and familiar
in his manners.

And her own dreadful behavior. Unthinkable. Unfor-
givable.

And his revenge. He had planned it all, moment by
moment. She could clearly see that now. Everything, from
that first encounter in Lady Clancy's drawing room, had been
directed toward achieving his revenge.

But why? That was the question that had revolved and
revolved in her brain since the afternoon. Wounded pride
and consequence? Would that account for all he had done?
Would not some public humiliation have been more appro-
priate to a revenge from that motive? This revenge would
surely not be public enough for such a man, even though
there were undoubtedly several people who were expecting
them to marry. She did not believe that he would make public
the fact that she had given herself to him and declared her
love for him.

But if not that motive, then what?

If he had not changed radically in the past eight years, if
he had been then in character what he was now, then what
must he have been like beneath the harsh exterior? She had
never tried to find out at the time. How must he have felt
about his betrothal? About her? He was a man now who loved
to give happiness, a man who loved children. He loved her
own children even though they were hers—and Andrew's.

She had not thought him quite human eight years before.
And yet even if he had changed in that time, he had still been
human then. He had been a man engaged to be married and
within one month of his wedding. A man who had since
proved himself to be fond of children . . .

Judith dashed a tear from her cheek impatiently and
continued to stare upward into the darkness.

* * *

The Marquess of Denbigh sat in his library for a long time after his guests had gone to bed. He was not really thinking. He was just allowing sensation to wash over him and felt too lethargic to drag himself off to bed.

"I love you," she had told him when they had first arrived at the cottage. And during the following couple of hours she had loved him indeed with all of herself, with her body and with the part of herself that had looked at him through her eyes.

"I love you," she had told him again, lying warm and relaxed in his arms beneath the bedcovers, smiling at him with love and trust and the full expectation that he would return her words.

A Christmas flirtation! I thought you understood. I am so sorry, Judith.

And this was what sweet revenge felt like. He had waited eight years for this. This was what it felt like. So empty, so very very empty that there was pain.

She had smiled at him almost throughout their second loving and teased him about having to watch her. Was he afraid she would run away if he did not keep an eye on her? And she had told him what she liked and had gasped and bitten her lip and smiled again when he had done it.

"Tell me what else you like," he had told her, "and I will do it."

"I like all of it," she had said. "All of it. All."

He had given her all and they had both laughed until passion had taken away the laughter and replaced it with ecstasy.

He had filled her with his seed—twice. Perhaps even now there was new life beginning in her. His life. Hers. Theirs. A new life. She was going away in the morning. He would be as greedy for news of her as he had ever been. He would want to know, he would need to know if she showed signs of swelling with child.

And if the news of such came back to him, then what would he do?

And if no such news ever came, then what would he do?

He had brought a single candle with him from the drawing room. But he had not lit the candles in the branched candlestick on the mantel with it as he had intended. It stood on his desk, the berry-laden sprig of holly twined around its base giving it a festive glow.

A Christmas candle. All that was left of Christmas. A single frail light in a dark room. He could snuff it with one movement of his fingers. And then there would be total darkness. No Christmas left at all. Nothing left at all.

He jerked to his feet and wondered belatedly and in some surprise why he had not touched the brandy decanter.

He was not the only person in the house still awake, he discovered as he reached the landing at the top of the stairs, holding his single Christmas candle. There was a little figure in a long white nightgown standing there, obviously frightened to stillness by the sight of the approaching light.

"You cannot sleep?" he asked.

"I was on my way to Mama," Rupert said. "To see if she was all right."

"She has probably been asleep for hours," the marquess said. "Will I do instead?"

"I could not find Papa," the child said.

"Couldn't you?" The marquess stooped down and picked up the little boy, who wrapped his arms about his neck and shivered.

"He kept going through doors," Rupert said. "But when I went through them, he was not there. And they all said they had not seen him. Some of them said they had never heard of him. But I could see him going through another door."

The marquess let himself quietly into the nursery. The doors into Kate's and Mrs. Webber's bedchambers were open. Mrs. Webber was snoring loudly. Obviously, she was too elderly a lady to have the night charge of two young children. He went into the boy's bedchamber, pulled a blanket from the bed, and seated the two of them in the nursery again. He wrapped the blanket warmly about the child.

"I knew your papa," he said. "I saw him many times."

Rupert looked up at him hopefully. "They said they had never heard of him," he said.

The marquess smiled. "That was because they were dream people," he said. "Dream people are always remarkably stupid. How could anyone with any sense not have heard of a man who was once on the first eleven at Eton?"

"Uncle Maurice said he once hit three sixes in one inning," Rupert said.

"Did he?" The marquess shook his head. "Then he was a greater champion than I ever was. The best I ever hit was one six and two fours."

"Was I dreaming?" Rupert asked.

"You were," Lord Denbigh said. "The next time you meet those foolish people in a dream, you can tell them that the Marquess of Denbigh knew your papa very well and envies his record at cricket. And he could skate like the wind too, could he not? I am afraid I can skate only as fast as the breeze."

The boy chuckled. "Tell me about Papa," he said.

"Your papa?" The marquess looked up and thought. "Let me see. Did anyone ever tell you how he charmed all the ladies? How he charmed your mama and whisked her away to marry him when I fancied her myself?"

"Did he?" Rupert asked. "Tell me."

Lord Denbigh told a tale of a handsome, charming young gentleman who could dance the night away long after everyone else had collapsed from exhaustion and drive a team with such skill that he was known as the best whip in London and spar with any partner at Gentleman Jackson's without once coming away with a bloodied nose.

Andrew Easton's son was sleeping before the marquess had finished.

16

Amy was hurrying down the driveway, wondering whether she had the courage to do what she had planned to do or whether when she reached the village she would merely step into the shop to purchase some imagined need. There had been no problem with Judith. She too apparently had something she wanted to do before the carriage was called.

Amy rounded the bend, head down against the wind. It was a chilly morning. There was no sign yet of the cold spell breaking. She lifted her scarf up over her mouth and nose.

"Good morning," someone called. "You are up and out very early."

Her head snapped up and there he was, walking toward her, his chin buried inside the neck of his coat, his cheeks reddened by the cold, his mustache whitened by the frost. And everything she had rehearsed fled from her mind.

"We are leaving," she said. "At noon. I was walking into the village to—to buy something."

"Leaving?" He stopped beside her and hunched his shoulders. "All of you? So soon?"

"Yes," she said. "We need to be back. We have engagements, you know. And Judith's parents will be returning from Scotland soon. She is eager to hear news of her sister from them. And I love town. There is so much yet to see there."

"We are going out to collect firewood this afternoon," he said. "We always make a festive occasion out of it. I thought that perhaps you would care to come with us. But I said good-bye yesterday, did I not? It would have been better to have left it at that, I suppose."

"Yes," she said.

He offered her his arm. "May I escort you to the village shop?" he asked.

"Thank you." She took his arm and they began walking

211

toward the village, exchanging opinions on the weather and guesses about when it would begin to warm up and predictions on whether it would snow again.

"I was not on my way to the shop," she said in a rush all of a sudden. "I was on my way to call on you. I remembered that the rector would be busy with the boys this morning."

"Yes," he said quietly. "That was why I was free to walk to the house."

She drew a deep breath. "I have had material comforts and a large home and a protective family all my life," she said, fixing her eyes on the roadway ahead. "And though I have always counted my blessings, I have been unhappy, Spencer. There has been nothing to give my life purpose. Nothing to warm my heart."

He was patting her hand.

"The only bright moments in my life have been the times when my brothers and some cousins came with their children," she said. "I always loved to play with them and talk with them. I used to think that I would give up every last thing, every last brick of the house and rag of clothing just to extend those times. It was foolish, of course. One cannot in reality live without even the basic necessities of life. But I felt it and believed it and still believe it in part."

"Amy," he said. They had stopped walking and he had turned to her.

"You were wrong," she said, her voice agitated. "You said that it would not work. Perhaps it could not from your point of view. But you were wrong about me, I . . ."

He laid two gloved fingers against her lips. "Don't," he said. "Don't say any more."

But she pulled back her head. "Yes," she said, "I will. It is not fair that just because I am a woman . . ."

"Sh," he said, and he set his hands on her shoulders and pulled her against him. "Don't say any more, Amy."

"I came to say it." She looked earnestly up into his face. "I will be sorry forever after if I do not. For once in my life . . ."

"Sh," he said, and he kissed her briefly on the lips. "You

are a woman, Amy, like it or not, and we live in a society which would make you feel ashamed of having to say such a thing. And you do not need to say it when I can just as easily say it myself and propriety will not be outraged. Will you marry me, my dear?''

She gazed mutely back into his eyes.

"I do not need to explain that it will not be a brilliant or even a very eligible match for you. You know that already," he said. "I have an independence, Amy, in the sense that Max does not pay me a salary, only all the expenses of the home. But I cannot offer a wife any sort of luxury. And I cannot give up this work I have begun. I am too selfishly happy doing it. But you would not want me to, I know. I can only feel sorry that I cannot offer you a better life. But the decision must be yours. I am offering myself and my life to you for what they are worth."

"Only because I was going to ask?" she said wistfully. "Only because you are a gentleman, Spencer?"

He chuckled. "I have avoided matrimony for almost forty years," he said. "I do not think I would consider entering it now just to be gentlemanly. I am not much of a romantic, am I? It should have been the first thing I said. It will have to be the last. But it is the most important. I love you, dear."

"Do you?" She put her arms up about his neck and looked earnestly into his face. "Oh, but you can't, Spencer. Look at me."

"A little bird," he said. "A cheerful little singing bird. Will you give me your answer? If it is no, I shall escort you back to the house without further delay. If it is yes, we had better go and break the news to the boys—if you are prepared for a great deal of noise and commotion. But it is dashed cold standing here. A foolish place for a marriage proposal, is it not?"

"Yes," she said.

He raised his eyebrows.

"Now we can go to tell the boys," she said.

"Ah." He threw back his head and laughed. "It was yes to the first question, was it? And would you care to tell me why you are accepting?"

She looked somewhat taken aback for a moment. And then she smiled brightly. "Because I love you, of course," she said.

Mr. Cornwell seemed to forget that it was far too cold a place for such a scene. He caught her up into a tight hug and swung her once around. And then he kissed her soundly and quite unhurriedly.

"Perhaps we can think about taking on that home of boys and girls together," he said.

"Yes," she said. "An instant and large family, Spencer. I would like that."

"And a large bundle of problems to come with them, I warn you," he said.

"Something to challenge the mind and give a reason for living," she said.

"How old are you?" he asked her.

"Thirty-six," she said.

"Quite young enough still to have what you most want out of life, then," he said, and watched her flush quite outshine the glow of coldness in her cheeks. "Perhaps a child or two of our own, Amy."

"Oh." She hid her face against his broad shoulder. "I'll not be greedy. I already have the promise of heaven."

"Heaven!" He chuckled. "Are your feet numb yet? Excuse me, but I am going to have to look down to make sure that mine are still there. Here, let me tuck my arm about you like this. You will be warmer and you fit very snugly there, do you not?"

"Yes," she said. "Oh, yes. Oh, Spencer, has this not been the most wonderful Christmas?"

Fortunately, he had not been at breakfast with his guests. He had ridden out on some errand, Lord Clancy explained, but he would be back soon. And they had all been invited to a neighbor's home later for dinner and an evening of cards.

"What a shame it is that you have to leave today, my dear Mrs. Easton," Miss Edith Hannibal said. "You will be missed, and your dear little children too."

"Thank you," Judith said. "But I am eager for news of my sister. I have not seen her for an age."

"And the bond between sisters is a close one," Miss Frieda Hannibal said.

No one seemed to have thought to question the fact that Lord and Lady Blakeford were expected back from Scotland so soon after Christmas, far too soon for them to have celebrated the holiday there, in fact.

"Maxwell must be disappointed," Aunt Edith said. "It seemed . . . We thought . . ."

"Doubtless he will go up to town for the Season and meet Mrs. Easton there again," Lady Clancy said. "And talking about the Season . . ."

Judith returned her attention gratefully to her breakfast and excused herself soon afterward to go to the children in the nursery. They were not at all pleased at the prospect of going home that day. But children were resilient. They would be happy again once they were back in London.

"Papa was the best whip in London," Rupert told her. "And everybody at Gentleman Jackson's was afraid to spar with him because he was so handy with his fives."

Judith smiled. "Mr. Rundle told you a great deal yesterday," she said.

"No," he said, "it was not Mr. Rundle who told me. It was Lord Denbigh."

Judith gave him her full attention.

"Last night," he said. "He was in here. I was having that dream about Papa. But I won't be afraid of it any more, Mama. He says I am to tell those people that the Marquess of Denbigh knew Papa very well indeed and wishes he could have knocked sixes like Papa did. He said you would be asleep."

"Did he?" Judith said. "And you did not dream any more afterward?"

Rupert shook his head. "I don't remember his going," he said.

Judith had been relieved to find that he was not at breakfast. But she hoped he would not be gone all morning. She wanted to be on her way. She wanted to start on the rest of her life. She hoped that Amy would not be gone long. Or else she hoped that Amy would be gone forever. She had guessed her sister-in-law's errand from the set look on her face that morning.

If only Amy could come to an understanding with Mr. Cornwell, then something good would have come out of this Christmas after all. And Amy deserved happiness more than anyone else in the world. More than Judith did. Far more than she did.

She went into her bedchamber and summoned a maid. She sent the girl with a message requesting a private word with his lordship at his convenience. And she sat down in the windowseat, heart thumping, to wait.

Over an hour passed before the summons came. It was amazing, Judith thought as she descended the staircase, shoulders held firmly back, chin high, how resolution could falter in the course of an hour and how knees could weaken and heartbeat accelerate. She had not exchanged a word directly with him since before getting out of his bed at the cottage the afternoon before.

She stepped inside the library and stood still while the footman who had admitted her closed the doors behind her. And her resolution almost fled entirely. He was the Viscount Evendon as she had known him eight years before and the Marquess of Denbigh as she had known him in London a few weeks before. He stood before the fire, one elbow propped on the high mantel, one Hessian boot crossed over the other. His face was harsh, thin-lipped. He looked at her steadily from keen and hooded eyes.

I have summoned the carriage for noon. Her mouth opened to speak the unplanned words and closed again, the words unsaid.

"It was not a Christmas flirtation," she said. "It was revenge."

He said nothing.

"I have asked myself," she said, "why you would wish to take revenge. Because you were the Viscount Evendon and heir to the Marquess of Denbigh and very high in the instep? But such a man would plan some public humiliation, would he not? You will not be able to boast of this particular triumph. So your plan for revenge must have had a more personal motive.''

He turned his head sideways to look across the room away from her.

"I think," she said, "that I must have hurt you. Did I?"

His jaw hardened. He said nothing though she waited for several silent seconds.

"Whether I did or not," she said, "I behaved very badly. And that understates the case. I behaved abominably. I could not bring myself to face you at the time because I feared you and because—oh, because everyone under such circumstances, I suppose, is tempted to play the coward and I gave in to the temptation. And I have never been able to face you since over that particular matter, though the guilt has always gnawed at me. I suppose I have persuaded myself that what happened was of no great significance to you.''

She found herself being regarded suddenly by those steel-gray eyes again.

"After yesterday," she said, "I know that I was wrong. I have come to beg your pardon, inadequate as the words are."

He laughed, though there was no amusement in the sound. "You still have the power to amaze me," he said. "I expected that you were coming here to rave at me and accuse, perhaps to demand that I do the decent thing. You ask my forgiveness after what I did to you yesterday?"

"I am right, am I not?" she said. "I did hurt you?"

"I loved you," he said. "Does it surprise you that a man who had none of the charm or easy manner of an Andrew Easton could love? And feel the pain of rejection? And try for a whole year literally to outrun his pain?"

She swallowed and closed her eyes. "I did not know, Max," she said. "I had no idea."

"You are forgiven," he said shortly. "There, does that make you feel better? Now what must I do to win *your* forgiveness? Marry you? I owe you that after yesterday. Is there a chance that you are with child? Should I summon the rector here to speak with both of us? Or should I ride in to the village alone after luncheon?''

''Max,'' she said, ''don't.''

''My apologies,'' he said. ''You are a romantic, I suppose. You want sweet words and bended knee? Well, you can have them if you wish, Judith.''

She took several steps toward him across the room. ''I did not sleep last night,'' she said. ''I don't think you did either. Certainly you were awake and not even in your room when Rupert awoke with his usual dream. I did a great deal of thinking last night.''

''You need not have worried,'' he said. ''I am giving in, you see, without even a fight.''

''I hated you when I left you yesterday afternoon,'' she said. ''I thought it had all been a plot of revenge. I thought it had all been cold calculation. I thought I had been right about you from the start. But I was wrong. You still love me, don't you?'' She could feel herself flushing, but he was not looking at her. He had turned his head away again and set his forefinger against his mouth.

''Perhaps you did not hear my words,'' he said, ''or fully comprehend their true meaning.''

''Oh, yes,'' she said. ''Loud and clear. But they were just words, spoken at the end of it all. I think perhaps they were what you had planned to say and so you said them. But what happened before you spoke those words was not part of your plan, Max.''

He laughed again. ''That good, was it?'' he said.

''You know it was,'' she said. ''And thinking about it last night and remembering, I knew that I could not have been mistaken. I could not have been. Even if I had had no experience with such matters I would know beyond any doubt that I was not mistaken. But I have had experience. I was married for almost seven years. I have been made love to many times. But yesterday you were not making love to me or I to you. We were making love with each other. That has never happened to me before, and I could not possibly be mistaken. It was no game you were playing, Max. It was love. I know it.''

"So." He turned his head to look at her, and his eyes were weary, bleak. "What do you want me to do about it?"

"I don't know." She shrugged her shoulders. "Forgive me in your heart as well as with your mouth. Forgive yourself. Let go of all the bitterness. Move on into the future. There is so much goodness in your life. I will be gone within the hour. Let me go—right out of your life. Start again."

He stared at her, nodding his head slowly. "And you?" he said. "You will move on too?"

"Yes," she said.

"And if you are with child?"

"I will know," she said. "Whatever you may say, I will know that the child was begotten and conceived out of love. That is all that will matter. I do love you, you know, and it will always hurt me to know that I was pain and shadow and darkness in your life for eight years. But you can be free of me now, partly because you got even, but more importantly because you have forgiven me. And I you."

"Judith," he said. "We have given each other so much pain. That can have nothing to do with love, surely?"

She shrugged. "I don't know," she said. "It obviously has a great deal to do with life."

He reached out his free hand toward her and she took a few steps closer to him until she could set her own in it. He drew her closer until she was against him, and his arms closed loosely about her and hers about him. She turned her head to lay against his chest and closed her eyes.

They stood thus for many minutes, comforting each other wordlessly for pain and guilt and for all that might have been.

"And so," he said finally, "in one hour's time you will be gone and we can both start to reconstruct our lives."

"Forgiven and forgiving," she said.

"Pardon and peace," he said.

"Yes."

His cheek rested against the top of her head briefly. "It cannot be done together, Judith? Is it too late for us?"

She heard a gulp of a sob suddenly and realized in some horror that it had come from her. "I don't know," she said, and she tried to push away from him.

But she was pulled back against him by arms that were suddenly as hard as steel bands and when she raised her face to avoid suffocation against his neckcloth it was to look into eyes that were themselves brimming with tears. He lowered his head and kissed her fiercely, a wet and breathless kiss.

"Let us do it, Judith," he said. "Let us give life and love and peace a chance together, shall we? I cannot contemplate any of the three of them without you. Not again. I don't have the strength to do it again. I love you. Is that what I told you with my body yesterday? Did you recognize the language? I am telling you with words now. I love you. I always have."

He took one of her hands and held the palm to his mouth. She stood smiling up at him until gradually he relaxed and smiled back.

"I think we had better get married and be done with it," he said. "Don't you?"

Her smile deepened.

"You are holding out for the poetic speech and the down-on-one-knee business, aren't you?" he said.

But before her smile could give place to laughter they were interrupted. One of the doors opened slightly and two little figures appeared around it.

"Mama," Rupert said, "Aunt Amy is not back yet and it is beginning to snow again and Mr. Rockford said he would take us sledding if we had nothing else to do. May we stay?"

"The dog was sick all over the floor," Kate said.

"Oh, dear," the marquess said, keeping his arms firmly about Judith when she would have pulled away. "You must have been feeding him muffins again, were you?"

"And toast," Kate said.

"May we, Mama?" Rupert asked.

"How would you like to stay forever and a day?" the marquess asked. "If your mama would just consent to marry me, you know, you could do so. And go sledding and skating and have plenty of company from the children in the village.

And I could teach you to ride a real horse, Rupert, and to play cricket as well as your papa. And Kate could see the puppies when they are born in the spring and train one to sleep on her bed all night without once wetting the blankets or being sick all over the floor.''

"Ye-es!" Rupert yelled. "Famous. Will you, Mama?"

Kate had crossed the room and was clinging to a tassel of the marquess's Hessian. "A black puppy?" she asked. "All black?"

"I shall see what I can arrange," he said.

"Will you, Mama?" Dark and pleading eyes gazed up at her from beneath soft auburn curls.

"Will you, Judith?" Lord Denbigh's eyes smiled into hers. "Will you make it unanimous? It is already three against one."

"One thing I have noticed about you from the start," she said, "is that you will quite unscrupulously get to me through my children."

"Guilty," he said.

"And it works every time," she said.

"Does it?"

"Yes."

"This time too?"

"Yes."

"You will marry me?"

She smiled broadly at him.

He sighed. "Kate," he said. "Stand back if you will. And watch carefully. This is going to happen to you one day. And you watch too, Rupert, my lad. You are going to have to do this one of these fine days. I am about to get down on one knee to propose to your mama."

"My Christmas beau," Judith said fondly, smiling down at him as he suited action to words.